IN$URED
TO THE
HILT

IN$URED
TO THE
HILT

A JOHN SMITH MYSTERY

CHARLOTTE STUART

LEVEL
BEST BOOKS

First published by Level Best Books 2023

This novel is entirely a work of fiction. The names, characters and incidents portrayed in it are the work of the author's imagination. Any resemblance to actual persons, living or dead, events or localities is entirely coincidental.

Charlotte Stuart asserts the moral right to be identified as the author of this work.

Author Photo Credit: Faye Johnson

First edition

ISBN: 978-1-68512-340-6

Cover art by Level Best Designs

This book was professionally typeset on Reedsy.
Find out more at reedsy.com

To Elizabeth, Michael, Sammy, Jill and Mark. Thank you for sharing chortles, smirks, giggles, snickers, guffaws and laughter. It's contagious and inspiring.

Chapter One

BUZZZZ. BUZZ. BUZZZZ. A persistent drone interrupted my mid-morning nap.

"Are you in there, Mr. Smith?" a voice snapped at my left elbow. The sleepy haze slowly lifted, taking with it the scantily clad women dancing to the refrain of *Fanta, Fanta! Don't-cha wanna wanta Fanta.*

"Mr. Smith!"

I blinked at the angry red light on my Intercom. Groggily punching buttons, I managed to announce to half the staff that I was in my office before finally hitting the right one and putting an end to the buzzing.

"It's about time you answered." Emma's short-order cook voice left no doubt that she was displeased. "Your door is locked. I've been trying to let you know that Mr. Van Droop wants you in his office in fifteen minutes." Click.

That was Emma's urbane way of telling me that employees have no right to privacy, that she didn't like me any better than she had ever liked anyone, and that I'd better hustle because you don't keep the vice president in charge of claims waiting, especially if you are an insignificant "trainee in claims," barely above an amoeba in the corporate ecological food chain.

Dazed but determined, I pushed myself away from my desk and willed my body to unlock the door. Then I stumbled back to my chair just in time for Emma to open the door, poke her head in and say, "That was fifteen minutes from fifteen minutes ago, and you have a red spot on your forehead."

She disappeared before I could open my mouth to reply. The door shut with a whoosh followed by a muffled click.

1

Fifteen minutes from fifteen minutes ago didn't sound so good. And something was definitely wrong with my forehead. I could feel an indentation, right in the middle, where I had been resting on my class ring. But the important thing was that the vice president wanted to see me. Right now.

I leapt up, swaying unsteadily like the proverbial sailor on shore leave. Unless we were having an earthquake, I was not yet fully functional. Mother always says that if you are groggy after coming out of a deep sleep you should have a drink. Of course, she probably means water, but if I was going to meet with the vice president, I needed something stronger.

In the bottom drawer of the ancient battleship gray filing cabinet that fills about a quarter of my modest office was a locked wooden box with a tiny hair positioned across the lid as a security measure. I glanced over my shoulder to make certain I was still alone and reached for the box. Even in my stuporous state, I remembered to check the hair before fumbling in my pockets for the key. Inside was a bottle of vodka and a single unwashed glass. The only secret I've managed to keep from Emma's lyncean watchfulness.

The two-gulp shot I poured myself brought the contents down to half a bottle. Not bad. Eight months with the company, and I had only required half a fifth of reinforcement. Of course, I had never been called before the vice president. If there were going to be many such meetings, I'd have to get a larger box. Unless he was going to fire me. In that case, I'd be packing up my half-empty bottle and my unwashed glass and saying goodbye to Universal Heartland Liability and Casualty Assurance Company of America, Incorporated. Not in one breath, of course.

Just the thought of being fired was disconcerting. I didn't want to say goodbye. My job with Universal had saved me from food stamps and generic peanut butter. How can you expect to get any nutritional value from something labeled Product 438 Crunchy!

The only other job I'd been able to land after joining the ranks of the educated unemployed was as a private detective. I always wanted to be a detective. Even as an undergraduate philosophy major, I read every classic mystery in existence, from hard-boiled to cozy. Unfortunately, things didn't turn out as rosy as the brochure promised. Despite my unremarkable appearance, one irate ex-boxer husband had no trouble at all remembering my face. And he didn't like me tailing his wife to get evidence against her lover. I almost had my nondescript face made descript, spent two weeks in the hospital, and promptly retired from the private detection business.

No, I didn't want to say goodbye. I wanted to stay right where I was. So I needed to get my act together and hotfoot it over to Van Droop's office pronto. Feeling better, I hurriedly locked up the bottle, replaced the hair, and took several loud breaths with my mouth open to dissipate the liquor odor. Worried that there might still be a slight alcohol aroma, I looked for some mints in the top drawer of my desk. Finding none, I settled for an allergy pill. They have a minty flavor and melt in your mouth. And they last for twelve hours.

There's a mirror just to the left of my door. I paused on the way out to check how I looked. The red spot Emma mentioned was still there. I tried pulling my hair forward to conceal it. That looked stupid. Lazy or stupid—those were my choices. I brushed my hair back in place and headed for Van Droop's office. Maybe he would think it was a birthmark.

Emma pointedly looked at the clock on the wall across from her desk as I rushed by. Van Droop's office is just a short sprint away in the "new" section of the building. As the most recent addition to the company, I had a tiny room between a broom closet and an alcove that housed some hard copies of closed files that had not been transferred to a digital format and probably never would be. The rest of the employees on my floor were billeted in cubicles ringed with brightly colored, half-wall partitions that allow you to scratch unseen but amplify coughs and whispered confidences. It's the kind of place that makes you aware that you are part of a team.

As I emerged from the gloom into the corridor leading to the corporate offices, heads surreptitiously turned, and curious eyes followed my progress. Feeling self-conscious, like someone caught blowing in the vichyssoise, I looked straight ahead as I marched toward the door marked, "Martin van Droop, Vice President, Claims." I could almost hear my mother's voice ordering me to keep my shoulders back, stomach in, chin up. Sometimes she gives good advice.

Van Droop's office, like mine, has walls that reach the ceiling. You can't get his attention by coughing or clearing your throat. You have to take positive action. I had read somewhere that when knocking on the door of an executive, it should be soft enough so as not to seem aggressive, yet loud enough to be heard. To get it just right requires practice and fairly fleshy knuckles. I rapped a shade too loud and didn't have to look around to know that eyebrows were being raised. Then, after being told to "Enter!" I inadvertently let the door slam behind me. Van Droop looked up and scowled. Before I could apologize for slamming the door, for being late, or for just being me, he waved me to a seat. My knees didn't need to be asked twice.

Once seated, Van Droop's basset eyes roamed over me as if he'd lost something I might have. "I don't think we've met..."

"At the Christmas party," I meekly corrected. "And at my interview." I didn't take his forgetfulness personally; no one remembers the thousands of extras in B movies.

"Christmas party?" he echoed uncertainly.

"Yes," I said. "The one for the employees." Van Droop had made an appearance at the company "social hour" the Friday before Christmas. His present to the junior staff had been to let them rub elbows with him while they munched green bonsai Christmas tree cookies and drank weak punch that made some of the admins giggly. My elbows had been among those rubbed. Perhaps my elbows were as forgettable as my face.

"Ah, yes, of course," he murmured. "You're, ah..." He fumbled among some papers on his desk.

"John Smith," I said. If he didn't even know my name it seemed unlikely that I was in much trouble. Maybe I'd only needed one gulp of vodka.

"John Smith, John Smith," he repeated, as if wondering why the name sounded familiar. Then his eyes wandered to my forehead and lingered there a moment. With luck, the blush I felt creeping up my neck would camouflage the spot.

Van Droop looked down again, found the paper he'd been searching for, and started reading. "It has been called to my attention, Mr., ah...Smith, that

4

you have been with the company eight months now." Once he got past my name, he knew his lines. I slowly began to relax. He hadn't called me in to chew me out about something; he was congratulating me for making it through the company's probationary period. If I hadn't been awakened from a sound sleep, I might have considered this possibility sooner. Oh well, you can't complain about happy endings.

Van Droop rambled on, pausing now and then to lick his lips and glance at my forehead. Whenever his eyes went to my spot, I reached up and rubbed it as if concentrating on what he had just said. Finally, he reached the dénouement. "So,...Mr. ... Smith. We are happy to consider you a permanent employee of Universal Heartland Liability and Casualty Assurance Company of America, Incorporated." He took a deep breath to replenish his lungs, folded his hands on his desk, and smiled.

I smiled back. I liked the sound of what he said: *permanent*. A permanent position with a nice safe company. I definitely had to buy some mints to make sure I didn't ruin everything the next time I needed a pick-me-up.

After thanking him for his kind words and for the job of claims adjuster, I scurried back to my own office, made dearer by the word "permanent." It wasn't much. A little bigger than the closet next door, with a tiny window facing a brick wall splotched with white bird droppings. The khaki-colored paint was peppered with nail holes, an occasional nail still in place, waiting for someone to come along with a family portrait or a Demotivators Calendar. Cobwebs hung like dirty cotton candy from the high ceiling, but there didn't seem to be any spiders, so I didn't care. The bottom line: it was a comfortable job with a nice steady income. Who could ask for more?

Emma had invaded my domain during my absence and had left a file on my desk labeled "Marshall, Vivian." Since this was my first case as a permanent employee, I opened the file immediately. There was a thin line between "permanent" and "adios" in an "employment at will" environment; I didn't want to let them down.

The question was whether Universal had an obligation to pay for an accident under Mrs. Marshall's $100,000 family auto policy, an adequate but low-limits policy. The facts seemed straightforward, but people always managed to bend them a little this way and that. Mrs. Marshall's son Mark Jr., age 16, had been driving what he claimed was a borrowed '91 Ford when he collided with a car driven by a woman named Pearl Rosenblatt. Rosenblatt had been well into the intersection when the Ford ran into her 2000 Corolla broadside. Two old cars, racing to their final destinations.

Rosenblatt claimed Mark had been speeding and, according to the police report, the tire marks indicated she might be right. But that would be difficult to prove with certainty. In any event, the Corolla had the right of way, so Mark was clearly at fault. The company was on the hook, but only IF the '91 Ford was borrowed. According to Mrs. Marshall's insurance agent, it was his understanding that the car had been purchased, not borrowed. Although no paperwork was completed before the accident, and Mrs. Marshall said that she had only asked the agent about what it would cost IF Mark decided to purchase the car. A simple accident, but too many if's to make it an open-and-shut case.

In addition to the issue of coverage, there were a few other complicating factors. The initial medical report on Pearl Rosenblatt looked bad. She claimed that her neck had been injured in the accident, and she had already been operated on. Talk about speed! Presently she was unable to walk and was confined to a wheelchair. Some notes taken by one of the admins on a phone call to the hospital suggested there might also be a malpractice suit against the doctor who performed the operation. Universal would join the queue when the limits for the other policies were reached.

To top it all off, the Corolla wasn't insured. That meant we would be dealing directly with Pearl Rosenblatt rather than with another insurance company. Depending on what she was like, that could either be a plus or a minus. Although I would have preferred a quick and easy win, this was definitely the most interesting file to cross my desk so far, a case befitting my new status. If I did a good job, maybe they would ask the janitor to start picking up my wastebasket instead of requiring me to dump its contents in the lunchroom garbage can and scrounge for new plastic liners.

Time to talk to Mrs. Marshall and her son.

In claims adjusters' school, we were taught that you should surprise people by dropping in on them unannounced. That supposedly throws them off balance and makes them pliable and easier to manipulate. Of course, they didn't use those exact words. They talked about "fast response times" and "negotiation skills." But everyone knew what they meant. In the long run, it seldom makes much difference. The people you try to drop in on are rarely home anyway. Still, it's company policy, and it was a beautiful day for a drive.

Universal does not issue smartphones, but it provides a city map that spans an entire wall in the fourth-floor foyer. The theory is that you can chart your route on the map and write out the directions if necessary. You can't get reimbursed for a normal-sized map, but you can make as many copies as you want of your handwritten directions using company paper. You can also google a map and print the directions, but often times you end up going from one place to another and are then on your own. I've considered taking pictures of the map and piecing them together, but it seems like a lot of work. And it would be hard to spread out in the car and even harder to fold into a manageable size.

Fortunately, I was familiar with the area where the Marshalls lived, so I informed Emma that I would be out of the office on business and departed. The sun was riding high, I was on a new case, and I had been made a permanent member of the claims adjusters club. This was clearly my lucky day.

Chanting, "a-weema-weh, a-weema-weh," I wheeled out of the parking lot and headed toward the low-income residential district where the Marshalls lived. I sang along to the song as I tapped the gas pedal to the rhythm of my music. I couldn't remember the second verse, so returned to a few more choruses of "a-weema-weh's." The drive went quickly, and once in the area, it didn't take long to locate their house.

"Marshall" was scrawled in bold, uneven letters on a mailbox in front of the gray remains of a picket fence. I pulled into the unpaved driveway and stopped just inches from a rusted pink tricycle. As I got out of the car, I noted that the unmowed lawn was competing with a host of dandelions for dominance, and a tangle of ivy and weeds had taken over the flowerbeds. But there were bright floral-patterned curtains in the windows and a welcome mat on the doorstep.

I tripped over an anatomically correct Barbie doll and started up the steps. A large calico cat was slumped over the second step, two paws hanging limply down, head turned upward into the sun. Her tail twitched as I stepped over her, but her eyes remained closed. Next to the door, there was a sign that read "Beware of the Cat." I glanced back to make sure I hadn't disturbed her, but she hadn't moved. Then I pressed the doorbell.

Nothing happened. I pressed again. It's hard to know whether a doorbell is working. If it is and you also knock, it can seem pushy. On the other hand, if it hasn't rung and the occupant suddenly decides to leave via the front door, it can be a bit awkward for them to find you just standing there with your hands in your pockets. I opted for pushy. I knocked softly on the screen door. No one answered. I knocked just a little louder, glancing over my shoulder to make sure I wasn't disturbing the cat. Still no one answered. Surprising people can be a drag.

I was just about to give up when a small girl peeked out the front window. I smiled broadly at her and pointed to the door. She shook her head and stared at me. I showed her a few more teeth and made an exaggerated motion indicating that she should go to the front door. She remained immobile. After trying a few more hand signals, I decided to look around for someone capable of more sophisticated communication. Where there's a child, there's usually an adult nearby. As I turned to leave, the child suddenly disappeared from sight. Then the door rattled. She had correctly interpreted my hand signals, after all. Or so I thought.

The door opened about two inches.

"Hi," she said in a thin, diaphanous voice.

I've never been adept at talking with children, but I was prepared to give it my best for Universal. Bending down to speak through the narrow opening at her level, I said, "Hi there." I sounded like someone trying to make conversation with a parakeet. "Is your mommy home?" She gazed back at me with blank blue eyes.

"You talk funny," she said after a few moments.

8

Straightening my shoulders, I got up from my crouch and peered down at the little urchin. Then I cleared my throat and addressed her in a no-nonsense, adult tone. "I'd like to speak with your mother."

"She isn't home."

"Well, what about your brother then?" I caught myself wanting to stoop down again and snapped to attention.

"I'm not supposed to tell you they aren't home."

"That's good advice," I found myself agreeing. "You shouldn't talk to strangers."

That did it. She closed the door and went back to the window. *Not ME,* I wanted to yell. I'm not a stranger; I'm a claims adjuster. She stood there staring at me. What should I have done? I asked myself. Tell her it's okay to talk with strangers?

I glanced around the sides of the house but didn't see anyone. It was a nice day for waiting around, so I decided to do just that. Either her mother or brother would probably return soon.

I was leaning against my car, lulled by the sun's warmth and the distant sound of a dogfight, when a car turned into the driveway so fast I felt like I was stalled on the track at the Indianapolis Motor Speedway. Startled, I lost my balance and rammed my elbow into one of my car's fenders. If the car's body panels hadn't been made of some dent and ding-resistant polymer, I would have damaged my car instead of rearranging the skin on my arm.

A long-haired teenager jumped out of the other car and demanded, "You looking for somebody?" He sounded like he was trying to be tough. No, on second thought, he sounded tough. He wasn't much to look at—all bones, faded blue jeans, and acne. But he had his Clint Eastwood imitation down pat.

"Are you Mark Marshall, Jr.?" I asked, rubbing my injured elbow.

"Who's asking?" He tried a swagger, but it came out more like a stumble. He pushed up his sleeves to give me a glimpse of a tattoo to emphasize his point. I tilted my head to see what it was, but I couldn't tell.

"I'm with Universal Heartland Liability and Casualty Assurance Company of America, Incorporated," I said quickly, wishing for the umpteenth time that the name was shorter.

"That's supposed to be *insurance*, dude," he challenged with a snicker.

Jeff Bridges isn't scary like Clint Eastwood can be, but he was still trying to impress me with his ability to sound like someone he wasn't. I needed to cut to the chase. "No, we are an *insurance* company," I explained, "but the word in our name is *assurance*. It means we assure you of certain forms of *insurance* coverage."

He seemed to accept my explanation but still looked dubious. "You don't look like an insurance man," he said, giving me the once-over. People always expect anyone who works for an insurance company to look like a short-haired version of the Quaker Oats Man.

"I left my ascot at home," I quipped, but the comment was obviously lost on him. He probably ate pop tarts for breakfast. "I just have a few questions."

"Well, I may have a few answers…or I may not," he countered in a slow, nasal voice. I wasn't sure who he was mimicking with that one. Maybe John Wayne. He needed to lay off the macho movies and watch some *Leave It to Beaver* reruns.

"Can I come inside?" I asked. I've never been good at taking notes while standing. Besides, my elbow hurt, and the sun was in my eyes.

"Do you want to ask your questions, or don't you?" He was back to Eastwood again.

I was about to point out that it was *he* who wanted something from me, not the other way round, when a voice yelled, "Mark, who is that man?" I turned and saw a woman standing in the front doorway of the Marshall house. Had she slipped past us or come in from the back? Or had she been there all along, and her daughter was an incredibly good liar?

"Some man from the Universal **Ass**urance Company," Mark called back, his dark eyes laughing at the fine joke he'd made. Ignoring him, I headed toward the house. He tagged along, flexing his fingers as if in preparation for a karate chop in case I got out of line.

"Mrs. Marshall?" I asked as I tripped over the Barbie again. She had her son's dark brown eyes, but the resemblance ended there. She was soft and smooth looking, no visible tattoos, no acne, and no apparent attitude. "I'm from Universal Heartland Liability and Casualty Assurance Company of America...Incorporated," pausing after "America" to take a breath.

The little girl came from behind her mother, pointed a plump pink finger at me, and cried, "That's the strange man!"

"If I could just ask you a few questions..." I began.

"About what?" Mrs. Marshall interrupted, sounding anxious.

The little girl started hopping up and down in front of me, waving her finger and chanting: "That's him, that's him."

Meanwhile, Mark was cracking his knuckles, one loud crunch at a time. In spite of the distractions, I was still smiling, an unnatural smile, as if I'd been waiting too long to have my picture taken, but a smile nonetheless. Trying to display patience and strength without gritting my teeth, I finished my sentence: "About the accident your son had in the '91 Ford."

"Oh. That."

"I already told him he could ask me anything he wanted," Mark interjected, trying to make *me* out to be the difficult one.

"I'm afraid I didn't catch your name."

"That's him, that's him, that's him..." the little girl repeated in a singsong voice. It was sounding less accusatory and more like a nursery rhyme set to music.

"Smith. John Smith."

Mark stopped cracking his knuckles and offered up a mirror-practiced, lip-curling smirk. "Where'd you leave Pocahontas?"

Wondering what enterprising history teacher managed to instill that bit of scholarship, I stepped around him and pulled on the screen door. I didn't realize it was locked and pulled on it hard enough to make an unpleasant screeching sound, almost ripping it off its hinges.

"Easy, man, easy." Mark held up his hands, palms out.

I took a deep breath and waited until Mrs. Marshall opened the door and invited me in. Once inside, things improved. She offered me coffee, which I gratefully accepted. Then she perched on the edge of an overstuffed chair across from me, hands demurely folded in her lap. I noticed that she was wearing an apron. Not one with a cutesy saying appropriate for someone about to barbeque, but a retro June Cleaver apron covered with bright flowers. Surely a woman wearing an apron wouldn't be difficult to deal with. I took a sip of lukewarm, bitter coffee.

Then the blue-eyed girl stopped singing and thrust a stuffed elephant covered with what looked like dog drool and smeared chocolate at me. I tried to decline, but she insisted. Finally, I thanked her, took it, and ditched the beast behind the couch. She retrieved it for me—three times. It was no use. In the end, I managed to balance it on the arm of my chair while the faithful retriever waited patiently for the next opportunity to fetch.

"Mandy just adores her elephant," Mrs. Marshall said, beaming at her daughter like she had done something clever. In a way, I felt honored. Children don't usually like me.

Mark had switched on the television, dividing his attention between what looked like men wearing camouflage struggling to make their way through a swamp and my conversation with his mother. I found my eyes irresistibly drawn to the men in the swamp. What were they up to, anyway?

As if she had been waiting for the right time to make her attack, Mrs. Marshall suddenly leaned forward and said in a firm voice, "Mark just *borrowed* the Ford." As my eyes darted back and forth between the men on the screen and the woman in the apron, she repeated her assertion. "He *borrowed* the Ford." Then she explained that she couldn't afford to buy her son a car on her small income, and although he was free to use the family station wagon whenever he wanted, there were times when he needed the use of another car.

Mark corroborated his mother's testimony with occasional grunts. "Unh," the Ford had been borrowed. "Unh," she couldn't afford to buy him a car. An extra "unh" seemed to indicate that he couldn't afford to buy himself a car either. "Unh," he was free to use the family station wagon. But his face said *who would want to?*

When I addressed him directly, I also learned that "humph" he didn't have a job, and "humph" he had no prior tickets for speeding.

There were no surprises or hiccups until I asked about Frances Metzker, the man from whom Mark allegedly *borrowed* the Ford. As soon as I mentioned the name, Mrs. Marshall leapt up to get more coffee, and Mark clicked the television off with the remote. Just when things were getting interesting in the swamp.

"He was confused," Mark complained in a whiney voice that was probably his own.

"You mean he claims that he sold you the car?" It was hard to keep the sarcasm out of my voice. Unfortunately, the information in the file wasn't complete.

"Definitely confused when the agent first talked to him. He knows I was just borrowing it. I told him if I liked it that I MIGHT consider buying the heap, but I didn't make any promises."

"The report says you had the Ford almost two weeks before the accident," I persisted. As they apparently knew, as an "additional insured," he was probably covered for a borrowed car under his mother's insurance, but most likely not for a purchased one, especially since he'd had it longer than the usual grace period.

"So?"

"And that you replaced the filters."

"They needed replacing." He was glaring at me as if he wished he could put me in a swamp with a few gators.

"Isn't that rather a long time to borrow a car when you don't really need one and aren't serious about buying it?"

A red line was creeping up his neck, but he wasn't about to back down. When the going gets tough, Clint's jaw turns to steel. "He wasn't in any hurry to get it back. I told him I'd do some work on the engine in exchange for driving it awhile. I like to work on cars, and he didn't say no."

It sounded a bit rehearsed, but a reasonable explanation. I'd seen cases like this before. The policyholder feels victimized and sees the insurance company as an amorphous rich uncle who can make everything all right. What they fail to realize is that an insurance company is a business like any other business, and it isn't good business to pay out on phony claims. That's where I come in. That's why I have a permanent job in a company with a future.

It was time to talk to Frances Metzker and get his side of the story.

I flipped my notepad shut and stood up. Mrs. Marshall had come back into the room and was leaning against the side of the couch. She wiped her hands on her apron and took one step toward me, beseeching me with her eyes. "Is everything going to be all right?" It was enough to melt your heart, but claims adjusters have to be strong.

"We try to be fair," I said. To do the line justice, I would need to turn slowly and walk off into the sunset, but it was still morning. Then, before I could say or do anything more, Mrs. Marshall began making little hiccupping sounds like she was about to lose control. Clutching my notepad to my chest, I backed away. I'm defenseless against a crying woman. Especially one wearing an apron.

The age lines around her mouth quivered. I was almost to the door. Then suddenly, her demeanor changed. Nostrils flaring, she angrily shook her head and practically shouted, "That awful woman. She's not really hurt, you know. She just wants to make some easy money off us."

Smoothing out her apron, she regained her composure. "Being alone with two children isn't easy. And all I have is a little savings." She lowered her head, tilted it to the side and peered up at me. Was she about to try the sexual come-on other adjusters were always talking about? It had never happened to me before, but I was ready with the appropriate response. It was going to be a bit awkward, though, in front of the kids.

"I couldn't afford to buy him a car," she repeated. Then she sighed and turned away. Mandy took that opportunity to push her favorite elephant at me again, and I took another step back. The aging mesh in the screen door made a horrible crunching noise as one corner pulled away from the metal. Stammering an apology, I pushed the pesky pachyderm aside and hastily made my exit.

The cat raised its head as if considering whether I was worth attacking, then collapsed back into her original pose. I was about to step around her when something Mrs. Marshal had said made me pause. I turned back to the house and saw her silhouetted in the doorway as if anticipating my return. Well, she needn't get her hopes up. I definitely wasn't going back inside.

14

Through the screen door, I asked, "Do you have any specific reason to believe Ms. Rosenblatt is faking her injury?" Mrs. Marshall's face was a mosaic of thousands of tiny squares as I looked at her through the mesh. "Well?" I prompted.

After a brief hesitation, the words poured out of her as if her complaints had finally reached flood stage. "Mark told me she was fine when she first got out of the car. It wasn't until they started talking about insurance that she grabbed her neck and began moaning."

I started to interrupt, but she anticipated my question and continued. "It wasn't shock."

"You can't know that for sure."

"Well, I can certainly tell when someone is trying to work the system...." She paused, blinking guiltily.

"You've talked with her, haven't you?" It wasn't exactly a Holmesian deduction, but a damn fine guess, nonetheless. Why didn't clients trust the insurance company to take care of matters for them instead of muddling things up? "You shouldn't be getting in touch with her," I said. "That's what I'm here for."

"*She* called *me.*" Mrs. Marshall protested. "She told me that I couldn't weasel out of paying for what my son did. I didn't know what to say. Mark did run into her. But why should I have to pay for it out of my savings? That just isn't fair." Then, remembering the key issue. "Especially since he only borrowed the car."

I considered informing her that it was doubtful she was personally liable for Pearl Rosenblatt's medical claims, but some people do sue everybody and anybody they consider even remotely responsible. And I didn't want to get into a complicated discussion of the possibilities when the lines around her mouth were starting to quiver again. It was time to make a run for it.

As I drove away from the Marshall residence, I thought about what she'd said about Rosenblatt's injuries. Not that I trusted anything Mark told her about the accident. He had lots of reasons to lie. But there might be witnesses who could either verify or disprove his story. And if the policy *did* apply, I would sooner or later have to determine whether Pearl Rosenblatt was, as Vivian Marshall implied, a sly old fox who was trying to take advantage of Universal. If so, it was my job to make sure she didn't. After all, as Mrs. Marshall had so aptly put it, "That just isn't fair."

Chapter Two

As I bumped over the potholes in Metzker's driveway, my 2001 Saturn started acting up. It sounded like a bronchial attack. Most of the time, I love my car, but it can be temperamental. I pounded on the dashboard and swore. The glove compartment flopped open. I'd been trying to get that thing open for weeks.

All I wanted was to get through my interview with Frances Metzker and call it a day. Then, after a good dinner and a hot bath, I looked forward to settling in with a rerun of The Office. I liked the older shows when Steve Carell was still Regional Manager of the Dunder Mifflin Scranton Branch. I'd seen most of them more than once and enjoyed being able to anticipate what was going to happen next.

Metzker's back yard looked like a used car lot. He was either having quite a party, or he was an insurance man's dream. I jerked to a stop as smoke started spewing from under the hood like a pulp mill smokestack the day after the federal inspector's quarterly visit. Then it gave a gasp of pain and made a couple of loud farting sounds. That had never happened before. Without waiting to find out if it was going to erupt into a volcano of flaming auto parts, I leapt out of the car and made tracks.

A young, grease-covered man stood about two feet away, calmly watching the show. "Car trouble?" he asked.

The Saturn was shivering in what I feared to be its death throes.

Before I could stop him, the young man bravely approached the car, opened the hood, waved away some steam and smoke, and began tinkering. I opened my mouth to call out a warning, then changed my mind. Judging by the number of cars around, he had more actual experience with older vehicles than I did. Then again, I didn't know if any of them actually ran.

"Are you Frances Metzker?" I asked, loud enough to be heard over the sizzling, tapping, and clanging.

"Frank," he corrected without looking up. My car was obviously more interesting to him than I was. How was I going to explain to Universal that a star witness had been blown up by a car? *My* car. Maybe I wouldn't have to admit that it was my car that had exploded. In any case, I'd better hurry up and ask my questions.

"I'm with Universal Heartland Liability and Casualty Assurance Company of...America, Incorporated. And—"

"Oh, you're here about Mark's accident." He briefly glanced at me before returning his attention to my car's motor. "Just a minute, I think I about have this." He plucked a few wires, tapped a thingamajig or two, and probed a whatsis. Then he straightened up and announced, "That ought to do it. Go ahead and shut it down. Then see if it starts up okay."

"Are you sure?" It did sound better. And there was no more smoke coming from the engine, although a thin ring of haze hovered above the car.

"Yeah, try it."

Seeing no alternative—it *was* my car, after all—I got inside and turned off the ignition. After taking a deep breath, I turned the key back on and held my breath. The engine turned over, caught, and buzzed contentedly, like a swarm of bees in a field of flowers. "Hey, it sounds good," I exclaimed.

Metzker grinned. "I like cars. And it's good to maintain ones that aren't being made anymore." He affectionately rubbed some grease on the Saturn's fender with a dirty palm. "But the color is a bit much."

"Yes," I admitted. "It was my mother's. She called it Bee. Yellow is one of her favorite colors."

"Hope you got a good deal on it."

"I did." At the time I bought the car from Mom, I needed transportation and didn't have much money, and I actually liked the color. I even continued to think of the car as Bee, although I never said it out loud. At least not in front of anyone. But I admit to being a little tired of the yellow car comments.

Maybe a new car in a more macho color should go on my wish list now that I was a permanent employee.

I shut down the engine and offered to pay Metzker for his help, but he turned me down, explaining that it was a simple fix. I gave in but felt guilty. If I had taken it to a car repair shop, I bet they would have claimed it took hours to diagnose and more hours to repair, resulting in a whopper of a bill and a short-term fix. It always made me wish that I had tinkered with cars as a teen instead of spending all of my time daydreaming about girls and playing video games.

"Well then, about Mark's accident," I began awkwardly, concerned that I had compromised my position by letting him help me for free.

"First, I have a few questions." That was *my* line, but I could hardly object. "If Mark 'borrowed' the Ford, then his insurance policy covers the accident, right?"

"Yes…" I tentatively replied. I didn't like the way this conversation was heading.

"But if he bought it, then he's out of luck, right?"

"Well, it depends on his coverage."

"But it's likely he isn't covered if it's a limited, minimum coverage policy, right?"

He'd been doing his homework. Or someone had done it for him. "Yesss," I admitted reluctantly. You had to pay extra to get extended coverage when you are driving another purchased vehicle."

"On the other hand, if I had sold it to him, then he wouldn't be covered for liability." He looked at me for agreement. I nodded.

"But, *your* insurance might cover both collision and liability…" I began. "That is, IF you have insurance?" It started as an explanation and ended as a question that I was sure I already knew the answer to.

"I hadn't actually been driving that car, so I wasn't worried about insurance." Translated, that meant no insurance.

"Do you buy and sell cars?" That was a loaded question in more ways than one, but I tried to make it sound like an innocent inquiry.

"Oh, I'm not in the business." He shook his head for emphasis. The area probably wasn't zoned for commercial use, and chances were he didn't have a dealer's license. Most likely, he sold cars without paying taxes to people not too concerned with the finer points of the law.

"You plan on keeping all of these cars?"

"You have an eye on one of them?" He smiled. "There's no law that says a private party can't sell a car now and them." I looked around. It was tempting. But that wasn't what I was there for.

The situation was becoming clear. Mrs. Marshall had most likely talked to her agent, who had obviously said enough to make them start thinking about the best way to escape financial responsibility and get the insurance company to pay. She, or Mark, had, in turn, talked with Metzker. Initially, Metzker had probably been upset because the Ford was almost demolished, and without collision insurance, there wouldn't be any money for repairs. But once he realized that the only way he was going to avoid a series of inconveniences and possibly some legal problems was to say that Mark had borrowed the car, he got on board with "the story."

Then there was the potential for a claim from Pearl Rosenblatt. If she didn't have sufficient coverage, and it was established that Mark was negligent, then she would go after him. When it became clear there was no money there, the whole mess would land in Universal's lap.

"When I talked with Mark, he seemed to be under the impression that you may have indicated to the agent that you thought he had purchased the Ford."

"Well, there may have been some confusion about the matter, but that's cleared up now." *Confusion.* It was such a convenient word. I'd have to remember that.

"Look, just to be clear. Was there a Bill of Sale?" Even if the deal was only made orally, it would still be a legitimate sale.

He shook his head no.

"Was the title transferred?"

He shook his head, no, again.

"What about price? Had you agreed on a price?"

He tugged at his ear, leaving a dark smudge on the lobe. "Well, we discussed price…but it wasn't a done deal yet."

I had no doubt that Frances Metzker was making some money buying and selling cars under the pretense that it was just an occasional private sale, not a business. And I had no doubt that Mark was one of his customers. But they had obviously come to some sort of understanding and weren't about to do or say anything that wasn't to their mutual advantage. I'd reached what appeared to be a dead-end.

Unwilling to admit defeat on what had started out to be my lucky day, I decided to try one more angle before returning to the office. The Lady of the Lamp Memorial Hospital was right on my way. If Dr. Leon Oliver, the orthopedic surgeon who had operated on Pearl Rosenblatt, was available, I could clear up a few issues concerning her injuries. To get the full medical report, I'd have to get a release from her, but the doctor might give me a few tidbits gratis. He was part-time staff at the hospital with an independent practice in the city, so I was taking a chance on catching him at the hospital, but that was better than trying to track him down at the ninth tee.

It turned out to be a day for medical miracles: first, the Saturn was brought back from the brink of death, then I arrived at the hospital while Dr. Oliver was on a coffee break. I didn't even know doctors took coffee breaks. So instead of cooling my heels reading month-old sports or gardening magazines in the waiting room, I got a free cup of coffee and a chance to talk with Dr. Oliver without delay.

As hospitals advertise more aggressively, they ought to consider using Dr. Oliver in an ad. He could rival any television doctor, even McDreamy. Distinguished looking, in his early sixties, with a mane of wavy hair and a low soothing voice. The perfect prototype.

"You're here about Mrs. Rosenblatt," he said in a confidential tone that implied he knew all about my weak kidneys, and he understood.

"Yes, I'm a claims adjuster, and I'm interested in learning more about the nature of her injuries and her present condition."

"As I'm sure you know, I can't share the details of a patient's medical condition with you." He softened the statement by raising his arched brows a quarter of an inch to let me know that he understood that this was inconvenient for me. "But I can tell you that she had a pinched spinal cord nerve, and I operated to relieve the pressure."

It seemed to me that he *was* giving me details, but I wasn't about to complain, "My understanding is that she is confined to a wheelchair at this point..."

He didn't wait for me to finish my sentence. "She seems to feel that it's necessary."

"But you don't?"

"All I can tell you is the operation was a success." He shook his head sadly from side to side. "Unfortunately, Mrs. Rosenblatt refuses to come in for further testing and examination."

"Oh." I couldn't think of anything else to say. When I fell silent, he again breached confidentiality without prompting.

"She's a very emotional woman, and she has succumbed to feelings of self-pity about being the victim of another person's careless act. She, therefore, refuses to try to stand and walk. But physically, she should be capable of both." The laugh lines around his eyes were beginning to look as though they had been etched in stone instead of earned through laughter. "She is no longer responding in a rational manner," he continued. As if suddenly realizing that his bedside manner was slipping, he added, "Ah, in my opinion, that is." He glanced quickly around. 'You realize, of course, that this is strictly off the record. I'm just trying to be helpful."

I nodded. I had been hoping for a scrap of information. Instead, his venting had given me a number of suggestive facts to chew on. Maybe Mrs. Rosenblatt was also putting the squeeze on her doctor. He obviously thought Mrs. Rosenblatt's injuries were psychosomatic, or possibly faked.

"So, you believe that she is, ah, deluding herself regarding the seriousness of her injuries." Even if it wasn't for the record, I wanted to be clear on that point.

"What I am saying is that there is no way of knowing the extent of her disability without further tests and perhaps therapy. One doesn't get up and walk away from the operating table, you know."

It crossed my mind that Frankenstein had done just that, but I would reserve judgment until after I'd met Pearl Rosenblatt. For the present, I would hold off judgment on whether she was the victim of teenage recklessness or simply a greedy hypochondriac.

"Is she under another's doctor's care that you know of?"

"Not at this hospital."

That was the last question I got the opportunity to ask. Dr. Oliver was called away to an emergency. An orthopedic emergency didn't sound good to me. Visions of crushed bones and twisted backs haunted me as I hurriedly made my way down several long white corridors and out through the glass doors at the hospital entrance.

The sun was still shining, and my curiosity was piqued, so I decided I might as well make one more stop. The sooner I determined whether Pearl Rosenblatt's injuries were fact or feigned, the easier it would be to make a recommendation about the claim. And even if her injuries were serious, it was possible that she had outstanding insurance that would limit our exposure.

"My bologna has a first name…." I stopped singing the instant I realized *what* I was singing. That's an insidious ad. It captures mind space and pops out when you least expect it. I like to sing, but I can never remember the words to songs. Commercials are different. You get so many opportunities to memorize them. But singing about bologna feels demeaning. I switched to "I'd like to teach the world to sing in perfect harmony." At least it was about global goodwill.

Pearl Rosenblatt lived in one of those cheap development areas where a bulldozer had systematically removed every tree and bump, leaving the terrain flat, brown, and somewhere south of uninteresting. Then an architect had been called in to complete the project by designing one house as a clone for all the others. The only way to tell them apart was by color and which side the garage was on. White, cream, brown. Left, right, left, right. A code to help people find their way home while preserving uniformity.

The Rosenblatt house was the fifth brown house with a garage on the left. But it was also distinguished from its counterparts by being just a bit dingier, drooping at the edges, slowly losing the battle against the elements. One of the house numbers was missing, but its outline was clear against the faded paint of the rest of the house. I pulled up and looked around. The only activity was a young girl playing hopscotch on the sidewalk. I got out of my car and headed up the walk. One of the front window curtains moved as if drawn aside by an invisible hand, but I didn't see a face.

Shortly after I knocked, the door was flung open, and a woman in a wheelchair sat there staring at me. She had spikey dyed red hair, a large red nose, and a red blouse that was buttoned wrong. Her perfume was straight bourbon.

"Pearl Rosenblatt?" I inquired.

"Yes?"

"I'm from Universal Heartland Liability and Casualty Assurance Company of America, Incorporated. I have a few questions." I paused, waiting for her to invite me in.

"Yes?" she repeated.

"I was wondering if I might ask you a few questions." I could repeat myself too.

"Yes," she said again, only this time it wasn't a question. But she made no move to let me come in.

I pulled out my notepad, tried to balance it on one knee while standing, became irritated, and plopped myself down on the front steps. If she didn't care what the neighbors thought, why should I?

In a voice that admitted no prior break of etiquette, she finally asked, "Would you like to come in?"

I quickly got up, dusted off the seat of my pants, and followed her into a cluttered living room full of worn, musty-smelling furniture. Not the kind of stuff that ends up in antique shops with high-priced tags, but the kind that ends up at thrift stores. The rug was thin and spotted, a matrix of aging flowers and years of living. Everything in the room had the look of a second-rate motel, except for the large television in the corner. It hunkered there like a primitive god waiting for the evening sacrifice.

After removing a magazine and a slipper, I settled into a faded chair and turned toward the potential claimant. "As I said, I'm with...the insurance company investigating the Marshal accident." She nodded for me to continue. "I understand that you were injured when the cars collided." I wanted to keep my description of the incident as neutral as possible. "Could you tell me about the nature of your injuries?"

"It was his fault. All his fault. He did this to me." She recited the words in a low, whispery voice, like she was putting a hex on Mark for what he had done. For just an instant, I had a flicker of sympathy for him. Pearl Rosenblatt was a bit scary.

"But about your injuries," I prompted. "We have not yet decided to take an adverse position on liability."

"What does that mean?" Her crone's eyes narrowed. I half expected her to whip out a wand and turn me into a toad.

"That means we haven't yet determined whether Mr. Marshall was negligent. Nor do we have a position on any potential claim that you might make."

"*Mister* Marshall! What a crock." She started to laugh, but it turned into a full-throated cough that seemed to drive all the humor from her body. When she recovered, her voice was loud and hard and determined. "He's going to pay. He's definitely going to pay for what he did to me." I pictured a straw-filled effigy of Mark with pins sticking out of uncomfortable places.

"Universal is not trying to shirk its responsibilities," I assured her. "But we have to investigate first. That's why I would like you to explain the extent and nature of your injuries." It occurred to me that she wasn't quite sober. That would account for her peculiar behavior and the two empty liquor bottles on the kitchen table.

She suddenly became teary-eyed. "Look at me," she ordered. "See what he did to me? Just look…." A tear streaked the white powder on her face, followed by a drool of mascara.

"I assume you are unable to walk," I said. I was reluctant to discuss how she looked and didn't know what to say to discourage more tears.

"If I could walk," she challenged, "why would I be sitting in this thing?"

Trying to reassert control of the conversation, I asked, "Were you unable to walk immediately after the accident?"

"I was in shock." She paused and licked her thin lips, her eyes darting to the empty bottles on the table. "I was in a great deal of pain, but I didn't know how bad I'd been hurt. Moving around just made things worse." The statement sounded rehearsed.

"Then you had an operation."

She leaned forward in her wheelchair, gripped the armrests, and glared at me. "And that bastard screwed things up but good. If it hadn't been for that operation..." She ended in mid-sentence, as if aware she was off script. "Not that I wasn't hurt bad before the operation."

"But your current condition is not the sole result of the auto accident."

"Don't twist my words." She looked around, saw a half-full glass on an end table and wheeled over to it. She drank down its contents with a loud slurping sound. After wiping her mouth with the back of her hand, she turned back to me. "They're both going to pay. That no-good doctor and *Mister* Marshall. Both of them are going to pay for what they did to me."

"You do have full use of your arms and hands," I observed.

"This is a good day. Not every day is a good day."

Using my official let's-get-down-to-brass-tacks tone, I said, "Mrs. Rosenblatt, you cannot expect an insurance company to pay for an injury unless they are appraised of the nature and extent of that injury."

Mimicking my let's-get-down-to-brass-tacks tone, she said, "I can't walk. I can't work. My life is ruined. Does that tell you what you need to know?"

"Well, yes and no. It doesn't tell me why you are no longer going to see your doctor about your injuries."

"Because he's a quack, that's why."

"There are other doctors. Have you considered getting a second opinion?"

"No doctor can do me any good." Her hands moved restlessly in her lap, searching for a glass that wasn't there.

"You do realize that we can't pay a claim without medical evidence and an independent medical exam. And if you go to court, a judge might compel you to undergo a medical examination to ascertain the validity of any claims you make." Universal agents were not supposed to threaten potential claimants, but someone needed to let this woman know that her current course of

26

action would not be all beer and Skittles.

"No judge is going to let you push me around." Threat for threat. A draw. Getting a generous settlement out of a judge or jury by playing on their sympathy was a common fantasy, like winning the Irish Sweepstakes or finding a wallet full of money in the gutter. But if she was going to play that game and win, some lawyer would have to earn his or her contingent fee by transforming her into everyone's favorite grandma, no easy task in my opinion. On second thought, instead of getting a lawyer, maybe she ought to try a trip to Lourdes.

"No one is trying to push you around. But even a judge or jury will need to hear expert testimony." I paused, counting to six so as not to sound too eager. "Perhaps we could expedite settlement for a quick payment of, say, $1,500? And you would still be free to sue the doctor if you want." It was too early to settle, but I had a bad feeling about how this was going to turn out if I waited.

"$1,500?!" The offer was low, but it was company policy to start low. And I had offered up Dr. Oliver as a way to get more. However, I felt a little guilty about that. Now it was her turn to propose a counteroffer.

"Get out!" she screamed. She apparently didn't know the rules of negotiation. "Get out NOW!"

I tried to pacify her with "there, there's" and "there's no need to get excited," but it didn't work. When her face became the color of her nose, I leapt to my feet and bolted for the door. The lawyer who took her case would have to work on her manners as well as her appearance.

Once outside, I tried to act normal, hoping no one heard her screaming. It's against company policy to create a scene. Universal employees are supposed to maintain a dignified appearance commensurate with the Universal tradition established over fifty years of service to its clientele. But neither the training nor the manual covered what you were supposed to do when someone continued to scream at you as you hurried away. I couldn't quite make out the words, but the intent was clear. Fortunately, the only one around was the girl who'd been playing hopscotch. She stood there, knee socks sagging around thin ankles, enjoying my discomfort in the way only a child can enjoy adult chagrin, unabashedly staring, the glitter of braces flashing as the sun caught her unrestrained smile.

When I got in my car, I glanced at my watch. I knew it was old-fashioned to wear a watch, but I'd tried using only my cell phone, and it was never in the right place when I wanted to know what time it was. There was something I wasn't doing right. According to my timepiece, it was too late for lunch and too early for dinner. But I was hungry, so I pulled into one of those plastic palaces with bright orange fixtures and a menu full of pictures of high-cholesterol food. I ordered a number forty-seven and a cup of coffee with cream. The cream was twenty-five cents extra.

I dumped the cream into my coffee and stirred vigorously. It refused to blend, the cream at odds with the coffee, like my client refusing to cooperate. Symbolic? Or just bad coffee? I added sugar and stirred some more, trying to decide whether it was worth it to ask for a fresh cup.

The number 47 was greasy and had too much salt even for me. But I ate it anyway while mulling what I had learned about the case so far. I was certain that Mark and Frances were lying about the car being borrowed, but I was doubtful that I could prove it. I also strongly suspected that Pearl Rosenblatt was out to make a buck off real or fake injuries. We wouldn't know which until when and if she filed a claim against us. And if she did and it went to a jury trial, she might be able to get a jury to believe her, no matter what the medical testimony turned out to be. Jury verdicts were difficult to predict. I'd been right to offer her an early settlement to avoid a higher cost later on, but obviously, she didn't think so.

Perhaps the easiest thing for me to do was to turn the case over to one of the senior claims adjusters. It was not only the easy thing to do, but from the company's point of view, probably the correct thing. Still, I felt dissatisfied. Maybe I should have ordered number forty-six.

I chewed on my thoughts and number forty-seven some more. If it hadn't been my very first day as a permanent employee, I might have opted for the easy way out. But it felt wrong to give up so quickly. I needed to at least talk with the two witnesses to the accident. And it might not hurt to snoop around Pearl's a bit. Although that was undoubtedly outside the scope of my investigation. But she had riled me. Maybe I could catch her doing something athletic, like climbing a tree or hanging out the laundry. It's not that I enjoy invading someone's privacy; I'm basically a nice guy. I don't cheat on my income tax (except for occasionally declaring an iffy charitable deduction), I don't let my dog poop on the neighbor's lawn (I don't have a dog), and I never jog around the neighborhood in a fancy sweat suit before going to work. But I have been known to spy on people in the line of duty. Somebody's got to do it.

Chapter Three

"Is this some kind of joke?" a gruff voice asked as an eye filled the peephole on the door of apartment 201. I'd knocked, but no one had answered. Feeling frustrated, I jammed my card under the door, scrunching it between the threshold and whatever was on the other side. Before I could leave, it had magically disappeared. Now it was being thrust back at me by a bodiless arm that had appeared as the door opened just barely enough for the arm to reach through. I smoothed it out and realized the problem: "Good for $1 off on any box of Frosted Flakes at participating grocers."

"Wrong card," I mumbled apologetically, reaching into my other pocket. Collecting coupons is a habit I've picked up from my mother, although I never use them. I'm too embarrassed. But I have quite a collection. "Here," I said, reaching in through the narrow opening. Someone plucked the card from my fingers as I explained, "I'm from Universal Heartland Liability and Casualty Assurance Company of America, Incorporated." My voice almost gave out before saying the full company name.

"What's this?!" the voice asked as the arm slipped back through the door again, my card held distastefully between two fingers. "I don't want any 'assurance.'" The arm hung suspended in space, waiting for me to take back my card.

"I called you at five o'clock, but you weren't home."

"I work for a living." My card fluttered to the floor as the hand on the end of the arm dropped it. The arm withdrew, and the door started to close.

"I need to talk with you about an accident you witnessed," I said, putting my face against the tiny space that was fast disappearing. The door stopped moving, as if I had stuffed something between the door and the jamb to keep it open. Fortunately, it wasn't a body part that had stopped the movement, although my lips were in danger if he decided to finish closing the door. I straightened up and took a step back.

"I've given a statement to the police." The door opened a couple of inches.

"I just have a few questions. It would be easiest for both of us if you could answer them now." It was an empty threat, but hopefully, he didn't know that.

The door slowly opened while he explained that he could only spare a few minutes. One glance around the fancy apartment told me why. A table just off the kitchen was set for two, wine glasses gleaming in readiness next to an open bottle of red wine. Soft, sensuous music filled the room, coming from strategically placed, expensive-looking speakers. Pillows on the sofa were plumped, the shag rug quivering in anticipation, the door to the bedroom invitingly half open. The lights probably dimmed automatically or on a voice command such as, "You look beautiful this evening."

As for Malcolm Chillquist, he was impeccably dressed in a casual, but not too casual, outfit. Snug-fitting pants and tapered silk shirt with just a few dark chest hairs peeking through his open collar, poking up between the links on the gold chain necklace circling his neck. A sophisticated tiger waiting to be unleashed.

"This won't take long," I assured him.

"Good."

Uninvited, I sat on the couch, careful not to disturb the fur-covered pillow. Tan cheetah faux, I noted. I'd seen them advertised online. "Now then," I said, pulling out my notebook. "Would you mind telling me in your own words what you saw?" I always thought that was a strange thing to say—whose words would he use other than his own? "I'm especially interested in what you saw *after* the crash."

"You don't want to know about the one car blasting the stop sign?"

"Did the Ford fail to stop? Was he speeding?" I might as well know the worst, although fault was not the issue at this point.

31

"I don't know if he was speeding, but he hardly paused at the stop sign before entering the intersection."

"And the other car?"

"I wasn't looking at the other car."

"So, afterwards, what did you see when the two drivers got out of their respective cars?"

"Well, let me think." His eyebrows moved toward each other, and his eyes closed slightly, replaying the scene in his mind. "I don't know which one got out of their car first. Both got out pretty fast. They were both mad and lit into each other right off the bat." He opened his eyes and relaxed his brows.

"Lit into each other?"

"You know. They started arguing about who had the right of way, whose fault it was, that sort of thing."

"Were they standing?"

"Yes, about halfway between the two cars."

"Both were standing?" I asked just to be sure. Although it seemed unlikely that Mark would have been arguing with her if she had crawled out to meet him.

"Yes." He seemed puzzled by my question, then filled in a few details. "The old woman kept pointing at the stop sign and waving her arms up and down. I thought she might hit him. He was all red-faced and mad. Claimed he didn't see her. But he would say that, wouldn't he?"

"What do you mean?"

"Well, if he had seen the other car, he wouldn't have run into it."

"So, both were angry, and neither appeared to be injured?"

"It didn't look like it. But then the woman started complaining that her neck hurt." He paused. "Victims in shock often don't realize how badly they've been hurt."

I didn't write that down. "I just need to know what you actually saw," I said.

"Well, I think they realized at this point that there were a number of people watching, so they quieted down. Then she slumped onto the pavement and lay there moaning. It was awful."

"What happened next?"

"Well, there was nothing I could do. You aren't supposed to move people with neck injuries, you know, so I told the young man that I would call the police and he should wait where he was. A woman bystander offered to watch over the old lady while I made the call. I had to walk over and take a look at the street sign so I could give them accurate directions. They arrived within minutes of the call. Pretty impressive, actually. Then I gave them my name and went on my way." He glanced at the door to suggest that he had told me all he knew, and it was time for me to leave.

"Before she slumped to the ground, did the woman seem to be having any difficulty walking or moving around?"

He gave me an "I know what you're hinting at" look but seemed to consider my question carefully before answering. "Not that I could tell." Before he could lecture me again on the effects of shock, I asked another question.

"Did she say anything about the nature of her injury or the location of the pain?"

"No, nothing too specific. Just that her neck hurt like hell, and it was the kid's fault, and he wasn't going to get away with it. She kept rambling like that." His eyes darted to a piece of art on the wall, possibly a clock without referent points, two black hands snaking from the center pointing in the same general direction as the hands on my watch. "As I said, I've already given a statement to the police."

Thanking him for his time and cooperation, I stood up and let him herd me toward the exit. As we reached the door, he glanced anxiously around, checking to make sure that my presence hadn't in some way made his trap less inviting. Whoever she was, she didn't have a chance.

One witness down and one to go. If Vicki Martinelli's version of what had happened after the accident matched Chillquist's, I would definitely spend some time and effort trying to disprove Ms. Rosenblatt's injuries. Saving money for the insurance company is a form of "adjusting," and any claims man who expects to move up in the company has to become an expert in this field.

When I called Vicki Martinelli to see if I could drop by with a few questions, she didn't seem particularly thrilled, more like underwhelmed and resistant. Witnesses often act as though they are doing you a favor by cooperating. Somewhere along the line the concept of civic duty has been lost, replaced by making a quick buck or looking out for number one. To top it all off, witnesses are supposed to be neutral, but they are, after all, only people. Each one brings their own baggage to the table, seeing events and people through their personal filters. I knew this in advance but was still somewhat unprepared for Vicki Martinelli.

At first, she was convinced I was a telephone pervert, insisting if I wasn't, I should prove it. I didn't know whether she expected me to say that I was an Elks member in good standing, would settle for knowing I had a library card, or wanted me to recite the Pledge of Allegiance. Having company identification wasn't good enough. Apparently, even perverts carry cards.

Finally, I suggested that she call Universal in the morning to verify my credentials. Then we could set up a time to meet at her convenience. To my surprise, she seemed disappointed with that option. Instead, she suggested I come by after dinner, about seven-thirty. Did I have her address?

That worked out perfectly. Although I hate to cut into my evenings, I didn't have any plans, and I was anxious to talk with her. Besides, if she *had* called Universal, it was just possible someone would have said, "John who?" Then even a letter from the Pope wouldn't have helped me gain admittance to Ms. Martinelli's apartment.

I had just enough time for a quick Subway sandwich and a cup of coffee before heading to her apartment in a modest but aging section of the city. Her brick building with the chipped gargoyles above the entrance looked about ready for demolition, but it had probably looked that way for fifty years plus. It could be argued it was more of an eyesore than an historic landmark.

She had one of those chain safety locks that allows someone to open the door about an inch and a half to take a look at a would-be attacker before they kick the door in. "Who are you?" I could see her eyes above the chain. They were large, brown, and weary.

"John Smith. We spoke earlier."

"Is that your real name?"

"Yes." I never get anywhere arguing about my name; people automatically assume it's an alias.

"And who do you work for?" She sounded like one of my old grade school teachers about to criticize me for getting an answer wrong.

Taking a deep breath, I said: "Universal Heartland Liability and Casualty Assurance Company of America, Incorporated."

"You mean insurance, don't you?" She was helping me get my answer right. A kind teacher.

"No," I said, reaching into my pocket for a card.

"Watch it," she said. The chain grew slack as she inched the door closed a notch. I whipped out a card and slipped it to her, thankful to retrieve my fingers intact. At first, she acted as though I'd handed her a miniature bomb, but just moments later, she released the chain and invited me inside. I had the feeling she was holding a rolling pin behind her back, just in case.

My interview with Ms. Martinelli—Vicki—went well. I was served weak tea from a flowered porcelain pot that played some unrecognizable melody every time she lifted it to pour. She also served some crumbly cakes that were awkward to eat but quite tasty. Then, one delicate pinkie gracefully gripping the handle of her china cup with her little finger aiming off into space, Vicki happily chatted about the accident. She gave me more detail than a play-by-play sports commentator. Then she concluded, "She wasn't really hurt, you know."

I gulped too much weak tea and sputtered, "What?" as water dribbled out one side of my mouth.

"She's faking."

"What makes you say that?" Trying to be discreet, I coughed so I had an excuse to wipe the tea off my chin.

"Weren't you listening to what I said?" She sounded like my A grade had just been changed to a C-.

"Yes, of course, but I'm not sure how you can be so certain."

"Well, as I said, she was able to move before and after she laid down on the pavement. And note that I said 'laid down.'" I assumed she wasn't referring to her grammar. "She didn't collapse or fall down. She simply got down on the ground and sprawled out. It was an intentional act."

"But—"

"And, as I already explained, she complained about being uncomfortable, so I slipped a blanket under her." She looked expectantly at me, but I wasn't sure what she expected. "You can't 'slip' a blanked under someone just like that." She paused, waiting for me to catch up.

"Oh."

"The woman held herself up while I slipped the blanket under her. You can't do that with an injured spine." She gave me a self-satisfied smile. "I know. I used to be a nurse's aide."

Suddenly I saw a different side of the prim and quaint Vicki Martinelli. "You did that deliberately, didn't you?"

"Well, it did cross my mind that someone might ask me about what I witnessed, so I wanted to be sure."

I left Ms. Martinelli's needing to go to the bathroom from drinking so much tea, but happy. So what if Frances and Mark conspired to sluff off the responsibility for what they had done. At least Pearl Rosenblatt wasn't going to take us to the cleaners. Not with a resourceful woman like Vicki in our corner.

Chapter Four

The police officer was polite enough, although he scared me half to death, sneaking up on me like that. It was nine o'clock, Thursday morning, just an hour after I'd begun my stakeout watching the Rosenblatt house. It seemed that someone had reported a peeping Tom in the vicinity. It couldn't be me, I explained to the officer; peeping Toms didn't do their peeping from parked cars. Then I showed him my card and told him I was on a case. He didn't make me get out of the car but leaned in the open window and lectured me on a citizen's right to privacy, and informed me that loitering was against the law. That apparently satisfied his legal obligations when responding to a neighbor's complaint. He left as quietly as he had come.

As I followed his departure in my rearview mirror, I noticed the police car parked a few spaces back. How had I missed it? Was it possible that I had dozed off? I *was* feeling a bit sleepy. What I needed was a stroll around the block to get my blood circulating.

It was a beautiful spring day, the soft grass of the parking strip lent a spring to my step, and the scent of flowers and freshly mowed lawn mingled with the faint aroma of fertilizer. It's too bad green lawns, flowers, and fertilizer so often go together. What one needed was a nose filter to let in the good smells like coffee and fresh bread, and keep out the bad, like fertilizer and vomit. But I wasn't complaining. It's a great job that gives me an excuse to commune with Mother Nature while putting in my hours.

I returned to my car refreshed, alert and hungry. I opened another bag of chips and popped the lid on a lukewarm Coke while humming a classic

Coke ad, hoping for something to happen soon.

The rest of the day passed slowly and unproductively. It took two more strolls just to make sure I stayed awake.

Friday was another lovely day, but by late afternoon Mother Nature and I weren't getting along too well. I had hay fever, and my nose was sunburned. There had been too many walks needed to stay awake. In addition, the holster-like camera case looped over my belt kept flopping around. Nothing serious, just irritating. I needed to learn how to retrieve a camera quickly from my pants pocket so I could do away with the case. But whenever I put a camera in my pocket, it always seemed to get caught on something just when I needed to take a picture. Until I figured out a better way, I'd have to put up with the case. Step, flop, step, flop.

My only relief from the monotony of forced walks and sitting was eating. I'd probably gained five pounds already. That's two and a half pounds a day or point two pounds per hour for each twelve-hour shift. Or, figured another way, each hour was costing me about $2.50 in supplies, i.e., food, and there was no way I was going to be able to pad my expense account to cover it all. Especially since the stakeout was something extra I was doing to demonstrate my value to the company.

To top it all off, the only action I'd seen was Pearl lifting a glass to her thin lips. No reason to even flex my camera finger. If she didn't actually need that wheelchair, she was putting on a good act. Of course, it was possible that she'd made me and that each time she saw me drive off to use the john at the gas station down the road, she jumped up, ran outside, and danced a jig on the front lawn.

On the third day of surveillance, I suffered from an advanced case of the yawns. My mouth kept stretching open, forcing my eyes closed. Not even eating or walking around the block seemed to help. I longed to exchange my car seat for a double bed and clean sheets, but as a permanent employee wanting to prove himself, I remained committed to the proposition that if I just waited long enough, I would catch Pearl using her legs for transportation. It's like trying to gamble just a little in Vegas. You can't quit, because the minute you leave your machine, someone will sit down and hit the jackpot on it.

The only picture I took during my first three-day vigil was of the nose of a very angry dog. He charged me during one of my walks, yelping like I was out to steal the family jewels. He chased me down an alley and around the block. I accidentally snapped a picture as I scrambled back into the car just ahead of his snapping, slobber-filled, toothy jaws.

Sunday, it rained. A real downpour. I hauled out my rain gear, but I didn't put it on. Instead, I crawled back into bed and slept until noon. No one really wins a jackpot in Vegas; it's a myth perpetuated by casino owners who want to part you from your hard-earned cash.

First thing Monday morning, I called the Lady of the Lamp Memorial Hospital and asked to speak to the person in charge of the hospital's insurance. I had decided to change tactics. Before wasting any more time on Pearl, I would find out if she had made claims against either the doctor or the hospital to see if there would be another contributor to the settlement. And I might also save some time by talking to the insurance adjuster for the hospital to see if they would share any medical data on Pearl. I'd had it with the outdoor approach.

After cutting me off twice, the operator put me through to the assistant director's office. Byron Cheever was attending a conference, his admin informed me, but she obligingly gave me the name of the firm that handled the hospital's insurance: Babcock-Chalmers Brokers of Insurance. The agent's name was Wallis Conklin.

Babcock-Chalmers is a nationwide firm with a small branch office in one of the modern downtown buildings, a steel and window structure that made me feel cold the minute I stepped inside. I glanced up, half expecting to see ice stalactites hanging from the high ceiling in the lobby.

The elevator trip from the lobby to the thirty-third floor was nonstop, my ears popping in protest at the rapid ascent. The bouncy, abrupt stop threw my equilibrium out of whack and made my stomach do a U-turn. I've always been sensitive to motion. I was carsick a lot as a kid and distinguished myself as a teenager by spewing vomit over everyone when I went on a zero gravity ride at the state fair. Still feeling slightly unsteady and queasy, I had another unsettling moment when I caught sight of the blond receptionist at Babcock-Chalmers. She was all soft angles and dimples with a smile that could have been the inspiration for *When Irish Eyes Are Smiling*. She was definitely capable of stealing *my* heart away.

"May I help you?" I had the impression she was repeating the question. Had I been just standing there staring?

"I'm sure you can," I said with feeling, grinning foolishly, wishing I could spend the next ten years nibbling the dimples on her knees. "I'm here to see Wallis Conklin."

In a voice as soft as cotton candy, she directed me to another desk further down the hall. I had no choice but to move on.

At the next desk, there was a small sign attached to an inbox that read: "Miss Zelda Gunnar." I was still grinning at the thought of getting it on with the receptionist when I came face-to-face with Miss Zelda Gunner. As I took in the lean woman's stern features and Norman Rockwell hairdo, I felt the smile slide off my face.

"May I help you?" Her tone made it clear that she didn't have a single dimple on her entire body. I asked if I could see Mr. Conklin.

"Do you have an appointment?" She glanced at her computer to verify that I was an unwanted drop-in.

"No, I'm sorry, I don't. I was in the neighborhood." That sounded lame even to me.

"Mr. Conklin is a busy man."

"Yes, I'm sure he is. But this is about an important matter concerning hospital insurance that was just called to my attention, and since I was in the neighborhood—." I stopped when I realized I was repeating myself.

"Please have a seat. I'll see if he has time to see you." I was dismissed in a tone that brooked no argument. She was the gatekeeper, and I was a person to be let in if and when she decided I was worthy.

Pretending I was fine with waiting until she granted me admission, I strolled over to a chair, prepared to sit it out. Although it was a standard issue office chair with a straight back and not much padding, it was still better than sitting in the car in front of Pearl's, whiling away the hours waiting for her to do something besides drink.

By the time I sat down, Zelda had disappeared. Either she was taking a break or she had gone to tell Conklin in person about the guy in the waiting room who thought he could just waltz in and get an appointment with him.

To my surprise, moments later, Zelda returned with a paunchy "oh dear" type in an expensive suit following in her wake. He introduced himself as Wally Conklin and ushered me down the hall and into his office with a flurry of arms and apologies for keeping me waiting. Before I could utter a word, he began explaining the ins and outs of hospital insurance. I had to interrupt and break the bad news about not being there to purchase insurance. "It's about the coverage for the Lady of the Lamp," I said. "I'm a claims adjuster and am hoping you can give me some information about their coverage."

He immediately went from sell mode to irritated. "Well, that's, well, their policy information is confidential."

"Perhaps it would be best if I talked with Mr. Cheever," I said, implying that I had come to him as a courtesy, and if he didn't give me what I needed, I would go over his head.

"No, that won't be necessary, depending on what you need to know." He started going through some files on his desk. "I believe I have that file right here." After a few more minutes of checking the same pile of folders several times, he pulled one out and announced, "Ah, here it is." Then he started explaining the finer points of the policy, points I didn't need to know.

"I'm only interested in your errors and omissions coverage," I interrupted.

"I'm almost there." He continued to tick off benefits and read obscure clauses out loud.

After a while, I became suspicious. "Are you reading from the actual Lady of the Lamp policy?" I asked when he paused to catch his breath.

"Well, not exactly."

"What does 'not exactly' mean?"

"It's a standard policy."

"But it could differ from what the Lady of the Lamp has in place?"

"Only in minor detail."

"Do you have a copy of their policy?"

Without responding directly, he started reading again, trying to snow me with fine print and subclauses, making me very suspicious that something was not right. He would have been better off sticking with his "the policy is confidential" approach and escorting me back to the lobby.

I stood up. "Look, all I want to know is whether Pearl Rosenblatt has filed a claim against the hospital." Well, I wanted to know a lot more than that, but that was a start.

He stared at me for a moment. "I'm afraid that name is not familiar." Then why had he read the policy to me? Unless all of my instincts were as dead as the bounce in last year's tennis shoes, there was something fishy going on.

I left with more questions than answers. Why was Conklin so nervous? Why didn't he ask me more questions about why I was there? And, if he was going to read policies to people, why didn't he take a drama course? Not only was he a lousy reader—no inflection, just a boring monotone—but he wasn't a very good liar.

As I went by Miss Zelda Gunner's desk, her eyes roamed over me as if checking to make sure I hadn't stolen anything. To make matters worse, my dimpled blond wasn't at her desk when I passed through the reception area. The place was empty as only a place once blessed with beauty can be empty. Doubly disappointed, I headed for the elevator.

A hunger pang and a glance at my watch told me it was almost lunchtime. That gave me an idea. I decided to hang around to see if Conklin left his office to get a bite. I pulled out a few pieces of paper I had in one of my pockets, a grocery list, and an ad for a tire sale, and pretended to be studying them. For good measure, I also got out a pen. People are suspicious of someone standing around, not doing anything.

When the first person arrived at the elevators, I faked scribbling a note on the top paper. Glancing at the look on her face, I decided I didn't look sufficiently occupied to justify hanging around, so I put the paper and pen away and got out my cell phone. That seemed to work as several people passed me without a second glance until it rang while I was talking. I quickly turned off the ringtone and continued my phony conversation.

After a dribble of early birds, people began pouring out of offices at noon, rushing to catch elevators. I didn't need a ruse to be standing there. I wouldn't have been aggressive enough to get on one of the elevators anyway. Neither my dimpled blond nor the ominous Miss Gunner was among the participants in the mass exodus. But Wally Conklin was. I turned away as he hurried past, then waited until his elevator reached the lobby before making my way back toward his office.

The reception area was vacant, but I could see Miss Gunner's elongated shadow through the glass door of the office next to Conklin's. Hoping she wasn't looking, I tried not to call attention to my presence, sprinting the last few steps before lunging into his office. Then, heart pounding, I pressed my ear against the door and listened for the sound of pursuit. It crossed my mind that I would probably be better off standing to one side in case she had seen me and pushed the door open, but it was too late for that maneuver and, fortunately, I didn't need it.

There were still files on his desk, and his computer was also on. I hit a key to see if he had logged off. Unbelievably—he hadn't. He probably didn't think anyone would have the nerve to try to get past Miss Gunnar. I typed in "Lady of the Lamp," and a folder obediently came up. Inside the folder, there wasn't anything labeled Rosenblatt. I also checked under Marshall. Then I did a general search for those names. Nothing.

Conklin's desk was my next target. As my eyes moved across the disorganized desktop, I caught a glimpse of movement at the door. I stood frozen in place as it slowly opened, leaving Zelda Gunnar silhouetted against the light like a statue guarding the entrance to a tomb. Telling myself there was no need to panic, I mumbled something about leaving my pipe on his desk. Oh my god, did I say pipe! No one smoked anymore, especially pipes.

"Your 'pipe.' You left your pipe on Mr. Conklin's desk?"

"No," I said. "I put my sunglasses on his desk when I was searching for my card." Did that even make sense?

"Your sunglasses?"

"Yes. Have you seen them? Pricey, Ralph Lauren, automotive collection." I pay attention to the ads, but I wouldn't spring for expensive sunglasses. I was always misplacing them. "Thought I might have left them here. But…" I pointedly looked around. "I don't see them anywhere. Do you?"

Miss Gunner stood there, silent as death, her eyes probing me, waiting.

"Well, that's that, then. I'd better be going." As I tried to step around her, she reached out and grabbed something off my head.

"These what you are looking for?" They didn't look pricey at all, but they were sunglasses.

"Oh, I feel so stupid," I said, meaning it. "Thank you so much. They're prescription, you know." Of course, she didn't know. When I'm nervous, I talk too much. "Well, I'm off. I have a lunch appointment."

I rushed to the elevator and pushed the button, expecting at any moment to have security guards appear and ask me to accompany them to wherever they take people who make up stupid excuses and do stupid, illegal things.

When no one appeared to stop me, I *did* go to lunch, but for a solitary meal at a nearby deli. Poking at my potato salad while cursing my luck, I asked myself for the umpteenth time why I hadn't just waited for the case to play itself out instead of thinking I could somehow prove my worth by being proactive in handling what I still believed to be a questionable potential claim. Universal didn't employ me to follow hunches, especially ones that turned sour. I was not only under no obligation to take chances, Universal was a conservative company that frowned on taking chances.

I took a couple of bites of salami sandwich, followed by a sip of acidic coffee. What if Zelda Gunner called the police? Worse yet, what if she called Universal? I had to face facts: I had bungled my assignment. And for that, I could lose my job. *At-will* employment really didn't mean "permanent." It means that they *will* keep you around until they have an excuse to get rid of you. And I may have just given them a very good excuse.

Emma scowled at me when I returned to the office. Was the scowl deeper than usual? Was there a tiny gleam of triumph in those colorless cold eyes? On the other hand, she never seemed friendly. Maybe she was just letting me know that she didn't approve of my being out of the office so much. After all, it was possible Zelda hadn't reported me yet. It was possible she wanted to talk to her boss before calling the police. Was Conklin the type to take long lunches? Did I have time to clear out my inbox?

The telephone rang incessantly all afternoon. Each time, the riiinnnnggg went through me like a knife. Each time, I was sure "this was it," the call that would end my employment, maybe even send me to jail.

I spent the afternoon tidying everything, readying things for my successor. They could accuse me of being reckless, but not inconsiderate. Then, when Emma announced that she was leaving for the day, I breathed a sigh of very welcome relief. For some reason, I'd been given a stay of execution. But why?

That was the evening I'd promised to make my weekly visit to Mother's. I vary the night so as to avoid creating a regular expectation, but I do have to warn her a day in advance so she can cook up a storm. It's a small concession for being allowed a life of my own without constant comments about how seldom she sees me.

"Johnnie," she said as though surprised to see me when she opened the door. It's her standard greeting. Her gray curly hair tickled my cheek as she gave me a motherly embrace. Then she stood back and wiped her hands on a bib apron with a quotation on the front: *I like cats, too. Let's exchange recipes.* "Son, you've been working too hard." Translated, that meant you should take more time off to visit your mother. Not that she really wants me hanging around; it was just a well-practiced guilt trip. Between going to the casino, her volunteer work, vacations with friends, and her mystery book club, she doesn't have much time to spare.

"That isn't funny, Mother." I pointed at her apron.

"Yes, it is," she countered. The matter was settled.

Her sharp blue eyes glanced down at my smudged shoes, traveled up to my wrinkled shirt and my mussed hair. "You need to take better care of yourself." She didn't expect a response. Her idea of me taking better care of myself has nothing to do with polishing my shoes, ironing my shirts, or combing my hair. She wants grandchildren. And that involves me finding a wife. At my mother's instigation, all of the middle-aged women in the neighborhood are involved in a search for my mate.

We didn't talk much during dinner. I happily consumed everything that was set before me, not hesitating when offered seconds. Obviously, the day's troubles had not affected my appetite. Or it could be that I was subconsciously thinking of this as a last meal before a steady diet of prison food. It wasn't until we retired to the living room with our coffee that Mother, in her all-knowing motherly way, asked, "So what's troubling you?"

I could have tried to argue that everything was just fine, but I knew I couldn't fool her. "It's a case I'm working on."

"What's the problem?"

"Well, it started when I decided I needed to prove that the so-called injured party isn't really injured."

"And?"

"I can't prove it."

"What have you tried?"

"I staked out her place for three days, but I couldn't catch her out of her wheelchair."

"She's in a wheelchair?"

"Yes, she claims she can't walk."

"What do the neighbors say?"

"I didn't want her to know I was asking around while I was watching her place. I could try that next..." I hesitated. She was right. If Zelda Gunnar gave me another day of grace, I would see what the neighbors had to say. Maybe I had a chance to go out in a blaze of glory. *Call me young gun. I'm a young gun.* Yeah.

Chapter Five

"We don't want any." The door slammed in my face. I never even had time to get out a single word. Resolutely, I knocked again, carefully keeping my feet and fingers clear of the door and trying desperately to look less like a salesman. Wiping the smile from my face, I hunched forward, like an accountant on April 14th. It may not have been the best ploy, but at least it wouldn't look like I was trying to sell magazine subscriptions or aluminum siding.

"I said…" she began when she saw that it was me again.

"I'm not a salesman," I quickly explained.

She hesitated, one hand on the doorknob. "Well?" She had shiny brown hair and smelled like fresh baked bread.

"I'm with Universal Heartland—" I began.

"Thought you said you weren't a salesman."

"I'm not selling anything. I just have a few questions." The door started to close again. "I'm with Universal Heartland Self-Help Corporation," I blurted out. "We're a nonprofit organization dedicated to helping the handicapped, and we are doing a study." It wasn't much of a cover, but I was pleased to have come up with such a self-sacrificing sounding purpose on the spur of the moment.

She frowned. "Like the March of Dimes?"

"No," I ad-libbed. "We're supported by a government grant. We ask nothing except information from people." Damn clever idea, I said to myself.

"No one handicapped here."

"I know. But you have a neighbor in a wheelchair, and I'm working up a profile on her. To know how we can be of help."

"Then why not talk to her?"

"I intend to. But to get a complete picture of the prospective recipient, we also interview neighbors in a position to observe the individual's particular problems and adjustment needs." I was on a roll. "So, if I might ask a few questions, you would be doing me and your neighbor a service." How could any self-respecting citizen refuse to donate a few minutes of their time to help someone get money from the government?

"Well—"

"Fine. My first question is…" I consulted a blank page in my notebook. "What is your relationship with the individual? That is, do you have any social contact with her? Or would you describe her as a casual acquaintance?" I stumbled over a few words like I was having a reading problem rather than trying to make things up as I went along. Fortunately, government questionnaires seldom sound like something written by Gallup.

"No, no social contact. We exchange a few words when we run into each other in the grocery. That's about it."

"So, you see her at the store." She nodded. "Have you observed her having any difficulty with her shopping?"

"Not that I've seen."

"How about when she needs to reach for things? How does she manage?"

"She just reaches for them, I guess."

"She does have full use of her arms, then?"

"I'm not sure."

"But you've seen her reach for items in the grocery?" She made me feel like I was asking her to donate blood instead of spending a few minutes answering questions about a neighbor.

"I'm sorry, but I don't pay much attention." Her eyes looked guiltily in the direction of Pearl's house. "You don't like to stare at someone with an, ah, affliction, you know."

"Of course. I understand." Great. But I wasn't going down for the count yet. "Has she ever asked you for assistance?"

"No."

"And you haven't noticed her anywhere but in the store?"

"That's correct."

Okay, I was getting nowhere. "Is there anyone else in the neighborhood that you can suggest I talk to?"

"Not that I can think of."

I glanced at my blank page again. "Well, thank you for your time. You've been very helpful." Not really, but what else could I say?

"You don't want a donation?" she asked as I turned to leave.

"No, as I said, I just had a few questions." The door closed with a jarring bang. Maybe I should have asked for a donation. It would be a way to make up the costs incurred during the failed stakeout.

No one answered at the next neighbor's house, and by the time I found someone else at home, I was better organized. I had the name of the nonprofit down pat, and I was prepared to snow the resident with my dedication to helping the disabled.

A middle-aged woman with sagging breasts and too much lipstick answered the door. Her black dress was about two sizes too small for her ample body and looked out of place in the neighborhood, more like something you might see in a bistro or cabaret. Before I could say a word, she invited me in.

Once inside, I tried to explain my mission, but she didn't seem to want to carry on a conversation, and she was standing a little too close for comfort. She definitely wasn't my type—I've never cared much for lavender eye shadow and glitter fingernail polish. But I didn't want to be rude. I accepted the offer of a drink. It wasn't until she sat down next to me on the couch and started running her hand along my thigh that I decided something had to be done to clarify my intentions.

"I'm from—"

"That's not important," she whispered in my ear as her hand moved higher up my thigh.

I stood up, sloshing the drink in my glass on her dress. "You don't understand."

"You want to skip the drinks?"

"Ahhh."

"Just say the word. I don't care either way."

"Either way?"

The doorbell rang.

"Shit," she exclaimed. "Who could that be?" There was another male at the door. An overweight business type who looked like he was in disguise with his oversized sunglasses and a black turtleneck jersey under a checkered black and white sports jacket. I saw them exchanging a few whispered comments. Then, as he stood in the background, she turned to confront me. "I thought you said you were sent by Harry?" Her flaccid breasts wobbled indignantly as she pointed accusingly in my direction.

"Nooo." I wanted to explain, but she didn't give me a chance.

"Get out of here, you imposter," she demanded loudly. I spilled more drink on the rug as I hurried toward the door, apologizing for not knowing Harry. At the last minute, I handed her my half-empty glass.

On my way to the next house, it occurred to me that my luck had gone on holiday. Not only wasn't I getting answers to my questions, I wasn't even getting many opportunities to ask them. At least the police hadn't appeared yet with an arrest warrant and a pair of handcuffs. And you never know what life has in store. Maybe I could resurrect my luck at the next house.

Or maybe not.

An old man wearing an obtrusive hearing aid answered the door. He stared blankly at me while I went through my spiel. Then, when I asked him if I could ask a few questions, he smiled, said goodbye, and closed the door in my face.

As I made my way down the block, I wondered what kind of reception these neighbors gave to someone actually trying to sell something. They probably called out the National Guard. I remembered something W.C. Fields said: *If at first you don't succeed, try, try again. Then quit. There's no point in being a damn fool about it.* I would try two more houses. Then I would quit.

My next stop produced a talkative teenager with an overactive imagination and a 19th Century melodramatic view of the world. To her, Mrs. Rosenblatt was a Dickensian character, doomed to unhappiness by a fated accident. I tried, but I couldn't get anything out of her except dire predictions about Mrs. Rosenblatt's unfortunate future. Some English teacher might have found her interpretation fascinating, but it wasn't helpful to me. I thanked her and departed stage left.

At the last house, I not only found someone at home but also someone who appeared to be a normal human being. If it hadn't been for the baby slung over the young woman's shoulder, I might have made some headway. But first, the baby burped, then it cried, and heaven knows what else it was up to. The woman had her hands full, but I give her credit for trying to answer some of my questions.

Yes, Mrs. Rosenblatt seemed to have the use of her arms. "That's a good 'lil' boy." Yes, she seemed to get around all right. "There, there, Billie. Momma's here." No, she never seemed to have any—"Hush now"—difficulty in the grocery. "Momma's big boy shouldn't cry." Although she did remember one time when she saw her almost lose her balance trying to reach for something. But no, she hadn't stood up.

Finally, Billie decided I'd asked enough questions. He began bawling for all he was worth, beating tiny clenched fists against his mother's neck. I quickly made my exit.

So much for interviewing the neighbors. Although it wouldn't look bad in the report: *Interviewed representative sampling of neighbors. Although claimant*—the potential claimant, that is—*has been observed on the street and in stores, no one has noticed anything to indicate that she is able to get about without the use of a wheelchair. She does, however, appear to have full use of her arms and hands.* Yes, it sounded pretty good except for the fact that without some proof that Pearl was faking her injuries, I had no reason to be investigating her in the first place.

The sign over the drive-in said, "Almost 2,000 Sold." I stopped there for lunch; that was the kind of mood I was in. I stayed in my car to eat, pulling down the armrest to spread out my French fries. The glove compartment door hung at a tilt on one hinge, but I put my coffee there anyway. What the heck?

When my lunch upset my stomach, I wasn't surprised. I headed back to the office to find out if Miss Gunnar had ratted me out to my bosses yet. I hoped they would let me pick up my personal belongings in private. It would be embarrassing to remove the bottle of liquor and unwashed glass with an audience watching.

Emma scowled at me as usual as I passed by her desk, but she didn't call out for me to "halt!" Nor was there an eviction notice on my door. And inside, everything looked just like I had left it. I checked for phone messages. Nothing. Maybe Miss Gunnar's idea of a good time was to let me stew over the inevitable, like telling the turkey, *Only five more days until Thanksgiving.*

After writing my report, I leaned back in my chair and looked around. I was already feeling nostalgic. A picture of the first building Universal had occupied hung crookedly on the otherwise bare wall across from my desk and to the right of the door. The cobwebs overhead hung undisturbed by either spiders or cleaners. The filing cabinet would be considered vintage in a few more years. It wasn't much, but it had been all mine.

What was I thinking?! I couldn't sit around moping, waiting to be excommunicated. For all I knew, Miss Gunnar had bought the sunglasses act. Or maybe she harbored an ounce of pity in her tiny heart. It *had* been two days. If I hadn't already ruined everything, there might still be a chance to redeem myself.

There wasn't much to go on, but I did know that Pearl had been able to move around immediately after the accident, and her neighbors agreed that she had full use of her arms and hands even though she claimed that was only on "good" days. Of course, it was always possible that the operation had made things worse instead of better. But if I were a betting man, I'd place my money on Pearl being the con rather than Dr. Oliver having committed malpractice. Besides, I had already invested a lot of time trying to prove that Pearl was faking her injuries. A few more hours couldn't hurt. I jumped in my trusty Saturn and headed for my favorite parking spot.

The sunshine from the last few days had been replaced by a damp mist that didn't flatter the row of matchstick houses in Pearl's neighborhood. It also made it extremely difficult to see, especially when what you were hoping to see was across the street and inside a house. I got out for a stroll, trying to blend in with the haze. What I needed was a tan Burberry with a turned-up collar.

When the dinner hour rolled around, I was glad for an excuse to leave my post. Watching Pearl drink had made me thirsty. I had run out of water an hour earlier but had managed to find one stray can of Coke under my seat. That hadn't been nearly enough, though. I was still thirsty.

Pho On U, the noodle shop that I chose at random, had the advantage of being slow. I didn't get back to my parking spot until dusk. A few more hours, and I would call it quits. Mark and Frank could dodge Universal's policy bullets, and Pearl could sue anyone and everyone she liked. I didn't care. I would go home, have a drink and a good night's sleep, and hope for a better tomorrow. Maybe even world peace.

When it got dark, and Pearl pulled the curtains shut, I decided to take one last look around. It was inevitable that it started to rain just as I approached the back of her house from the alley. Big splotches of water filled my eyes with unsalted tears. With a trench coat and a fedora, I would have been fine, but I was wearing an old ski jacket with a missing hood. I moved in closer. Might as well; no one could see me through the downpour. Even if she was running naked through her back yard, the chances of getting a good picture under these circumstances were, at best, iffy. Although maybe a light show from my camera's flash would make her think I got a picture, even if it wasn't clear enough to be considered conclusive evidence. I could use the act of taking pictures as leverage.

As I crept forward, my hair plastered against my head by the heavy rain, monstrous rivulets of water streamed down my face. It was like standing under a shower that was turned on full force, only I was wearing all my clothes, and the water was cold. I rubbed my sopping sleeve across my eyes to try to clear my vision, but no luck. The situation had become ludicrous. Time to throw in a very wet towel.

Just as I was about to leave, a tall figure moved past Pearl's kitchen window. Tall? People in wheelchairs aren't tall. Barely able to contain my excitement, I raced toward the window, bent over in typical spy fashion, not to be sneaky but to keep my eyes out of the sheet of rain that showed no indication of letting up any time soon. The window was streaked with water, fogged a bit on the inside, like glass in a bathroom. But I could tell there was someone standing next to the stove. I reached up and rubbed the window with my saturated sleeve and simultaneously fumbled with my camera. I had to try.

In my eagerness, I lost my footing and fell against the side of the house with a thump that seemed muted by the falling rain. But apparently, it was audible inside the house. I barely had my camera in position when the person at the stove turned toward me. Click. A dim flash of light. Another click. Another flash of hazy light. A woman shrieked, and the figure standing at the stove ran toward me, full bore.

Startled by her response, I stepped back, and my foot caught on something. The next thing I knew I was wallowing in the mud like a rutting pig. Even so, if I hadn't dropped my camera, I might have escaped. But by the time I located it, there was a woman standing over me with a gun in her hand.

"Okay, fella. Get up real careful like." She waved the gun in the direction of the back door. "Move it. Now!"

My dignity covered with brown slime, I humbly acquiesced.

Escorted by the gun-toting woman, I stumbled into the house, a soggy dispirited mess.

"Why, it's that insurance guy," Pearl exclaimed. There she was, sitting in her wheelchair, a drink in her hand. I turned and looked at my captor, a wild-eyed redhead, all sensuous lips and breasts. Her rain-drenched clothing adhered to her body like a second skin, revealing bikini panty lines and a very low-cut bra. For a moment, I forgot about the gun pointed at my midsection…but only for a moment.

"You know him?" the redhead asked Pearl. Then she turned to me and demanded in a gravely, although not unpleasant, voice, "What were you doing out there?"

"I'm afraid I owe you an apology," I began. Then I sneezed. The gun jerked up at the sound, and for a moment, I was afraid she was going to shoot me for sneezing. "Please," I said. "You don't need the gun. I'm just a claims adjuster, not a criminal." Well, maybe a criminal claims adjuster; it was hard to know at this point.

"That's what he said before," Pearl commented.

"A claims adjuster?"

I nodded, mesmerized by a tiny bead of water that hung suspended between the swell of her breasts. The gun wavered, but she didn't put it down.

"I'm with Universal Heartland Liability and Casualty Assurance Company of America, Incorporated." It's amazing what a shot of adrenaline can do for one's ability to spit out a long sentence in one breath.

"But what were you doing out there with that camera?" Her voice reminded me of pebbles being washed by waves.

"Yeah," Pearl chimed in, sounding slightly sloshed, "what were you doing out there?"

"I was watching."

"Watching? You some kind of peeping Tom?"

"No, I'm just a claims adjuster," I repeated.

"So, tell me what you were watching for, or I'll blow your head off." That didn't sound like a very good option, so I decided to come clean.

"I wanted to make certain Mrs. Rosenblatt wasn't faking her injuries. That's all."

"Faking?" The redhead didn't seem convinced.

"Yes."

"But you took a picture of *me*," she said. "Why did you do that?"

Now I was really embarrassed. "A mistake," I muttered.

"Mistake?" She had an annoying way of turning all of my statements into questions.

"Yes, a mistake." Just a little mistake. People made them all the time.

Pearl started to laugh, an open-mouthed roaring laugh. Then the real redhead started laughing. The gun wobbled up and down as she rocked back and forth. It was uncomfortable being the object of their combined hilarity, but it was better than being shot. Trying to recover some of my lost dignity, I wiped rainwater from my eyes and said, "So if I might leave now..." It was half statement, half question.

Then the doorbell rang.

Pearl wheeled about and headed for the front door. A few moments later, a tall thin police officer with a narrow face and a prominent nose, wearing a long black raincoat, came into the kitchen. He looked like someone who should be named Ebenezer. "So, nothing's wrong?" he asked, eyeing our wet demeanors with suspicion.

"Everything's fine, Officer," Pearl called from the living room. "I can't imagine why my neighbor called the police."

"She said there was a man looking in your window." He looked me up and down like I was standing in a line-up. I was about to confess when a pain shot up my leg. The redhead's foot was pressing down on my instep, and the gun had disappeared from sight. I smiled self-consciously and nodded, aware of the sound of water dripping off my clothes onto the floor. Plink. Plink.

"John here was kind enough to go outside to look for our cat," Pearl explained as she wheeled herself into the kitchen, an unexpected ally. Unless they just wanted the pleasure of disposing of me on their own after the police left. "That must have been what the neighbor saw." She sounded surprisingly sober, and I noticed there was no longer a drink in her hand.

"Weelll," the officer said, hesitating. He looked first at me, then Pearl, then the redhead, his gaze lingering on the redhead. Who could blame him? "If you're sure—"

"Quite sure, Officer. We appreciate your concern, but, as you can see, everything is just fine." He looked us over one at a time again, blinking as if to clear his vision. The redhead and I stood there in our drenched glory, trying to look just fine.

After he had gone, I turned to them. "I really appreciate what you just did." They both nodded. "I mean it, it was decent of you not to turn me in. Under the circumstances. The police and all...." There didn't seem to be anything more to say.

"I hope you're satisfied," Pearl said.

"I'm sorry, really sorry."

"You should be, spying on me like that." She squinted disapproval at me, and at the puddle I was making on the floor. Miraculously, she had a glass in her hand again. "I hope you've learned your lesson."

"Oh yes," I replied, feeling very much like a repentant sinner speaking to a priest. "Yes, I have." I wondered how many Hail Marys I had earned for my little stunt.

"Hand it over," the redhead demanded, gesturing at my camera. I gave it to her without so much as a murmur of protest. I wasn't exactly in the driver's seat on this one. She flicked through the pictures, then deleted all of them. Even the personal ones. But I didn't complain. "There," she said when she was finished. She wiped mud from the camera with a kitchen towel and handed the camera back to me. "Now leave."

"And don't come back," Pearl added for good measure. "Don't ever come back, you hear?"

Chapter Six

Wednesday morning, I didn't suspect a thing. When my alarm clock failed to go off, I didn't curse fate. I simply hurried through my morning ritual, skipped breakfast, and rushed to my car. When the car wouldn't start, I didn't see it as an omen. Methodically, I went about finding a neighbor to help me jump-start it. And the ticket I got for speeding didn't even phase me. The gods weren't out to get me; I was simply having a bad start to my day.

Mumbling to myself, I hurried past Emma with an obligatory "Good morning" and went to my office. Once inside, it took me a few moments to realize that something was wrong. My office is never locked when I'm away. If Emma or anyone else wants to check on something or leave something for me, they are free to do so. No one ever disturbs anything.

But today, things were definitely disturbed.

Papers and files were scattered everywhere as though blown about by a giant industrial fan. My desk looked like it had been the object of a drone attack. My file cabinet had been assaulted by some malicious vandals who knew how to pull drawers out but not how to close them.

Mutely surveying the mess that had once been my cherished home away from home, my eyes caught sight of my wooden box. It had been taken out of the cabinet and lay on the floor, its lid twisted off, its contents removed. The faint odor of alcohol mingled with the cologne of ancient carpet. The empty vodka bottle lay on my desk on its side, a stagnant pool of liquid in my paper clip container, the rest absorbed by the strewn and crumpled papers on my desk. The aging walls of my office had probably seen a lot of mayhem over the years, but nothing this crude.

I was still standing there, stunned, when Emma shook my shoulder and asked, not unkindly, if something was wrong. Then she looked past me into the room. "Oh my god," she cried, shoving me aside. She walked stiff-legged over to my desk, being careful where she stepped. "Oh…my…god," she said again.

Trying to pull myself together, I acknowledged, "It *is* a mess."

"Who would do such a thing?" I doubted her question came from a concern for me but the fact that she hates disorder.

"I don't know," I said truthfully. I took off my jacket and hung it on the hook behind the door. At least that was still where it was supposed to be. "It's okay. I'll clean everything up."

"They poured something on your desk." Before I could distract her, her eyes wandered to the empty bottle, then to the wooden box. I knew I was turning red. "Well!" she said with feeling. "Well!" She headed for the door, daintily trying to avoid stepping on things. "I shall report this at once." Giving me a departing glare, she warned, "And I shouldn't touch anything if I were you." Then she turned back, pausing like Columbo about to say *just one more thing.* Instead, she offered an explanation." There could be fingerprints."

With a mixture of confusion and helplessness, I looked around. It was too late to try to hide the vodka bottle. Besides, Emma was right. There might be fingerprints. Was there any chance they would think the perpetrators brought the vodka with them? Or was I going to be trapped into admitting that it belonged to me?

My desk chair had been pushed to the side. But it appeared to be intact. I sat down and looked around. Who could have done this to me? And why? It couldn't be a case I was working on because I had been concentrating on the Marshall affair, and no one involved had reason to want to hurt me. Mark would probably get his insurance coverage. Frances was off the hook and might be able to repair the car. Pearl had made a fool out of me. And Wally had stonewalled. No one connected with the Marshall case had any reason to vandalize my office. They should be sending me thank-you cards.

What about Emma? Had she discovered the wooden box while snooping around and flipped out? Could the rest of the mess be a diversionary tactic? Was that why vodka was poured all over my desk?

Suddenly it occurred to me that I might not be the only victim. Maybe it was part of a larger, senseless act against Universal employees. I roused myself and went down the hall to check. Everything seemed to be in order. Each cubicle a sterile, neat replica of the one before. Less hopeful, I made my way into the "new" section, peering over partitions and around corners. Everything was shipshape. I was the only victim.

As I mulled this over in my mind, another possibility popped up. Maybe it was a mistake. That's it, a mistake. Someone was mad at a person named John Smith. Some other John Smith. Not me. All I had to do was a little tidying up, and things would be back to normal. Except for the vodka. I had to give up my vodka. Emma would see to that.

When the police arrived, Emma hovered around my door, waiting to hear what they had to say. One of the officers, a barrel-chested fellow with a jowly face, got one of the vodka-drenched papers on the floor stuck to the bottom of his shoe. He tried to pry it off without bending over, putting one shoe on top of the paper and then lifting the offending shoe. The paper tore but remained stuck to his shoe. "Damn," he said under his breath.

"Careful," I admonished. "That could be important."

"You can tape it back together," he said as he ripped the remaining piece off. He had a low voice that sounded hollow, like someone talking in a cave. His lack of concern for my property irritated me.

"I took care not to disturb things," I said reproachfully. Although the officer I was talking to seemed oblivious to my concerns, the other officer caught the drift.

"Careful, Charlie." Charlie froze in mid-step. The hierarchy was clear, even if I couldn't tell from their titles.

"You can move," I said. "Just don't step on anything."

Charlie looked around, found a clear spot on the rug, and stationed himself there while the other officer checked out the mess. "Good of you not to disturb anything," the second officer said. The name on his badge was

Lapinsky.

"I told him to leave things as they were," Emma called from the doorway. "There might be fingerprints."

"They seldom leave fingerprints in situations like this," Charlie said. I wondered what kind of a situation he was referring to. Emma gave him a look that could have shriveled a ripe peach, but Charlie didn't seem to notice.

"Do you need me?" I asked, suddenly anxious to get out of there.

"I do have a few questions," Lapinsky said. "Charlie, you check things out. I'm going to have a talk with...ah—"

"John Smith."

Both officers suddenly stared at me, their police instincts alerted.

"It's my name. My real name. The name I was given at birth." I felt like adding, by inconsiderate or naïve parents. "We can talk in the reception area." Emma might be able to overhear, but I didn't care. Besides, she was usually pretty creative. She'd figure out a way to eavesdrop even if we had our conversation in the men's room. Why put her to all that trouble?

I sat down, and Lapinsky pulled a chair over close to mine so we didn't have to raise our voices to talk. I wasn't sure if he was being considerate or if he had forgotten his glasses and wanted to make sure he didn't miss any telltale nonverbals. "Well, let me ask the most obvious question first. Do you have any idea who might have done this?"

"No, none at all."

"How about an enemy? Someone with a grudge? Someone who dislikes you? Someone who would enjoy causing you a little trouble?"

His list of the categories of people who might want to tear my office apart didn't do much for my ego. Everyone ticked off a few people from time to time. People I honked at on the freeway because they failed to signal before pulling in front of me. The newspaper carrier, who I forgot to give a Christmas bonus. The meat market owner where I'd complained about a tough cut of meat. The religious fanatics I'd refused to listen to on the street corner. Still, in all honesty, I couldn't think of anyone with sufficient cause to wreak havoc on my office. "No."

"Come now, Mr. Smith, everyone has enemies." His bottomless eyes held mine, unrelenting, accusative.

"Weelll." Everyone has them. Like occasional bad breath or dandruff. It's the price you pay for being human. I tried to concentrate on my enemies. But I couldn't think of any. I'm not the kind of guy to acquire enemies; I have a hard enough time just making an impression. "Sorry, I can't think of anyone."

Lapinsky shook his head. "If you say so." Then he tried another tack. "What about a case you're working on. Any disgruntled clients?"

"I've considered that, but I can't think of anyone."

"It doesn't have to be recent," he prompted. "Sometimes these crazies harbor grudges a long time, then, one day, out of a clear blue sky, they explode." The look on his face suggested that he looked forward to these occasional explosions, probably a break from routine, a mind puzzle to brighten his day. But crazies? Was that how a professional should talk? Of course, he had more experience with this sort of thing than I did.

"I'll give it some thought." Then I added, "I don't handle what you might call 'volatile' cases. Just fender-benders and small P.I."

"Huh?"

"Minor car accidents and personal injury cases. Deaths and complex accidents are handled by people senior to me. And I've only worked here eight months."

The admission that I'd only been with Universal eight months resulted in questions about my life before I joined the Universal team. As Lapinsky waded through the tedium of my past, only one person stood out as a possible suspect—the irate ex-boxer who had gone after me once before.

"I thought you didn't have any enemies," Lapinsky said. He quickly fastened on this guy as the culprit. I didn't agree. He'd already had his revenge. But since I was getting tired of sharing my personal life with Lapinsky, Emma, and anyone else who happened to be in the area, I let him think he had a good suspect. Why not? It made him happy, and it didn't make any difference to me. As long as he didn't rile the guy too much. I didn't want to spend my vacation time in a hospital. Even if the nurses were cute.

When everything seemed to be winding down, I asked, "Do you need me anymore?"

"No, that about covers it for now. Just give us a little more time to look around your office. Then you can clean things up."

Emma seemed to be busy with something on her computer, but I felt certain that her shell-shaped antenna had been tuned to the frequency of our conversation and that she hadn't missed a thing. "Emma," I said as calmly as I could. "I have something I can work on without going back into my office, so I'm going to do just that." She nodded without looking up.

I didn't actually have anything to work on. All I wanted was to get away from Emma, Charlie, Lapinsky, and the shambles that used to be my office. I had a lot to think about: people with grudges, people who disliked me, people who wanted to cause me trouble—enemies.

When the Saturn headed for home, I didn't object. Maybe after some breakfast, things would make more sense. Besides, a man with enemies needs to keep up his strength.

When I saw the parking space labeled "Smith," I started to relax. Just a few hundred feet and I'd be home, safe in my rented houseboat. It was in a choice location at the end of a string of houseboats that stretched out along a long dock from land into the lake, a tiny community of people willing to walk to their homes in all kinds of weather for the privilege of being close to the water.

I was barely able to squeeze Bee past a Cadillac parked at an angle in the adjoining space. There were four cars on the opposite side of the Cadillac, each parked on an angle, invading the adjacent spot, like a disease spreading down the row of cars. Most of the parking for our houseboat community is on land, but my space was added on after they ran out of ground. It's on a raised wood platform supported by four-by-fours jutting out above the landlord's back yard. I got out and took a deep breath. The view from the parking area always gives me a lift. It's just high enough to have a view over the roofs of the houseboats to the lake beyond, a small body of water surrounded by city and industrial plants and ringed with marinas, restaurants, and houseboats. It's a great place to live, lots of atmosphere and friendliness. And the communal swimming pool—the lake—is big enough for all the kids and dogs who want to indulge themselves.

As I made my way down the wood-planked walkway past planters and pots filled with enough flowers and grasses to make up for not having yards, an occasional face peered out at me through ornate leaded and stained-glass windows. I could have waved, but I looked straight ahead instead. I always feel self-conscious around most of the other tenants, like they know I don't eat whole wheat bread or grow my own herbs. Even the plants I purchased to try it refuse to cooperate. Their withered appearance proclaims that I'm not really part of the community. All my attempts at bohemian end up looking schlocky.

In fact, I acknowledged, as I neared my end slip, that mess on my front porch was getting out of hand. It definitely needed to be cleaned up. I was still thinking about how messy my porch looked as I opened my front door. Even so, I was startled. Talk about a mess! Furniture was upturned, books were heaped in haphazard piles on the floor, rugs were pulled up. My home looked every bit as bad or worse than my office.

"Oh noooo." Heedless of fingerprints, I went inside and wandered from room to room, touching this and that in disbelief. Someone had ransacked the place. Vandalism? Theft? It didn't look like anything was actually destroyed, and it seemed like everything was still there, just moved around. Had someone been searching for something? If so, for what? Or were they trying to make a point? And, if so, what was the message?

Was Lapinsky onto something? Had the ex-boxer experienced some sort of psychotic break? I searched my mind for anyone else who could be angry enough with me to do this. I'd never heard of a waiter you didn't tip because of bad service seeking revenge, but I suppose it was possible. Or someone on the dock who felt I wasn't living up to their standards. Or the owner of the dog I had to keep chasing away because he wanted to take his daily constitution on my porch. Or, it could still be some other John Smith they were after. It just didn't make any sense.

I knew I should call Lapinsky, but I really didn't want to. Once he heard about my home being violated, he would be convinced that I was holding out on him. I continued roaming from room to room, almost hoping something valuable was missing so I could rationalize what had happened. Not that I had anything valuable. And even the small amount of cash I kept in my underwear drawer was still there. The television was intact. Too bad, with the insurance money, I could have upgraded. My liquor cabinet was untouched. Maybe whoever had done this preferred different brands or higher quality. Someone had gone through my desk, but nothing appeared to be missing. All of the receipts and bills were right where I'd left them.

"You're not a very good housekeeper," a husky female voice said, interrupting my inventory. I turned and saw the bosomy redhead whose picture I had taken the night before. Although the jeans and light cotton blouse she was wearing were dry, she still looked like she had been poured into them. I wondered briefly if she had to lie down to pull up her pants. But I had no complaints about how she looked or what she was wearing.

"Come in," I automatically said, although she was obviously already in. She hesitated, one foot poised to take a step if she found a safe place to put it down. "I've had a visitor," I explained.

"A messy visitor, I'd say." She looked around some more. "So, you don't usually live like this?"

I was too overwhelmed to feel insulted. "No." It didn't occur to me in the moment to be surprised by her visit. My world had been turned upside down in so many ways. If she had pulled out a gun and demanded that I leave my own house, I would have simply said, okay.

"Your secretary said I'd find you here."

"Secretary? Oh, you mean Emma, our admin."

"Old stone face, is that Emma?" For the first time that day, I found myself grinning. Then it struck me. "But how did she know I was here?"

"I don't know. She just said you'd probably gone home and gave me the address." Glancing around one more time, she said, "Maybe we could go somewhere to talk."

"You want to talk?" Although I still felt a bit muddled, my head was clear enough that I recognized a stupid question when I heard one, but there was no way to retract it.

"That's what I came for."

"I should call the police." She waited patiently for me to make up my mind. Oh well, the mess and the police could wait. I motioned toward the front door. As I left, I looked at the lock. It looked fine. Although I obviously needed to replace it with something more secure. Or had I left a window open? In any event, I didn't bother to lock up. If someone stole something at this point, it was one less thing to clean up.

We took her car; mine wouldn't start. I did, however, intend to pay for the coffee. Then as we settled into the booth and took our first sip, my stomach started making noises. The memory of skipping breakfast came back to me on a waft of bacon and eggs that drifted in from the kitchen. I waved at the waitress and put in an order. My companion declined an offer of breakfast. She apparently really did just want to talk.

"You see," she began, "Mother and I got to thinking about what happened after you left."

"Mother?"

"Haven't I introduced myself?" She seemed genuinely surprised. I shook my head. "I'm Rosemary, Rosemary Rosenblatt." Without the gun, she was even more appealing. "My friends call me—"

I interrupted. "Let me guess." I pretended to give the matter some thought. "Rose," I concluded. *By any other name.*

"No," she said solemnly. "Marie."

"Marie?" Now I was turning *her* statements into questions.

"Yes."

"Well, Marie, may I call you Marie?" She nodded. "What can I do for you?" The real question was what she could do for me, but that could wait. The waitress had placed my order of bacon and eggs in front of me, so I dug in, going by smell, not taking my eyes off of the dish across the table.

She took a deep breath, inflating her lungs, which in turn pushed out her breasts under the thin cotton blouse. "Mother and I were concerned about last night. And we were wondering..." I suddenly became aware that she was caressing my leg with her foot. She must have taken her shoe off. Her naked foot was caressing my leg. It felt good. "...if you'd been doing that sort of thing for very long." The muscles in my calf were quivering uncontrollably, and I was having difficulty chewing. "You know, spying on her."

"Ssppying?" I was trying to slip off my shoe so I could participate more fully in the under-the-table games, but my shoelaces were too tight. "Spying," I managed to say more precisely. Why deny it? "No, not long." Clenching my teeth, I pushed against the heel of my right shoe with the toe of my left, almost grunting with effort.

"How long?"

Her foot was sliding up to my thigh. It was driving me wild. "Oh, a few days," I managed to say. I've never been good at multitasking.

"Did you take any other pictures?" She was giving me that moist mouth look, lips barely parted, hints of delights to come. I knew that look; I'd seen it on the big screen often enough.

"No." As soon as I said the word, her foot stopped moving.

"None?"

"No, none." In desperation, I pushed at my shoe.

Her mouth closed, her bedroom eyes transforming into across-the-table-over-coffee eyes. "What's your position on all this?" I quit trying to remove my shoe.

"I have no position," I admitted. "No position whatsoever."

"What does that mean?" She leaned back, like a cat tired of attention.

"Well, the case is out of my hands at this point. I've made my report, and the rest is up to my superiors." I didn't add that I hadn't actually turned in the report yet and that it was probably a shredded mess on the floor of my office. I was beginning to suspect I was being used. It even crossed my mind that Marie had been the one to search my office and home, looking for incriminating pictures of her mother. I didn't want to believe that. After all, I'd offered to buy her breakfast.

"Thanks for the coffee," she said, slurping down what was left in her cup.

My "you're welcome" followed her as she stood up and rushed off. It was a few moments before I realized that my ride home had disappeared out the door. I left the rest of my meal untouched and hurried to settle the check, reaching the parking lot in time to see her pulling away. In response to my frantic gesturing, she smiled and wiggled her fingers in my direction. I hoped I was on a bus route.

I wasn't.

As I started walking in the direction of where I hoped I could find a bus stop or a taxi, I called Lapinsky and told him about my house being broken into. He wanted to know where I was, but I wasn't sure. I said I was having car trouble and would get there as soon as I could. He asked how I knew my house had been broken into if I wasn't home. When I explained that I had gone out for breakfast with a friend, he started shouting into the phone. I mumbled something about how he was breaking up and signed out.

My feet were killing me by the time I finally found a bus stop. And the bacon and eggs that I had managed to consume were coming back to haunt me. To top it all off, none of the buses that passed through this stop were going to take me anywhere near where I lived. I would have to travel miles out of my way, transfer twice, and still end up a fair distance away at the end. And government officials always wonder why people don't take the bus more.

When I reached the second transfer spot, I realized I was only a couple blocks away from Wally Conklin's office. In spite of concerns about running into Zelda Gunner, the draw was irresistible. I still didn't know whether there were other contributors to any potential claims that Pearl would undoubtedly make. If I got that information, I would have something to tell Emma that I'd accomplished this morning. She might think twice the next time she assumed I was shirking work.

Everything was quiet at Babcock-Chalmers Brokers of Insurance. A steaming cup of coffee was on the desk next to the receptionist's empty chair. Down the corridor, to my left, I could hear someone carrying on a one-sided conversation. To my right, all was still. Miss Gunnar was nowhere in sight. I went directly to Conklin's office as quietly as I could in case she was lurking nearby. His door was closed. I knocked gently and waited. Then I knocked again, this time a little louder. Still nothing.

My hand was on the doorknob. The door was open. I pushed it open a few inches with my toe and took a look up and down the hall before peeking into his office. There was no one there. I went back down the hall to make absolutely certain there was no one around. The receptionist's desk was still empty, the coffee on her desk steaming slightly less than it had been.

The library hush of the place was creeping me out. Where was everyone? I glanced at my watch: 12:15. I remembered the mass exodus at noon the last time I was here and relaxed slightly. Although the office next to Conklin's appeared to be empty, I decided to check it out just to make sure. Last time that was where Miss Gunnar had been lurking. I rapped lightly on the door of the office with no name. I was about to call it good when I thought I heard a noise from within. I stood very still for a minute, then knocked on the door again, a little louder. I didn't want to surprise Miss Gunnar in a compromising situation, like picking her nose, but I didn't want her surprising me again, either.

A noise that sounded like an animal in pain came from somewhere behind the door. I paused, waiting for a repeat to see if I could figure out what I'd heard. Was this a trick? Although my gut told me it was a bad idea to open the door, I found myself doing just that. "Miss Gunnar?" I said as the door creaked open. "Are you there?"

The blinds were drawn over the windows, leaving the room dimly lit and full of shadows. But everything seemed to be in order, nothing amiss. Except for one thing—a piece of paper on the floor to the left of the desk. How had the efficient Miss Gunnar overlooked that? I tiptoed over and bent down to pick it up.

Someone moaned.

My fingers stopped just inches from the piece of paper. Without straightening up I swiveled my head in the direction of the sound. There, just a few feet away, lay Zelda Gunnar. She was sprawled like a rag doll tossed aside by a careless child, one knee bent, one arm stretched out, the other grasping an ornate silver hilt that protruded from between her meager breasts. Dark thick liquid oozed around the hilt and through her white fingers onto the light brown carpet. It looked like…smelled like…

Blood!

Chapter Seven

"What do you mean she said 'Argghh.' What in the hell is that supposed to mean?"

The police officer pacing in front of me was a childhood buddy. Sergeant Bruno McGinty and I grew up together in the same neighborhood, played cops and robbers, swapped tall tales, were teammates, double dated in high school. All the things two young guys with absolutely nothing in common do together when the proximity of homes and ages make them friends. Physically and mentally worlds apart, we had shared confidences and dreams that still bound us by invisible threads of the past.

Bruno is a brawny hunk of a man, all angles and muscle, with a Dick Tracy chin and football mentality. If there's very little depth of thinking behind his clear brown eyes, that's his only shortcoming. He's smart enough, hardworking, committed, and loyal. But sometimes, he isn't too trusting.

"She said 'Argghh,'" I repeated for the umpteenth time. I was tired of trying to mimic the sound, although I felt I was doing a pretty fair job of it. "That's all I can tell you."

Bruno frowned, pounding his right fist into the palm of his left hand, an unconscious but impressive gesture of masculine frustration. He came over and stood in front of me and made one last attempt to appeal to my sense of camaraderie. "Come on, John. We've been friends a long time. You call tell me the truth."

"It happened just like I've told you, Bruno. She was laying there, one hand flopping back and forth, and when I leaned over to take a closer look, she said, 'Argghh.'" I tried to maintain eye contact, but my eyes didn't want to look directly into his. How could I tell him that I had asked Zelda if she was all right? But that was the only thing I was hiding. When I asked, she'd said "Argghh" as clearly as if she'd typed it. That was her last word, her final effort at communication. As soon as she uttered it, her head lolled to one side, and blood streamed from her mouth like lava from a volcano.

I called the police as soon as I was able. At least I had enough sense not to touch anything. They should have thanked me for that. Instead, there were complaints from all the officials on the scene about me vomiting on the body. I should never have eaten greasy bacon and eggs while Marie was running her foot up and down my leg. But could I help it if I had contaminated the murder weapon and body? It wasn't as if I'd thrown up on purpose. And it happened so fast I hadn't thought to turn my head to the side. Although one officer, in particular, told me more than once that you should never get close to a body unless you're used to the smell and sight of blood. Unfortunately, it was a little late for that piece of advice.

"Look, John." Bruno was about to switch from friend to officer in charge. I could hear it coming. I couldn't blame him for trying to pressure me. It was probably his first dying clue. And if it were a better clue, maybe it could have helped him solve the case. "Your office and home were broken into, and you rush right over to Babcock-Chalmers. Now you want me to believe this was just a coincidence? Do you think I'm stupid or what?"

I didn't want to answer that. Not that I think he's stupid, but the "or what" might require additional input as to my perception of his level and type of intelligence. It didn't seem like a good idea to go there. Fortunately, he didn't pause long but continued with his line of questioning.

"WHY did you come here to Babcock-Chalmers," he demanded forcefully, as if he thought he could scare me into a confession. It might have worked if I hadn't known Bruno since he was called Mikey…and if I had something to tell him. I'd helped him come up with the name Bruno when we were sophomores. We thought it sounded tough.

"Bruno, I'm giving it to you straight. I had forty minutes to kill…er, wait before my bus came, and I had a question to ask Wallis Conklin about a case I'm working on."

"And why were you taking the bus?" To him, that seemed like a singularly suspicious act. He had already asked me that question several times.

"My car's not running. A woman acquaintance gave me a ride downtown for an appointment, but she couldn't, ah, hang around to take me home." I didn't think he needed to know the part about being unceremoniously stranded at considerable distance from the nearest bus stop.

"We'll check out your story," he threatened.

"Do that." What would Marie tell them? She'd obviously corroborate my basic story, but when she told them where she had left me, would I look foolish? Could someone who had thrown up on a corpse be made to look any more foolish?

"Accepting that part of your story for a moment, don't you think it's a bit strange that instead of informing the police your home had just been broken into, you go off with some woman?"

Should I give him a locker room description of Marie's body to explain how lust had lured me away from the scene of a crime? Of course, if I did that, then I might have to admit that she'd used me and cast me aside like an expired coupon. It might be easier on my ego in the long run to simply let Bruno pummel me with questions than to admit my failure as a male. And if I eventually had to explain that Marie was Peal Rosenblatt's daughter, it was going to be even more awkward. To prevent having to discuss the unsavory details of my relationship with her, I was willing to take the chance.

"And why did you tell your admin that you would be working on a case if you intended to go home?" I groaned. That was such a tiny white lie. It didn't seem fair to have to explain it out loud. "I'm still not convinced," he continued, "that the case you're working on doesn't have something to do with all this." He made "all this" sound like an evil conspiracy conceived in a dark room in a sinister-looking Victorian building next to a fast-flowing river. Wherever evil people gather to plot.

"You're the police. If 'all this' is connected, feel free to prove it."

"Don't get smart with me, John."

"Sorry, Bruno. It's just that I find 'all this' tiring. And all I know about it is what I've told you. Believe me, I would like to know who ransacked my office and my home as much as you would. Maybe more." I was starting to feel sorry for myself. And I had a bad taste in my mouth. "Any chance you have a mint?" I asked.

Bruno stared at me like I had just said something crazy. Then he reached in his pocket and took out a roll of mints, and offered me one. "Thanks," I said. For a moment, he reminded me of the kid I used to play kickball with. He always carried Lifesavers back then. He liked the red ones, so I always ended up with yellow or green.

"Okay, John." He, too, sounded tired. "That's all for now." I got up to leave. "Oh, just one more thing. Lapinsky wants to see you."

"I *am* free to go?"

"Yeah, but let me remind you not to leave town without checking with me first."

"Jeez, Bruno. You know I wouldn't run out on Mother."

He flushed slightly, "Just doing my job, John."

Lapinsky didn't keep me waiting long, unless you consider forty-five minutes on an empty, upset stomach a long time. When I was finally called in to talk with him, I was surprised to find the room filled with smoke. Wheezing a little, I sank into a chair across the table from Lapinsky. "I didn't think you were allowed to smoke in government buildings," I said.

"Oh, smoke bother you?" He looked like he hoped it did. It was then I noticed the *Thank you for not smoking"* sign on the bulletin board behind him. And I noticed that he didn't have an ashtray; he was using his waste basket for his ashes. But under the circumstances, I certainly wasn't going to be a whistle-blower.

"Let's get right down to business, shall we?" He put out his cigarette on the side of the wastebasket and leaned forward. "Why did you leave your house after discovering it had been ransacked? Why didn't you call the police?"

"As I explained to Sergeant McGinty, someone dropped by to see me, and we went out for coffee."

After a lengthy glare, he asked, "Was anything taken?"

"I don't think so."

"Don't *think* so? What does that mean?"

"I haven't had time to check things out yet."

"You didn't take the time to check out whether you had been robbed." His tone made it clear that he found that hard to believe. In fact, it was clear he found the whole situation highly suspicious.

"I figured what had happened had already happened and that it wouldn't make much difference if I searched to see if anything was missing then or a few hours later." When put that way, I thought it sounded reasonable.

"And you left your door unlocked."

Phrases flickered through my mind, such as "Lightning doesn't strike twice in the same place" and "Don't lock the stable door after the horse is stolen," but I didn't think he would find these arguments very persuasive. Especially when he had already decided I was guilty of something. "It just didn't seem to matter at that point."

"Maybe whoever did it was interrupted. Maybe they intended to come back. And since you didn't check to see if they had taken anything of value…" He left the accusation hanging. "Do you have an alarm?"

"No, but I have nosy neighbors. And there are a number of dogs on the dock who bark at everything." He looked regretfully at the crushed cigarette in his waste basket. Maybe he thought I was blowing symbolic smoke and wanted to give me payback. Or maybe he just craved a cigarette.

"Let's set aside discussion of what may have been taken for a moment. What do you think they were searching for?"

"I can't imagine." Unless I was right about it being Marie.

"First your office and then your home is searched or burgled, and you 'can't imagine' what someone was after." He was beginning to remind me of a bully I hadn't much liked in grade school, a sarcastic kid with hair that stuck straight up like an abused paintbrush.

"That's correct."

"Really, Mr. Smith? How can you possibly expect me to believe that?"

"Because it's the truth." I probably sounded defensive. "Did YOU find anything?" My tone implied that it was his job to find clues, not mine.

"No. And unless we have your cooperation, Mr. Smith, I doubt that we will find anything." How quickly he had lobed the ball back into my court.

"I'll cooperate in any way I can."

"That's what I wanted to hear." His eyes were darting back and forth between me and a two-drawer filing cabinet on rollers to the left of the table. I had no doubt where he kept his illegal cigarettes. By prolonging our conversation, I might be prolonging his life. Or, he could want a cigarette so bad that he would let me go. It was a win-win. "So?" he prompted.

"I've told you everything," I repeated.

"Everything?"

"Everything."

He stood up. "Then there's nothing more I can do for you." He was a priest with an unrepentant sinner surely headed for hell, or at least a long stint in purgatory. I stood up too. Then I turned and headed for the door. "Just one more thing," he said to my retreating back. I didn't have to turn around to know that he had one forefinger raised, head cocked to one side, eyebrows elevated.

"What?" I asked, turning slowly back to him.

"Your mother wants you to call." My mother? What was he doing passing along messages from Mother? And how on earth did she know where to find me?

She answered after the first ring. "Hello, Mother?" I knew it was her, but for some reason, I always ask.

"John," she said excitedly. "What's wrong, John? What are they doing to you?" She went on for a few minutes before I managed to get in a word.

"Mother, everything's all right. Someone broke into my office and then into my houseboat, that's all."

"That's *all?* That's all?" Her voice would have carried all the way to where I was without using her telephone.

"That's all. Nothing stolen or damaged beyond repair." I hoped. "Every-thing's fine."

"But what about the bodies? That nice Polish police officer said something about you finding some bodies." Bigmouth Lapinsky. Why'd he tell Mother about the Miss Gunnar? And how much had he told her?

"Just one body, Mother. No one you know."

"Just one body, he says. Isn't one more than enough?"

"Yes, one is enough," I agreed, not entirely sure what I was agreeing to. Enough for what?

"Was there much blood?" she asked ghoulishly. Even the sound of the word made me nauseous. Darn that mystery book club she belonged to. She would probably want to hear all of the grisly details so she could share them with the other members. It would be their own version of a reality show.

"Look, Mother. I don't feel up to talking about it just now."

She quickly cut in. "I'll meet you at the houseboat."

"Ah, I'm not going home yet." I hadn't really intended to say that. I just knew I didn't feel like talking with Mother about Miss Gunnar's blood or anything else associated with my morning.

"Not going home? But where else will you go? Your office is a mess. You've discovered a body. Of course, you're going home. And I'll be there to fix you a nice cup of tea and help you straighten up."

I knew when to give in. After all, I'd known her all my life. "Okay, Mother, I'll be home as soon as I can."

She arrived before I did, of course. Her bus was faster. Or maybe it made fewer stops. She doesn't drive anymore, thank heavens. Not that she isn't capable, but she believes in using public transportation. Thankfully she doesn't feel it's safe to take a bus after dark because muggers ride city buses as soon as the sun sets. It's the only thing that protects me from evening visits. Of course, if the muggers knew her, they'd be afraid too. She carries pepper spray disguised as a miniature flashlight, and a couple of years back, she spent a summer taking a series of self-defense classes at the Y.W.C.A.

The living room was already tidied up, and she had started in on the kitchen. Two cups had been set on the kitchen table, and the teapot was whistling like a drunken canary. It was supposed to sound like a train, but it never sealed properly.

Once she quizzed me sufficiently to realize that I had lost what little I had eaten earlier, she set about remedying the situation. The welfare of her son was more important than the body of someone she didn't know. It was nice to be fussed over, and I found that in spite of everything, I had an appetite.

As soon as I finished eating, she started in on me, beginning with who had invaded my office and home. She lingered over the possibility of "senseless violence" for a time, quickly dismissed the "wrong John Smith" theory, and became fixated on the idea that I had something that someone wanted.

"It's all some kind of mistake," I insisted.

"Piffle," she said.

"Mother, no one says piffle anymore."

"Don't be silly. I saw the word just the other day in a whodunit I'm reading."

"Written in the 19th Century?"

"Don't try to change the subject, John."

"I'm not."

"Yes, you are. But it won't work. We need to go over everything that has happened the last few weeks. Because I don't care what you think, you're involved. And I can help you sort through the details. As you know, I'm very good at solving mysteries." She was using her *you-better-listen-to-your-mother* voice. I knew when I was beaten. "Now, let's start at the beginning. When did this all begin?"

"If I knew what 'this all' was, I'd be happy to start at the beginning." Well, maybe not happy exactly, but somewhat willing. Sometimes talking things over with someone did help. Even with my mother.

"Okay, let's start with today and go backwards." She poured us more tea and leaned back in her chair, the better to listen. I reluctantly started in on the highlights of my day. I told her about being late, skipping breakfast, the ticket for speeding, everything. Except for the part about being stranded by Marie, of course. A man has to have some secrets from his mother.

It got a bit tricky when I started describing what happened at Babcock-Chalmers. "Why do you need to know what the body looked like?" I asked, reluctant to live through that experience again.

"There is a lot to learn from a crime scene," she explained as if talking to a child. Well, in a way, she was. Once a child, always a child in a parent's eyes. So, I told her about the position of the body, the dagger, and the blood. When I got to the part about Miss Gunnar trying to speak, my mother could barely contain her excitement. "A dying clue," she said with awe. "You heard a dying clue." It made me feel like I had achieved something special. "And?"

"She said 'Argghh.'"

"'Argghh,'" she repeated with perfect intonation. "Hmmmm. I don't suppose that's a name." I had to give her credit; she didn't question me about what I heard.

We spent a few more minutes speculating about the meaning of "Argghh" before disposing of Zelda's body, metaphorically speaking, and moving on to a discussion of the Marshall case. I filled her in on the specifics and the issues, leaving out my blunders or glossing over them whenever possible. Once I had told her everything I could think of to tell her, I smiled and said, "Okay, Ellery, who did it?"

She tapped the side of her teacup with a spoon and chewed on her lower lip in concentration. For a moment, I almost expected her to name the murderer. Instead, she had another question. "Where were the receptionist and that Conklin fellow when you found the body?"

"I believe the receptionist was in with one of the executives, and Conklin was at a business lunch. My understanding is that they both have alibis."

"That doesn't mean a thing."

"Admit it, Mother. You don't know who the murderer is. You don't even know if the Marshall case is in any way connected to what happened to Miss Gunnar or to me."

"Well," she said, uncoiling from the chair like a python about to strike. "I may not know who the murderer is or what's connected to what, but I do know one thing: either that woman is lying or the doctor is."

"Huh?" I wasn't expecting that.

"That doctor wants you to believe that woman's injuries are phony. Either they are, or they aren't." My mother has an uncanny way of simplifying complex issues.

"But I haven't been able to prove it one way or the other," I complained, hating myself for sounding like a six-year-old whining about a lost toy.

"What do you know about the doctor?"

"Well, not much," I admitted.

"And you call yourself a detective!"

"He's an orthopedic surgeon with good credentials," I countered. "And furthermore, I'm not a detective; I'm a claims adjuster. It's not the same thing."

"Don't you remember me telling you about my friend, Jane? She hired the 'best' for her operation, but he still made a mistake. God rest her soul. And just last week on television there was this doctor who operated on the wrong person." She crossed her arms and nodded knowingly at me. Now *that* was proof.

"You've convinced me. I'll run a check on the doctor." It wasn't a bad idea, even if it had come from my mother.

"And the woman. Do some more checking on her, too."

"I already have, Mother. And I talked with the neighbors just like you suggested. It didn't get me anything I can use. In fact, what they told me suggests that she may be telling the truth about her injuries." I wanted her to know that although I had listened to her advice, the effort had been futile. "And I've spent a lot of time staking out her house. Days and nights, hour after long hour. For nothing."

"Son," she said, smiling sweetly. Oh, oh, she was going to bring out the big guns. "You don't sit back and wait for the mountain to come to you." She rolled her eyes at the ceiling and said to no one in particular, "What kind of an innocent have I raised?" Then she stared directly at me and said, "Set a trap."

"A trap?"

"Trick her."

"Trick her?"

She looked at the ceiling again. "Provide her with an incentive to walk. Plant some pennies on her sidewalk and be prepared to take a picture when she gets out of her wheelchair to pick them up.

"Pennies? Who cares about a few pennies?"

"If she is out to make a fast buck, she'll pick up the pennies. Believe me." I wasn't entirely convinced, but I said I would consider it. That seemed to satisfy her, for now.

While Mother busied herself getting things back in order, I made a phone call to a friend, Milton Davenport, an underwriter for one of the two insurance firms that handle most of the malpractice insurance for doctors in the city. After the usual small talk and promises to get together soon for lunch, I asked him if he would check to see if his firm handled the malpractice insurance for Leon Oliver and, if not, could he could find out who did. Although you can do a lot of research online, someone in the field can find things much faster. And if his firm actually handled Oliver's malpractice, well, that would be a plus. I wanted to know if he had high premiums due to other claims and, if possible, find out if Pearl Rosenblatt had filed a claim against him. If everything seemed normal, I would rule this out as a line of inquiry.

Milton said he would check right away and get back to me. We had exchanged favors in the past. It was nice to have a good working relationship with someone who would occasionally scratch your back.

After my conversation with Milton, there was only one thing left to do. I headed to the bank to purchase a roll of coins. If I didn't try, I'd never hear the end of it. And if the stunt worked, I'd be able to charge off the expense.

To my surprise, my bank doesn't give you rolls of coins anymore. But the bank down the street will sell you a roll of coins wrapped by a customer. That seemed a bit chancy, but I wasn't talking about a lot of money. When I learned they were out of penny rolls, I decided to spring for 40 nickels at $2.00. They were probably better bait, and it wasn't much of an investment, even if it didn't work.

Not long after picking up the roll of nickels, I was heading down the familiar alley behind the Rosenblatt house with my camera secure in its bag attached to my belt and the roll of nickels in my pocket. Fortunately, the mud bath didn't seem to have damaged the camera, and although I didn't anticipate having any luck with the current endeavor, it was nice to be doing something. Everything seemed peaceful. There were no barking dogs, no clamoring children, no noisy lawnmowers. Just silence.

I glanced around, wondering which neighbor had finked on me before, then, satisfied no one was watching, I crept up to the house and peeked in the kitchen window. When I didn't see anyone, I hurriedly tore at the roll of nickels. It was like trying to open a bag of potato chips. I poked at it with my fingernails, gnawed at it with my teeth, and clawed it like a wild animal. No luck. Finally, I smacked the roll against one of the back steps. The whopping sound echoed off the fence and down the alley. But the roll finally gave way. Nickels flew across the lawn. Cursing, I tried to collect them in little pools of faux silver to make them easier to pick up.

Just as I was about to retreat to begin my vigil, I noticed the screen door. It was open. The back door was also open a crack. That seemed strange. Of course, not everyone is conscientious about closing doors all the way, but for some reason, I was drawn to the opening, like a deer to a car's headlights.

I have no excuse for my behavior. I should have known better. But I went up the steps and pushed open the door.

Chapter Eight

She was sitting there in her wheelchair, staring at me. Feeling awkward, like a kid caught stealing apples off a neighbor's tree, I stepped inside. "I know you said not to come back, but, ah, I can explain."

The room was dark, a small utility area with blinds pulled over the windows. Light from the kitchen cast a pale shaft behind Mrs. Rosenblatt, but she remained in shadow. Shifting my weight from one foot to the other, I began making excuses. "You see, my insurance company doesn't like to pay for phony claims—not that I'm saying your claim is phony, mind you. But we get a lot of them, you see. And, well, as I said before, I have to make sure that everything is on the up and up before making my recommendation. Absolutely sure." I paused, waiting for a response: anger, reasonableness, empathy, hostility, something. But she sat there staring at me, her hard eyes two tiny pinpoints of light in the gloom.

"I'm sorry," I began again. "But you do understand, don't you?" When she still said nothing, I babbled on. "It's my job. Nothing personal. And my mother…." I hesitated. Maybe it was best to leave Mother out of it. "I mean, I thought, well, I have to be certain. I don't want to lose my job by making a mistake."

She remained absolutely still and silent. As silent and still as a figure in a wax museum. What did she want from me? Had she seen what I had done? Was it such a terrible crime to sprinkle nickels in someone's back yard? She could keep them, with my compliments. I would even pick them up for her if she wanted me to.

My conversation with Mrs. Rosenblatt was interrupted by a police officer who erupted into the room like a jack-in-the-box with an agitated woman and another officer flanking him. "That's him," the woman screamed, pointing at me. "That's him. That's the one."

"Oh no," the first officer said. "Not you again." It was the cop who had responded to the neighbor's complaint the evening I had tried to take a picture of Mrs. Rosenblatt. I blinked at the intruders, trying to get my bearings while the hysterical woman moved from side to side behind the officer, pointing at me.

"What are you doing here?" the officer asked.

"Talking to Mrs. Rosenblatt."

"Someone switch on a light." The second officer flipped a switch on the wall near the entrance to the kitchen, and there was light. The officer looked at Mrs. Rosenblatt, then turned to me and asked, "You were talking to her, huh?"

"Yes, I was just explaining…." He held up his hand for me to stop. The woman continued wagging a denunciatory finger in my direction. The second officer was watching the tableau with a look of disbelief.

"Call for backup," the first officer ordered.

"That isn't necessary, is it?" I asked. Was there a city ordinance against giving away money by tossing nickels on someone's lawn? In any event, they wouldn't need a show of force if they were going to arrest me. I would go quietly.

During all of the commotion, Mrs. Rosenblatt sat there stoically, eyes staring straight ahead. I turned to her to appeal my case. Something wasn't right. I took a step toward her.

"Stay where you are," the officer ordered. He moved alongside her and put two fingers on her neck. After a moment, he said: "She's dead."

"Dead?"

"He killed her," the woman screeched. "He killed her."

"Mrs. O'Lander, why don't you wait for us in the other room," the officer requested.

"Killed her…he killed her." She kept repeating herself like a needle stuck in a grove on an old 78 record.

"The other room, Mrs. O'Lander. Please." The officer turned her around and gave her a little shove.

"Dead?" I said again. "But we were just talking."

The officer cleared his throat. "I should warn you that anything you say can be used against you in a court of law."

It was unreal. Had I actually been conversing with a dead woman? I looked more closely. There was a tiny wound between her eyes. Blood had oozed out and dribbled in a thin stream down the side of her nose. "Oh my god," I said. "She's been shot."

"Looks like that's what killed her, all right," the officer observed. I let him lead me into the living room, too dazed to say anything more about who I was or what I was doing there. Pearl Rosenblatt was dead, shot between the eyes, and I had been talking with her while rigor mortis slowly set in.

The other police officer joined us. "The squad's on its way," he said. I sank into a chair across from Mrs. O'Lander. She was glaring at me with a malevolence I'm sure she usually reserves for the bad guys on the Sopranos.

In what seemed like only minutes, Bruno arrived with a host of other police officers who immediately headed for the kitchen. When Bruno saw me, his mouth fell open. "Not you," he said. I was getting the impression that I wasn't going to be given complimentary tickets to the Policeman's Ball in the next millennium.

"This is the man we found with the body," the first officer reported. Bruno drew him aside, and they went into a huddle, whispering and furtively glancing in my direction. When they broke out of the huddle, the first officer took a stand guarding the door so I couldn't escape, and Bruno confronted me, standing with his legs slightly apart, hands on hips.

"What are you doing here, John?" Mrs. O'Lander frowned. You could see the question written all over her face: why was a police officer on a first-name basis with a murderer?

"I think I mentioned to you that Mrs. Rosenblatt is, er, was a potential claimant in a case I'm handling." My voice was shaking. I still couldn't get over the fact that she was dead. "Well, I decided to try one more time to see if she was faking her injuries." Bruno shook his head as if appalled at the level I had sunk to as a claims adjuster. "You don't understand," I continued. "It isn't fair to the other insureds if someone fakes a claim. It just ends up increasing everybody's premiums."

"Mrs. O'Lander here says that you were lurking around the back door." I felt my face go red. "Well?"

"I was near the back door when I noticed it wasn't closed."

"But what were you doing out there?"

"He shot her," Mrs. O'Lander offered.

"I don't even own a gun," I protested. Suddenly I felt better. I didn't have a gun. I couldn't have shot Pearl without a gun. "Did you find one?" I asked. If there was no gun in the vicinity, then I was in the clear.

"Just tell me what you were doing snooping around out back." Everyone was waiting for me to reply.

"Could I talk to you about this in private?"

"He's going to confess," Mrs. O'Lander said gleefully. "I knew it—he shot her. He killed her."

"Do you want a lawyer, John?" Bruno gently asked.

"I don't need a lawyer, do I, Bruno? I didn't shoot her. I just want to tell you about what I was doing in private. It's a company matter. A private, company matter."

"Okay," he conceded. He turned to Mrs. O'Lander and told her she could leave, but to give the other officer her address and phone number. "I'll come by to get your statement as soon as I finish up here." Although he had clearly dismissed her, she didn't want to go. The other officer had to take her by the elbow and lead her away. "Now, John. Let's hear your story."

I explained the whole thing, right from the beginning. Bruno groaned and shook his head from time to time, but he didn't interrupt. If he hadn't known Mother as well as he knows me, he might have doubted my story, but when we were young, he'd spent almost as much time at our house as I had. Even as kids we had recognized Mother's knack for getting to the heart of an issue. We had both used her as a sounding board when we had a problem or a decision to make. "The nickels are still out there," I concluded. He called for one of his men to go out and check.

"John," he said in a tired voice. "You aren't making things easy for me these days." I understood what he was saying. I wasn't making life too easy for myself these days. "Two bodies in one day," he continued. "I understand bad luck and coincidence, but why were you *talking* to her, John?" The question was addressed to me, but he was staring at the wall as if the answer could be found there somewhere. Then he stood up and started to pace, doing that fist-in-palm gesture to punctuate each step. "Okay, so I *think* I understand, but how do I explain that to the Prosecutor? It looks like you are in it up to your eyeballs." He stopped pacing. "Although no one would be spreading nickels around if they had just committed a murder…unless it was a ploy," he said, not looking at me but going through the logic out loud. Then he glanced in my direction, apparently unable to decide whether I was a cold-hearted murderer or simply an unlucky and inept bystander.

"The gun," I said. "Did they find a gun?"

"No."

"Doesn't that prove I'm innocent?" Who would shoot someone, go somewhere to get rid of the weapon, and then return to the scene of the crime?"

"She's been dead for hours, John. I doubt anyone will think that you hung around all that time waiting to be caught. But you have to admit that it all looks damn strange. Damn strange."

She'd been dead for hours, just sitting there in her wheelchair, staring off into space, blood trickling down her face. And I hadn't noticed. It *was* hard to believe. Damn strange, in fact.

When Bruno left to talk to Mrs. O'Lander, I was escorted to headquarters. While I wasn't exactly given honored guest treatment, I wasn't abused either. There were no handcuffs, no glaring lights, no rubber hoses. And no one forced me to drink the rank brew they called coffee. I did that to punish myself for being stupid enough to carry on a conversation with a dead woman. Holy shit. Bruno was worried about how he would explain it to the Prosecutor, but I was starting to worry about what would happen if the press got hold of that tiny but juicy detail. What a great headline it would make. "Accused talks to dead woman, but she doesn't reveal her murderer's name."

No one seemed to need me for anything, but I had been warned not to leave. Not much was happening, a few officers here and there talking on the phone, filling out paperwork, or chatting with each other just out of earshot. There weren't even any six-month-old magazines to read. To kill time, I decided to see what was in the snack machine. Of course, once I started looking at the pictures of food on the packages, I wanted something. Even though I knew that whatever was inside would be a different size and possibly different color from the picture. But the implicit promise made my stomach growl.

A message on the machine flashed "no change." Wouldn't you know it, I didn't have any coins and nothing smaller than a five. I asked someone passing by if they had change for a five, but they said they didn't without even thinking about it. I tried again when the next person came by. He took out his wallet, said he had four ones and offered them to me for my five. I accepted. What can you do? Of course, the bag of ranch-flavored Doritos I wanted was a dollar and twenty-five cents. I put in my two dollars and watched as the bag moved slowly forward, stopping just a fraction of an inch away from the drop-off point. Since I couldn't exactly beat on a machine in a police station, I either had to put in more money or give up. In the end, the tiny bag of Doritos cost me five dollars. But they helped pass the time.

When the Doritos ran out, I was at loose ends again. I decided to call Mother. She was probably wondering what had happened to me. "Hello, Mother"? I asked when she answered.

"Well, did it work?"

"Not exactly."

"Not exactly? What does that mean?"

"It means she's dead."

"More bodies, John?"

"Just one more, Mother."

"Was it death by natural causes? She didn't have a heart attack or something while trying to pick up the nickels?"

"No, Mother. She was murdered. I, ah, discovered the body."

"How was she murdered?"

"A bullet."

"Where was she shot?" Only *my* mother would ask something like that.

"Between the eyes."

"Was there much blood?" The question seemed positively ghoulish to me. I would have to check what mysteries her club was reading. Or maybe I should be monitoring her television programs.

"Just a trickle." If I didn't tell her, she'd just keep trying. I suddenly remembered what it felt like standing there, talking to Pearl Rosenblatt, while she stared at me. Only she hadn't been staring at me after all.

"Nasty business," she said with feeling. Now that she had the key details, it occurred to her to ask about me. "Where are you calling from?"

"Police Headquarters. Since I discovered the body, they've asked me to hang around in case there are more questions. Bruno's handling the case," I added.

"And how is Bruno these days? He hasn't dropped by for a while. You tell him he should drop by for a cuppa one of these days."

"I'll do that, Mother." I could just imagine the conversation they would have about me and the dead bodies. "Well, I have to run now. I'll check in with you tomorrow."

"It would have worked," she said in parting. "If she hadn't been dead."

Yes, it might have worked. If she hadn't been dead. Damn. People were dying right and left, and they seemed determined to involve me in their messy departures. Why couldn't they leave me alone to deal with crumpled fenders and sore necks? If I wanted to look at dead bodies, I'd have become a mortician.

This time I made it to the john before I was sick. There was something about seeing or talking about blood and bodies that didn't set well with me. Maybe I was still reacting to my greasy breakfast. And the Doritos obviously hadn't helped. But immediately after emptying my stomach, I felt better. I returned to my assigned place and continued to wait. And wait. To my amazement, I started feeling hungry again. I checked my pockets again for money. Finding none, I looked around to see if there was any food on any desks in the area. Nothing. Not that I would have stolen food from someone in a police station. Well, maybe. I was getting pretty hungry. I remembered one time seeing a movie in which someone chewed on their shoe soles for nourishment, but I doubted there was any nutritional value in leatherette. It might pass the time, though.

When I had almost given up hope, Bruno finally showed up. "We need to talk," he said.

"I need to eat," I said. He looked at me as though I was out of my mind. "I'm hungry," I explained.

After only a moment's hesitation, Bruno herded me out of the building and down the block to a small café. He was an officer in charge of a murder investigation, but he was also a humane person, as well as my former friend. I say "former" because I was beginning to get the feeling that the past didn't count for much when it was a question of not one, but two corpses.

I ordered a hamburger and home fries, and Bruno ordered a bowl of chowder. Guiltily sucking in what I feared was a developing paunch, I suddenly envied Bruno's athletic physique and his square jawline. Maybe I should get a personal trainer.

We made small talk for a few minutes, as if Bruno wanted to postpone our conversation about the murders as much as I did. Finally, he stopped fiddling with his spoon, took a deep breath, and began.

"John, Wilhelmina O'Lander is anxious to testify that you have been hanging around Pearl Rosenblatt's house for weeks." Wilhelmina? No one was named Wilhelmina these days. "She also informed me," he continued, "that she reported you the other night, but for some reason, she can't explain. Both Pearl and her daughter Marie covered for you." Just as I was about to defend myself, our orders arrived.

I automatically picked up the ketchup bottle and turned it upside down over my hamburger, tapping the bottom with two fingers to get the ketchup flowing. A red glob oozed out and plopped on my hamburger. I quickly smashed the bun down on top. Red drool squished out and trickled down the side of my burger. I was suddenly not all that hungry.

"She thinks you were blackmailing them," Bruno said matter-of-factly. Like we were discussing the weather.

"Blackmailing them?"

Bruno took a sip of chowder, letting the tension build. "You have to admit that it does seem a bit strange that they didn't turn you in." Sip, sip. "I assume they caught you peeking in the window like Mrs. O'Lander claims?"

"Well, yes, I admit I was trying to catch Mrs. Rosenblatt standing up or moving around."

"So why didn't they turn you in?" He put his spoon down and stared at me.

My mind was as empty as my stomach, and just as uneasy. Why had they let me go? I didn't know for sure. "It was my impression that they didn't want any trouble or delay getting things settled as soon as possible."

He thought about that for a minute. "If Mrs. Rosenblatt was on the up-and-up, don't you think she would have been a little quicker to turn you in?"

"That's what I thought." Actually, it wasn't, but it made sense. "But they knew that I didn't have any evidence to suggest she was faking her injuries." I shoved a fry in my mouth. It was cold. They must have been sitting around awhile, maybe originally cooked for someone else who changed their mind.

"So, in other words, you're saying that you didn't have anything to blackmail her with?"

"Well, you might put it that way." Those wouldn't be the "other words" I'd choose, but the conclusion was the same. I was simply trying to explain that since I wasn't a threat, the Rosenblatts had no reason to turn me in. On the other hand, since I wasn't a threat, they had no reason NOT to turn me in. It was very confusing.

Sip. Sip. Bruno turned his attention back to his chowder. "But you didn't give up." Sip, sip. Sip. He finished the chowder, scraping the bottom of the bowl with his spoon. Scrape, scrape. It was a cacophony of eating sounds. Meanwhile, I hadn't been able to face biting into my ketchup drenched hamburger. And I'd only managed to consume a handful of cold fries. My stomach didn't know whether to ask for more food or scream "enough."

"The nickels were my last chance. If she didn't try to pick them up, then

I was going to call it quits. Frankly, Bruno, if it hadn't been for Mother, I wouldn't have gone back again." I didn't want to blame Mother, but I wanted him to understand.

Bruno nodded, pushed his soup bowl away, and looked at my plate. His eyes said "I thought you were hungry," but he didn't ask about my uneaten meal. It was just one more inconsistency to be chalked up against me. "You were reaching the end of your investigation?"

"Yes."

"And what were you going to recommend?"

"I was going to recommend that we cover the cost of Mrs. Rosenblatt's automobile through the Marshall's liability coverage. However, if Mrs. Rosenblatt decided to sue, then we might have done some further investigation. If she sued, there was a lot more money at risk. Of course, the amount would have depended on the extent of her injuries and who else was being sued. And there would still have been the question of fault, the accident, or the operation. As I explained before, I was trying to be thorough so that my recommendation would be comprehensive instead of limited to the Marshall claim."

"So, Mrs. Rosenblatt might have sued the doctor, the hospital, and Universal." It wasn't a question. Bruno picked up one of my fries, dipped it in some ketchup that had escaped from my hamburger, and chewed thoughtfully. "It seems like there were plenty of others with a motive for murder." A tiny fleck of ketchup clung to his lower lip. Please wipe it off, I silently pleaded. As if hearing my request, he picked up another fry that scraped off the ketchup on the way into his mouth.

"Mrs. Marshall is concerned about her savings," I said. "I don't think she realizes that she's probably not liable. But she doesn't seem like a murderer to me."

"Few ever do," Bruno assured me.

"No doctor likes to be sued," I continued.

"But they are sued all the time, right?" I nodded. "And they have malpractice insurance, right?" I nodded again. "What about the kid?"

"Mark?" He had nothing to lose; he could go bankrupt and not care a whit.

"No motive, no money."

"To save his mother?"

"Not the type," I answered firmly.

Bruno ate still another fry. "About your office and home—what do you think the connection is?"

"You mean between the break-ins and the murders?"

"Specifically, between the break-ins and the Rosenblatt murder. You said that was the only case you were working on."

"But why—" I began.

"*You* tell *me*."

"I don't think there is a connection. If there is, I can't imagine what it would be."

"So, what's your explanation for the break-ins?"

I felt like the kid who is suddenly pulled off the bench in the final minutes of the game and sent in to save the day. I wasn't warmed up. Worse yet, I'd never saved the day before and had no reason to think that I could do so now. Was it possible Mark Marshall had a soft spot in his adolescent heart for his mother? At least for his mother's money? Was Mrs. Marshall a villain hiding behind her vintage apron? Had the doctor become enraged over Mrs. Rosenblatt's charges, running amok to save his reputation? The only thing I knew for sure was that *I* hadn't killed anyone.

"I've told you everything I know, Bruno. Sorry."

"Everything?"

"Everything." This time I didn't avoid looking him in the eyes. He sighed, his fingers caressing the edge of my half-empty plate. He had devoured all my fries.

"I just hope you are telling me the truth, John."

As we were leaving, I said, "By the way, Mother said to tell you to drop by sometime."

Bruno smiled, and for an instant, I saw the Bruno of our youth with his lop-sided, mischievous smile. "Let her know that I'll do just that. Soon."

It was late when I arrived home. The place was neater than it had been for years. Mother had done a good job. Exhausted, I was torn between relaxing in a hot bath or dropping onto the bed fully clothed. The bath won out. I had one foot in the water when the phone rang. It was Milton.

"I have the information you asked for," he said.

"Shoot," I replied, then winced as I pictured the tiny bullet hole in Pearl Rosenblatt's forehead and the oozing red Heinz on my hamburger.

As it turned out, Dr. Oliver did indeed have coverage with Milton's company, but there was no claim pending. The doctor's premiums, however, were sky-high. They reflected a history of malpractice suits. "He could be canceled if he has any more problems," Milton continued. "Does he have a problem, John?"

"Not anymore," I said without thinking.

"Huh?"

"I appreciate you taking the time to check on this for me, Milton," I said before he could say anything more. "But you needn't worry about the coverage. The claimant involved is no longer, ah, in a position to sue."

"That's good news for Dr. Oliver," Milton said.

"Yes," I mused. "Good news for Dr. Oliver."

Chapter Nine

She stood there in the doorway to my office, her face expressionless. "Marie," I said, surprised to see her. "I'm sorry about your mother."

"Don't give me that crap," she snapped. "I didn't come here for sympathy." She plopped herself uninvited onto the straight-backed chair next to my desk and looked around. "Got anything to drink?"

"No," I replied truthfully with a regretful glance at the bottom drawer of my filing cabinet.

"Oh well, this won't take long." She crossed her legs and cleared her throat. "I want you to know that just because someone knocked off my mom doesn't mean your insurance company is home free."

"Well, technically, the case is closed." I didn't want to upset her further. Losing one's mother can be very traumatic.

"Not if I can help it." She glanced around as if expecting a waiter to come and take her order. "Look, I came here to let you know that I'm going to follow up on this insurance business on my own, so don't you go thinking that you can forget about my mother's money. She had it coming, and I've inherited everything. So now it comes to me. Got that?"

"Of course, we are responsible for the damage to your mother's car, but the rest is complicated."

"What about her injuries?"

"She didn't put in a claim—"

"We'll see about that," she interrupted. "I know what I'm entitled to, see? And I'm going to get my money." With that, she leapt up and flounced out of the room, panty seams protruding through tight white slacks.

94

And I had thought Thursday was going to be uneventful.

The Marshall-Rosenblatt file was on my desk. I flipped it open and tried to concentrate. If Marie pursued the claim on behalf of the estate, the company might make her an offer to cover medical expenses, lost wages, maybe even some for pain and suffering. Although the dead weren't supposed to suffer, at least not in this world. Unfortunately, the file was still incomplete. I needed to know whether Pearl had filed a claim against the hospital, and I needed a statement from her doctor about her injuries. Since I didn't feel up to tackling Conklin, I decided to try and accomplish both tasks by a trip to the hospital.

When I told Emma where I was headed, she gave me a "yeah, sure" look and went right on doing whatever she was doing at her computer.

The Lady was still holding her Lamp in front of the Hospital, towering over the expanse of well-trimmed lawn that stretched out before her like a green carpet. My eyes roamed over her shapely figure draped in a fetching version of an old-fashioned nurse's uniform. Nice, I thought. I've always liked big women.

Dr. Byron Cheever, Assistant Director, was out of town on important business, according to his admin. And she was unable or unwilling to provide me with the information I needed. She suggested I check with their insurance agent. I replied that I would rather talk directly with Dr. Cheever. Sounding very authoritative, she informed me that Dr. Cheever was a very busy man. He was second in command of the hospital, and with the Director about to retire, it was very difficult to get an appointment with him. He was available for fifteen minutes a week from next Monday at 11:45. Did I want to see him then?

I declined the appointment and decided to look for Dr. Oliver instead. As I wandered down one of the many antiseptic corridors in search of an information desk, it seemed like everyone I ran into was in a hurry. Workers in white or green uniforms rushed by me as if I were Chesterton's invisible man. Apparently, anyone either not wearing the team's colors or expiring on the spot wasn't worth noticing.

There were arrows directing me to grim-sounding locations like diagnostic imaging and gastroenterology and the renal unit. I wasn't sure about the first two, but I definitely didn't want to go to the renal unit. There were also official black and white signs posted on most of the doors: "Staff Only." "Keep Out." "Men." "Dr. Gill." "Television Room." "Linens." Didn't this hospital have any patients? When I finally found someone to ask and inquired as to whether it would be possible to talk with Dr. Oliver, I was told that he was in surgery. It looked like my only option was to call it quits and head back to the office.

The decision to locate Dr. Oliver's office came upon me slowly, like the tide gradually inching its way up the beach. It's my investigator's instinct. But I couldn't help arguing the decision with myself. So far, I wasn't scoring very high on the intrigue scale. Common sense told me I should let someone else do the snooping. From here on, the smart thing for me to do was lead a quiet life filled with routine cases and uncomplicated, cushiony women. On the other hand, a good investigator would definitely be interested in a look at Pearl Rosenblatt's file. It could be interesting reading, maybe even a motive for murder.

Of course, nothing is ever as simple as it seems at first blush. Did part-time doctors even have offices? Surely surgeons were important enough to claim some space as their own.

"Can I help you?" a quavery voice asked. Oh, oh, caught out of bounds. I turned toward the source and saw an ancient man wrapped in a maroon bathrobe slowly making his way toward me with the aid of a metal walker. The front legs of the walker ended in bright green tennis balls. His legs ended in brown slipper socks. One had a hole in the toe. His scant hair was unkempt, and he exuded a faint odor of age and illness that even a strong antiseptic couldn't mask.

"Thanks, maybe you can. Do you happen to know where Dr. Leon Oliver's office is?" The question slipped out before I knew I was going to ask it.

"Sure do," he said slowly, his voice as wrinkled as his skin. "At the end of the hall and to your right." He pointed with his nose, age-spotted hands tightly gripping the walker.

"Thanks. I appreciate that." I wanted to say more, something profound about aging and death. Instead, I set off at a brisk pace, embarrassed by my comparative youth and good health, fleeing from the future.

Perhaps I would have stumbled upon Dr. Oliver's office on my own. However, his office wasn't exactly on a well-traveled route. It was at the end of a short hallway, a dead-end that looked like it was devoted primarily to storage. But anyone who came anywhere near his office would have seen his nameplate. It was definitely an eye-catcher, with red economy-sized letters that proudly proclaimed his name and specialty, with a picture off to one side of a rod with a snake curled around it. I was pretty sure the rod and snake thing was a medical symbol, but no one who'd seen Snakes on a Plane would be reassured by a snake hugging a rod. Maybe Dr. Oliver should rent the movie.

Well, I couldn't just stand there gawking at his door, so I pretended I expected him to be in when I knocked. He wasn't. But the hall was empty. My fingers closed around the doorknob and turned. It wasn't locked. Before I knew it, I was inside, pleased to note that the prestigious Dr. Oliver had an office not much larger than mine, although there was a window with a view. It looked over the new wing of the hospital, floor after floor of hospital room windows looking back at him. Impressive.

Once inside, my mind and my heart started racing. A flurry of proverbs came to mind: "opportunity knocks but once," "if fortune knocks open the door," "make hay while the sun shines," the sort of things people tell themselves to rationalize doing things that common sense tells them they shouldn't. But instead of feeling buoyed by these thoughts, I remembered something Yogi Berra once said: *It's like deja vu all over again.* Here I was, in a place I had no right to be, doing something that was, at best, a bit shady, and most likely illegal. Why?

Oh well, I was already there, so why not?

Dr. Oliver's computer was turned off. I didn't bother trying to see if it was password protected. There was a huge file cabinet to the right of his desk that was beckoning to me. Older doctors still take a lot of handwritten notes. Probably so no one else can read them. Unfortunately, the good doctor left his office door open, but he had locked up his files. Sometimes I wished I knew how to pick locks, but that would probably lead me into temptation. Besides, like a lot of other people with locked drawers, Dr. Oliver kept his keys in the top drawer of his desk beneath one of those little insert trays. There they were, right next to his gum and his breath mints. Dr. Oliver was a very cautious guy. Who would think of looking in his desk for a key to his file cabinet?

The first drawer I opened contained files labeled A-L, as near as I could figure. The files were a mess. Maybe bone men don't have to be as precise as other medical specialists. Just pop a few bones back in place, and the patient is cured.

Then, much to my amazement, I found the Rosenblatt file under the "R's," just where it was supposed to be. I pulled it out and began wading through the pages of scrawled medical jargon. It was almost as bad as reading an insurance policy. I leafed through the file twice before concluding there were no post-surgery notes. There was, however, one piece of yellow lined paper scrunched under some of the forms that contained scribbled notations in some sort of personal shorthand. I smoothed out the sheet and tried holding it at various angles and distances to see if that improved its legibility. It didn't.

"X-rays so-so," one line seemed to say, if I squinted my eyes and used my imagination.

"Sue?" I deciphered off to one side. My heart started beating faster.

"GT RD RPT" was written in the lower left-hand corner with doodles around the letters, overlapping squiggles along the bottom of the page, and a smiley face with a crooked mustache in the margin above the cryptic message. GTRDRPT said rapidly altogether, out loud or uttered slowly in three separate chunks meant as much to me as Hilda Gunnar's last words. I gave up and returned to the routine forms in the file.

There was nothing of particular interest. What I needed were the post-surgery notes. Just in case they'd been misfiled, I rummaged through the adjacent files. Then I turned to his desk again. There, big as life, was another file labeled "Rosenblatt," the hospital file. Peeking from beneath the file was a sheet of paper with "Post Surgery Notes" written in a precise hand at the top. He may not have been organized, but he was a great labeler.

The notes were amazingly neat, with proper punctuation and literate phraseology. Surprising. Most post-surgery notes I'd seen were full of incomplete sentences and bad handwriting. They were frequently written in a hurry and had to be supplemented with verbal comments if a case went to trial. These were almost too good to be true. It was all there, the step-by-step procedure. A standard cervical spinal fusion. Supposedly successful. I borrowed a piece of blank paper from a side drawer and took a few notes of my own, summarizing the important points. I could have taken pictures of the pages with my cell, but then there would be a record that could be traced.

I was about to leave when I remembered the word "sue" written on the crumpled piece of paper. Had Pearl Rosenblatt contacted the doctor about a possible lawsuit, or was he just anticipating a potential suit based on her refusal to come in for a post-surgical checkup? I went back to the files and thumbed through the tabs. This was so much more satisfying than a computer search. You could see at a glance everything there was to look at. You didn't have to wonder what search term you might be overlooking or what complex hierarchy of files you needed to navigate.

Under "M," I found an unmarked folder containing insurance information. "M" for "malpractice"? "Marshall"? "Messy"? It was a thick file crammed with all kinds of handwritten notes and correspondence. What I found most interesting were two letters at the back of the file. One was a warning letter from his insurance carrier that discussed his history of malpractice claims, and the other was a copy of a letter he had sent to another carrier requesting information about possible coverage. The latter was dated two days after the first one. You could argue that looking for new insurance after receiving a warning letter was a wise precaution. On the other hand, it could have been prompted by the knowledge, or fear, of a potential claim by Pearl Rosenblatt. Her threat might have placed Dr. Oliver under the gun...or vice versa.

A cold chill ran down my spine. Not a good thing to have happen in an orthopedist's office. Here I was looking at what could be incriminating evidence. And it's a known fact that a man who has killed once does not hesitate to kill again. At least, I *think* that's a known fact. Even if it wasn't, I didn't think it was smart to hang around to test that particular hypothesis armed only with my wits and a very weak right hook.

After carefully returning all the papers and files to their proper, and improper, places, locking the cabinet, and replacing the key, I took one last look around to make certain I was leaving everything as it had been before my visit. Then I tiptoed to the door. With one hand on the doorknob, I paused. Did I hear voices? Yes, I did. There were voices in the hall. Someone was out there! Should I hide? Make a run for it? I looked around at the sparsely furnished office. Hiding was out of the question, and my knees were suddenly too weak to bolt. My only alternative was to wait and hope.

It seemed like they would never stop talking. Then, when they did, the sounds didn't drift away as if they were moving off down the hall. Rather, the conversation fell off suddenly, like flipping a switch. Had they sensed something was wrong? Were they standing outside in the hall waiting for me to come out? I pressed my ear against the wood surface and listened as hard as I could, but the only thing I could hear was a pulse beating in my ear.

When I couldn't stand it any longer, I turned the knob on the door and paused to wait for a reaction. Nothing happened. I pushed the door open a crack and listened some more. Still nothing. Each minute I waited was a minute closer to when Dr. Oliver might return and find me there on the wrong side of his office door. I had no idea how long it would be before he finished his surgery. At this very moment, he might be headed back to his office, still holding a bloody scalpel. There was nothing to do but go for it.

I opened the door and rushed into the hallway. There was no one there to thwart me. I almost ran into the opposite wall in my enthusiasm to get away. I had barely regained some of my composure when an intern and a nurse came out of a room a few feet down the hall. He was rubbing her left buttock and nuzzling her neck. She was busy buttoning her shirt. They seemed surprised and not too pleased to see me. They nodded as I strolled past. Somehow I didn't think they would be mentioning our encounter to anyone.

The nurse receptionist's head snapped up as I came out of the corridor marked "Staff Only." "Where have you been?" she challenged.

"Looking for a bathroom."

"The public restrooms are down that way." She pointed to her left, keeping her finger aloft, waiting for me to acknowledge her information with action.

"Thank you." I obediently headed in the direction she was pointing.

Before bypassing the restroom, I checked over my shoulder to make sure she hadn't followed me. The coast was clear. The problem was that I no longer knew where I was and didn't want to go back the way I had come. After wandering around awhile, I came to an information desk. The man behind the desk directed me to the entrance. By the time I found my way there, I had an idea. I stopped at reception and explained that I was trying to catch up with Dr. Oliver with a quick question and could they tell me the best time to do that. She looked up his online schedule and told me I should probably try tomorrow. He had back-to-back surgeries today and wouldn't be done until about eleven o'clock this evening.

Smiling to myself, I headed for my car, nodding cheerfully at the Lady with the Lamp as I passed by. GT RD RPT, huh? Well, Dr. Oliver, I said to myself, you might be able to fool your average claims adjuster, but I, for one, am onto you.

Chapter Ten

"Don't shoot!" I yelled. "I give up."

Why had the receptionist told me Dr. Oliver would be in surgery until at least eleven? Hadn't she realized that giving me that piece of information would tempt me to do something foolish? Of course, I had considered the possibility that Dr. Oliver had a large family and a live-in nanny, but if she hadn't told me he wouldn't be home until late that night, I never would have started thinking about a plan to search his residence. And now, there I was, hands in the air, staring down the wrong end of a .22 pistol.

The Oliver home was impressive by any standards, a huge white house that could have been a pre-Civil War mansion, except that it didn't have any pillars. It needed pillars to be authentic antebellum. Although everything else fit my romantic notions of what the world looked like back then. An ornate iron gate barred the entrance to a long, tree-lined driveway that curved through carefully tended lawns sprinkled with flower beds. I thought I could smell magnolias. Well, I could smell some kind of flower, and magnolias went with the rest of the setting.

The sun was just going down as I drove slowly past the front of the residence. A single streetlight winked on. Soft shadows flickered across the grass as flowers shivered in the early evening breeze. I parked across the street and down the block, waiting to see if any lights went on in the Oliver home once the sun set. None did. Even then, I played it cautious, in a bold sort of way. I went over to the iron gates, pushed one side open far enough to slip through, and walked up to the front door, and knocked. For good measure, I rang the doorbell. I could hear an old-fashioned ding-dong echoing somewhere deep inside the house. I rang it again, giving anyone inside plenty of time to answer. No one did.

It would have been easy right then and there to slink off the porch and creep around to the back of the house, but I was determined to play it safe. My blunder quota was filled. Instead of searching for a window conveniently left open or vines hanging from the second floor just begging to be climbed, I returned the way I had come, as if I were a legitimate visitor.

Once back at my car, I got in, drove around the block, and parked in a secluded spot away from streetlamps and the prying eyes of neighbors. From there, I was able to cut across a sparsely wooded area to the side of the Oliver home, masked from view by trees and gloom. Things went well until I reached the still unlit house. I couldn't find a single unlocked window. And unless I could scale the side of the house like a fly, there was no way to reach the second floor and remain out of sight. Things were looking pretty sad until I decided to try the back door.

It was unlocked.

I slipped inside and found myself in a dark room, unable to see a thing. That was when I realized I should have brought a flashlight. I searched my pockets and found a battered book of matches from the last time we had barbecued at Mother's. There was only one match left. I used it to get my bearings. After the flame died, I hesitantly headed in what I hoped was the right direction, swinging my hands in front of me to avoid smashing into something. That proved to be an effective tactic until one of my hands collided with something that fell to the floor and shattered into what sounded like a million pieces. Then I stepped on the rubble and ground the remaining chunks into dust with a loud crunching noise.

After standing there for a minute, frozen by my misstep, I decided it had been a blessing in disguise. Obviously, I had the house to myself. If I could find a study, I might even brave switching on a light.

Once I worked my way into the main part of the house, it was easier to see. The windows admitted just enough moonlight from outside to enable me to quickly pass through the kitchen into the dining room. From there, I found the living room, a bathroom, a game room and, finally, a study. It was at the back of the house on the opposite side from the door through which I had gained admittance. There were heavy dark velvet curtains over the windows, held back with what I imagined in the dim light were gold tassels. Scarlett O'Hara would have been in hog heaven. Unfortunately, when I tried to release the tassels in order to pull the curtains shut, I discovered they were fixed in place with large tacks. My fingernails weren't up to the job of removing the tacks, so I had to settle for hauling the curtains up through the tassels, a slow and tiresome chore.

When I finally located a switch near the door, the lights came on with a dazzling brilliance that blinded me. If the room had been filled with naked people, I would have been none the wiser. After my eyesight returned to normal, I was relieved to see that the room was empty. It was about five times the size of my office and looked like something left over from a movie set. One wall was lined with built-in bookcases filled to capacity with bound volume sets. There was a ladder that rolled along in front of the bookcase to provide easy access to the higher shelves. The adjacent wall had a series of expensive-looking paintings on display in gilt frames. I didn't much care for most of them, which probably meant they were worth a bundle. There was a knickknack shelf on the third wall, alongside a space filled with framed photographs. Family pictures. A younger-looking Dr. Oliver with a woman and children. An adorable young girl with a ponytail and skinny legs riding a bicycle. A towheaded boy, playing with a dog. An attractive woman beaming at the two children as they gaped with fascination at a magnificent cake glowing with candles. The stuff of family memories.

Feeling a bit guilty to be searching his study under the watchful eyes of his family, I nevertheless turned to the purpose of my visit: finding the missing post-surgery notes. If they hadn't already been destroyed, maybe they were here among the doctor's personal records. Of course, GT RD RPT might have meant something other than "get rid of the report," but I had other evidence to bolster my suspicions.

Right from the first time I saw them, I knew that the post-surgery notes I had found at the hospital were too good to be true. In fact, it hadn't taken much research to determine they had been copied almost word for word from *Hall On Orthopedics,* a standard medical text that Universal keeps in its claims library. I looked up the passages online by typing in phrases and sentences. Not exactly a feat of technical genius, but good enough to uncover the doctor's futile attempt at plagiarism. Why he hadn't simply paraphrased was beyond me. The bottom line was that he had not been trying to produce notes about what actually happened during the surgery. Rather, he had tried to establish beyond a reasonable doubt that he had followed best practices during his operation on Pearl Rosenblatt. In other words, he had lied. And I wanted to know why.

I went through his desk first. I found a few interesting items, but nothing pertaining to Pearl Rosenblatt. In one of the drawers, there was an ingenious corkscrew shaped like a miniature gun, and in another, tucked in behind a stack of notepads, was a lavender-scented envelope addressed in a feminine hand to "Leo." Obviously from a mature woman, someone who preferred a titillating scent to texting and who had learned cursive in school. I paused a moment to mourn the death of cursive writing.

Just as I was about to explore what was in a small wood cabinet to the left of the desk, I thought I heard a noise. If, at that point, I had anything resembling instinct, I would have made a hasty retreat out the window. Instead, I convinced myself it was my imagination and continued my search.

Moments later, a woman burst into the room, holding a gun in front of her in both hands like she was ready to take on the entire cavalry. Frosted hair sprouted from her head in unruly swirls, a modern Medusa without the snakes. She was wearing a long flowing gown, all hot pink and black. Elegant, but a bit flashy for my taste.

I took all of that in at a glance, but the thing that impressed me the most was the gun she was pointing at my chest. I couldn't be sure she knew how to use it, or even if it was loaded. For all I knew, it was a cigarette lighter. But I didn't need a light any more than I needed to be shot by this wild-looking, vaguely familiar woman. Faced with that unwelcome contingency, I did what any red-blooded American who hasn't seen a John Wayne film in eons would do. "Don't shoot," I yelled. "I give up!"

To emphasize my desire to surrender, I raised my hands in the air. That was a mistake. The Pekingese that accompanied her interpreted my movement as an intent to attack. It came lurching toward me like a fur toilet seat cover on the rampage. I automatically leapt back.

"Don't move," she cried, the gun wavering as she tried to keep it trained on my chest.

"Don't shoot," I pleaded, kicking at the dog to keep him away from my ankles.

"Don't you hurt FooFoo, or I'll shoot," she threatened.

"Call him off," I begged, continuing to take evasive action while keeping both hands in the air. Then I was up against the wall, and no further retreat was possible. The dog snarled and nipped at my legs like he meant business. I tried to ward him off by scrunching down and waving my left hand.

"Put your hands up," the woman screamed. She was standing almost on top of me, her trigger finger dangerously close to doing its worst.

"All right. All right." Both hands in the air once again, I nudged FooFoo away with my foot. Another mistake. He went for my ankle like a wolf for the jugular, his tiny pointed teeth penetrating my pant leg and tearing into my flesh. "Errgh," I whimpered, shaking my leg. "He's biting me."

"Good, FooFoo. Good dog."

The dog adjusted his grip, carving a jagged line in my ankle in the process. I couldn't stand the pain. In a frenzy, I grabbed the mutt by the ears and yanked him off my leg. When the gun went off, I was only numbly aware of what had happened. The bullet smashed into the wall where I had been standing just moments before. Holding the squirming tangle of fur and teeth away from me, I begged her to "Please take him."

She hesitated, a whiff of smoke emanating from the gun that was still hoping for more action.

"He bit me," I explained. "I'm bleeding." My leg felt like I had been attacked by a shark.

After an eternity, she relented. "It's all right, FooFoo," she crooned as she reached out and petted the beast. To me, she ordered, "Put him down."

"If I put him down, he'll just come at me again," I complained. The dog

106

continued to struggle. A sharp fang scraped along the top of my thumb, and droplets of blood started making a tiny pattern of dots on the otherwise immaculate carpet.

"FooFoo," she said loudly. The dog obediently went limp. "Give him to me." She extended one hand, the other still holding onto the gun, but it was unclear where it was pointing.

Relieved to get rid of him, I thrust the dog into her hands. "Look what he did," I said, showing her my thumb. She wasn't impressed until I also pointed out what my injury was doing to her carpet. It was no surprise when she blamed me for that. She reached into her pocket and handed me a Kleenex. I wasn't entirely sure that it hadn't been used at least once before, but I dutifully wrapped my thumb in it anyway.

"Now, what are you doing in here?" she asked.

Was it too late to claim I was in the wrong house, that it was all a mistake? Should I refuse to answer without a lawyer present? Should I ask to borrow a cup of sugar?

"You don't have a bag," she observed.

"Bag?"

"Your burglar bag."

"I'm not a burglar," I said. I was a lot of things, a bungler and a dog hater, but not a common thief. "And I'm hurt," I added, holding out my thumb as proof. If anything, my ankle felt worse. Maybe gangrene was already setting in.

"If you're not a burglar, then what are you doing here?"

I sighed, resigned to my fate. "I'm with Universal Heartland Liability...and Casualty Assurance...Company of America...Incorporated," I managed to spit out between spasms of shooting pain. "If you'll permit me to reach into my pocket, I'll show you my card."

"No funny stuff," she warned.

I definitely wasn't feeling funny. I got a card and held it out to her. "Put it on the desk," she ordered. She wasn't taking any chances. "Along with your wallet."

I put the card face-side up on the desk and placed my wallet beside it. She had a difficult time juggling gun, dog, and card, but she never took her eyes off me. Not that I would make a break for it leaving my card and wallet behind. And I was feeling too weak to run anyway.

"John Smith, harrumph," she scoffed. "You're going to have to come up with a better name than that."

"That IS my name," I insisted.

"Sure, and mine is Pocahontas."

"Look," I said. "Why don't you call your husband? He knows me." If I could prevent her from shooting me, maybe I could make a deal with the prosecutor. Plead guilty to hating Pekingese with sharp teeth and foul tempers in return for a light sentence.

"You know my husband?" Not surprisingly, her voice was tinged with disbelief.

"Yes. He operated on a claimant from a case I'm handling." My leg twitched convulsively, and I winced. Glancing down, I saw blood drooling down my shoe onto the rug next to the tiny droplets of blood from my thumb. "I'm getting blood on your rug," I observed. Blood. There had been entirely too much blood around of late, and I found the sight of my own blood pooling on the rug particularly distasteful.

"You're making a mess," she said, unfeeling.

"Sorry," I murmured. All that blood…and the pain. I was beginning to feel faint. "Urg," I said in an attempt to explain my worsening condition. I suppose some might consider it unmanly to faint from a Pekingese bite, but they've never been attacked by FooFoo. The last thing I remember before crumpling to the floor was the woman shouting, "Don't move, or I'll shoot."

When I came to, she was standing over me, still holding the gun. For a moment, I thought she'd followed through on her threat to shoot me. "Get up," she commanded. That was a good sign. She thought I was still capable of getting up. Maybe she hadn't shot me any place vital. I struggled to my feet, holding onto the desk for support. "I'm taking you to the hospital," she informed me. "My husband will meet us there."

Four items of information registered in my foggy brain. FooFoo was nowhere in sight. Nor were any police officers. The woman was, as I suspected from her resemblance to the younger woman in the pictures on the wall, the wife of Dr. Oliver. And she had talked with him about what had happened. I must have been out cold for a while. And, as the throbbing in my leg focused me on the reality of my situation, I began to wish I was still unconscious.

She wanted me to drive her car so she could keep the gun trained on me, but when I protested that I was in no shape to drive, I must have been convincing because she relented. She was all heart. Instead, she forced me to get down on my knees on the floor on the passenger side with my hands on the side window so she could keep them in sight, an awkward, back-twisting position. If I survived the dog bites, my back would probably be ruined. Well, I knew one doctor I wouldn't have operate.

Mrs. Oliver had thrown a coat on over her dressing gown and run a comb through her hair. Except for the gun, she could have been someone sneaking off for a tryst with a lover. And the way she put the pedal to the medal, you would have thought she was in a hurry to get somewhere. I crouched on the floor, banging into the door and all of the pointy things sticking out from it each time she careened around a corner, hands straining to stay on the window. I couldn't imagine how it looked to the people in the cars we passed. All I knew was that I felt damn silly.

Dr. Oliver was waiting for us at the emergency entrance. I rolled out of the car at his feet. He helped me up as he ordered his wife to get the gun out of sight. Then he ushered us past the woman behind the desk who was studiously ignoring everyone in the lobby and into a small examination room. He waved me to the examination table. I gratefully climbed up and laid back. Mrs. Oliver took a chair off to one side, the gun resting on her lap. If I didn't pass the examination, would she shoot me?

"So, Mr. Smith," Dr. Oliver said, a bit too jovial under the circumstances from my point of view. "I understand you had a run-in with FooFoo."

"Yes. He bit me on the ankle and the finger." I thrust my thumb at him.

"No problem. FooFoo de Banlieue has had her shots. You are not in any danger."

"FooFoo is a she?" That figured. "De Banlieue?" Was this some kind of examination room humor?

"She's got papers," Mrs. Oliver chimed in from the sidelines.

"And I should feel good about that why?"

"She's a very expensive dog. We make certain she is completely healthy."

Great, I was bitten by a healthy dog. Somehow that didn't make me feel any better. I leaned back with a sigh of resignation at the whole affair. Dr. Oliver slit my pant leg up to the knee to get at my ankle and said, "Of course, you'll need a tetanus shot just to be on the safe side. And there will be some forms to fill out." He probed the wound with an evil-looking silver weapon. Was he going to hurt me for revenge? Should I apologize for bleeding on his rug and thinking ill of his dog, FooFoo of the Suburbs?

"I think I've had a tetanus shot," I said.

"Most people fail to get updates when they should." He finished putting some evil-smelling ointment on my ankle wounds and wrapped it tight enough to cut off my circulation. Then he took out a wicked-looking needle filled with something sinister. Could I trust him? "It won't hurt much." It seemed unlikely I could hurt much more. At least, that was what I thought before he jammed the needle into my tender flesh.

"Can I get some painkillers?" I asked.

"Oh, I don't think you'll need any." What was that supposed to mean?

"You mentioned something about forms." A confession of some sort? Before whatever he had shot me with kicked in?

"For the emergency treatment," he said. "Technically you have to fill in the forms *before* seeing a doctor, but in your case, I've made an exception." That was either kind of him or...maybe he didn't want any record of my injuries before he worked on me. Maybe there would be some things he would add to my forms after the fact.

"Now," he said, motioning for me to sit up. "Perhaps you would like to explain what you were doing in my house." He sounded like this was nothing more than an amiable doctor-patient chat. But his wife was fingering her gun again, and his facial expression didn't match the friendly tone of his voice.

"Well, I was, ah, looking for something," I said.

"Me?"

"Yes, er, no. Well, you didn't answer when I knocked," I admitted.

"You knocked?"

"Yes, absolutely. I even rang the doorbell. Twice," I added truthfully.

"But you were here at the hospital earlier," he said. "And you asked about my schedule." He'd done his homework.

"I was hoping you'd be home by then."

"Really?" He began examining my thumb. "Does this hurt?" he asked, pressing on the tip.

"Yes, of course, that hurts," I complained, gritting my teeth to hold in the scream. How could I lie to him when he could torture me to get the truth?

"Just tell me what you were looking for." I was starting to sweat, whether from fear or pain, I wasn't sure. Maybe from the shot he had given me.

"Evidence," I blurted out. My threshold for pain is not very high. Ask my optician.

Dr. Oliver turned to his wife. "Estelle, I don't think it's necessary for you to stay. You might as well go on home."

"Are you sure I shouldn't call the police?" She caressed the gun as though regretting she wasn't going to get to use it.

"No, I know this man. I'll take care of the situation. You go home and make sure FooFoo is all right."

Jeeze. It sounded like they were worried that I had poisoned their dog with my flesh and blood.

As she moved toward the door, I almost screamed for her to stay. It might be better to die from a single bullet to the head than to submit to Dr. Oliver's ministrations. Besides, didn't he just say that he would "take care of the situation"? What did that mean?! No police. No witnesses. No emergency treatment forms. And just what was he planning to do with that needle? He'd already given me a tetanus shot. "What's that?" My voice was barely audible above the beating of my heart and the sound of sweat pouring off my body.

"You don't look too good," Dr. Oliver said. "I think you *do* need a little something for pain." He was concentrating on making sure the needle contained just the right amount of whatever it was, probably a fatal dose of an undetectable substance. Would it look like a heart attack? Would anyone even bother to check cause of death?

My will to survive overcame my inherent cowardice. I leapt off the table and staggered to the door. Dr. Oliver was taken by surprise. I made my escape and was in the hall before he could stop me. Although he recovered quickly, just moments behind me, motioning for help from a couple of interns. It took all three of them to subdue me. They finally managed to haul me back to the examination room. At least there would be witnesses to my demise. He wouldn't be able to pretend I'd never been there and smuggle me out in pieces in his little black bag.

"Mr. Smith seems to fear needles," he explained, smiling his toothiest smile. "If you'll just hold his arm down," he directed one of the interns. She obliged, muscles rippling along her smooth white arms. Helpless, I stared at the needle as he plunged it into my arm. The entry prick was followed by a feeling of numbness. I laid back and waited. I would know soon enough if I had just made the worst mistake of my life.

"That's fine," Dr. Oliver said to the two interns. "I can handle it from here." They left, shaking their heads in disbelief. As soon as the door shut behind them, he said, "Now, Mr. Smith, perhaps we can finish our conversation." He sat in the chair his wife had vacated. "What's this about some evidence?"

How long did I have? Did it make any sense to hold back? "I wanted to find out more about Pearl Rosenblatt's injuries," I began.

"Why didn't you simply ask me? There was no need for this cat burglar charade. I'd be happy to show you my file on that woman."

"Well, you never know how much a doctor holds back. Mrs. Rosenblatt seemed to think you were guilty of malpractice. That could affect what you told me."

I thought his eyes turned a steely shade of gray. Or was my eyesight going? "What's your interest in this? Why should you care whether she was going to sue me or not?"

"If her injuries were primarily the result of the operation rather than the accident, then Universal wouldn't have to pay," I explained. I was beginning to feel drowsy. And it was getting harder to form words and put them into sentences.

"But I understood that Mrs. Rosenblatt had, ah, died. If she's dead, the case is closed, isn't it?"

"No, her daughter intends on pursuing her mother's claims on behalf of her estate." On second thought, I was feeling good, calm, and euphoric. Perhaps dying wouldn't be so bad after all.

"I see." He didn't look pleased at what he saw.

"She's going to squeeze as much money out of the situation as possible," I said cheerfully.

"But why didn't you just come to me?" he asked again. I thought I'd already explained that. Had he given me a truth serum that took some time to work?

"I thought you might be hiding something," I admitted. I ran my hand across my sweaty, cold forehead. The euphoria was turning to dizziness.

"You might feel somewhat disoriented from the shot," he noted in his professional voice. "It's nothing to worry about."

"If you're hiding something—" I couldn't remember what I'd thought he was hiding. But I was pretty sure that I shouldn't tell him what it was. Not that I could tell him anything if I didn't remember.

"Evidence"? he prompted.

"That's it!" It was like coming across the answer to a crossword puzzle clue.

"What kind of evidence?"

I tried to think. "I don't remember." I tried to sit up. "And I don't care. I want to go home."

"Just tell me what kind of evidence you were looking for, and you can go home."

"I wanted to know…." For a moment, I thought I knew the answer to the question, but then it drifted away. Into the ether. Like a wispy cloud…or a ghost.

Dr. Oliver shook his head. "You're free to leave as soon as you fill out the forms. Do you want to call someone to pick you up?"

Does the body call its own mortician, I wondered? He handed me the forms on a clipboard along with a pen.

"And I don't think it will be necessary to name FooFoo in the report, do you?" My mind was barely able to grasp that subtle hint. "You were obviously bitten by a stray," he added firmly. "Well, I guess that concludes our business." He opened the door. "I hope I won't be seeing you again anytime soon."

That sounded like a plan to me. If I lived through this, I was definitely going to keep my distance from dogs named FooFoo, wild-looking women brandishing guns, and Dr. Oliver. And although I was grateful that he didn't turn me over to the police, I could only think of one possible reason why he didn't, and that seemed to me to be a motive for murder.

Chapter Eleven

"Your tie doesn't go with your jacket," Emma greeted me Friday morning. "What happened to your hair?" Before I could respond, she added, "And Mr. Van Droop wants to see you immediately." Her eyes darted to the clock above her desk. It said four minutes after the hour.

I headed toward my office.

"You don't have time," Emma advised, nodding purposefully at the clock.

Damn clock. I've often thought Emma has a remote-control system that she operates with her foot so she can make it say whatever she wants. My watch said it was three minutes to the hour. Still, I obediently turned and headed for Van Droop's office, running a hand through my unruly hair that was throwing one of those fits to which it is prone. Combing wouldn't help; the only cure was time.

Catching sight of myself in the reflection from a window as I passed by, I thought I looked pretty good. Was there something wrong with my gold-flowered tie and rust-colored jacket? Weren't rust and gold complementary colors? Perhaps the combination wasn't demure enough for Universal. They did advocate conservative dress, although I didn't think that meant drab. What I needed was a line of clothes with Universal approved coordination codes, like what they have for kids. I could be a tiger one day, a wolf the next, maybe an occasional grizzly. Oh well, it was too late to worry about what I was wearing.

My demure knock-knock on Van Droop's door was followed by an immediate "Come in." He didn't look up when I entered. I stood there like a raw recruit waiting for orders. Was this when my permanent status as an employee became as meaningless as the phrase permanent press? My left armpit started sweating like crazy. I've never understood why one pit would sweat more than the other, but I've always had that condition.

After a lengthy silence that drove home the point that he was the boss and I was an insignificant cog in the Universal wheel, he finally looked up as though surprised to see me standing there. Then he frowned, a deep frown that caused the sagging skin beneath his eyes to droop down against his cheeks.

"Sit," he said, motioning to the chair across from his desk. I did. He then stared at my tie as though trying to decide if he liked it or hated it. The creases on his forehead indicated he was leaning towards hating it. I looked down to avoid staring at him staring at my tie. There was a coffee spot next to one of the flowers. It was almost the same color as my jacket. Talk about coordinated. As I looked at the spot it seemed to be growing larger, spreading outward like liquid being soaked up by a paper towel. Perhaps I didn't deserve to be permanent.

Van Droop got tired of looking at my tie and leaned across his desk toward me, his eyes flickering with the next best thing to emotion. "What's all this about you finding one of our claimants dead?" he asked without any preliminaries. It sounded as though he was blaming me for Pearl Rosenblatt's death.

"I did discover Pearl Rosenblatt's body while I was investigating her Universal claim," I admitted, emphasizing that it was Universal's case, not just mine. They had drawn me into a rather unsavory situation, not the other way around. Besides, her death might end up saving them a chunk of change. Not that I intended to point that out. It sounded a bit mercenary under the circumstances.

He tapped his fingers together, elbows propped on his desk, like a creditor contemplating your ruin. "In your opinion, is the untimely death related to the case?"

Untimely death? That was quite a euphemism for murder, but I let it go. And, sure, I was suspicious of the arcane and scary Dr. Oliver, and I hadn't ruled out the possibility that Marie might be involved in her mother's death in some way, but I didn't have any proof. And every time I tried to get some, something terrible happened. There was a moral there somewhere.

"It may be possible," I said, choosing my words carefully, "that Mrs. Rosenblatt was murdered to prevent a successful claim being made, but not necessarily against Universal."

Van Droop had cringed when I uttered the word "murder." He considered what I had suggested, then asked, "You aren't saying that someone at Universal may have taken her life in order to avoid paying her claim?" He seemed truly offended by the thought.

"No, it's more complicated than that." I gave him a high-level overview of the complications. That seemed to relax him. He settled back in his ergonomic leather chair and nodded.

"Complications should be handled with speed and delicacy," he said as if reciting a company motto. He was very good at that sort of thing. Then he added, "We don't like our adjusters getting mixed up in unsavory affairs. It's bad for the image."

"Oh, I understand. Believe me, I don't want to be mixed up in this matter one whit. No, not one whit."

"So, how quickly can we extricate ourselves?"

I wanted to scream that if he wanted to resolve everything quickly, he should give the case to someone else, someone with seniority, someone with more experience, someone who could stand the sight of blood, *anyone*, as long as it wasn't me. Unfortunately, as the humblest member of the Universal team, I didn't think I had the right to suggest strategy to the top dog.

"Well, as I said, the daughter intends to pursue the claim, although she doesn't have much of a case for damages for injury. It will be my recommendation that we settle with her. Currently, she has some rather inflated ideas about how much she should get, but I think we can work with her to lower her sights." *Lowering her sights* was insurance jargon for getting the client to accept *the smallest settlement possible*.

"What about getting these other potential defendants to share the financial burden?"

"I don't know if she officially filed claims against them." How I hated to admit how little I knew. Van Droop rubbed a finger against his nose. I wasn't sure what that meant. Wasn't that something Santa did? Why? Maybe he just had an itch. "They are understandably being circumspect under the circumstances. If we don't want to have things drag out, it might be better to make her an offer now."

"Universal employees are expected to show initiative," he began, his voice trailing off as though he couldn't remember the rest of the statement. "You shouldn't be discouraged by a few minor setbacks," he said, taking a different tack. "Review the situation. Consider the alternatives. Then go out there and do your duty for the company." He seemed pleased with himself for having said the right thing to rally the troops. Maybe I should salute or click my heels together to indicate that I not only got the message but was sufficiently motivated to follow through.

I stood up. "Fine, Mr. Van Droop. I'll get on it right away."

"And remember, ah, Smith, Universal employees are loyal, discreet and, ahhh, always prepared." Hmmm, maybe I could earn a merit badge by being an exemplary Universal employee.

I almost made it to the door before he thought of one more thing he wanted to say. "I expect you to take care of this little matter posthaste. Preferably by first thing Monday. Understand?"

Did he realize it was Friday? Unless something had changed, there were only two days between Friday and Monday, and they weren't supposed to be work days. But from his point of view, it didn't matter if I had plans for the weekend. Universal came first. And since I had nothing in second place, why not?

Let's see, by Monday I could negotiate a settlement with Marie, perhaps identify her mother's killer, and then, for an encore, I could sail single-handed around Cape Horn. Oh well, there was no use wallowing in self-pity. At least I still had a job. The only question was whether I could accomplish enough by Monday to satisfy Van Droop. At this point, I could skip the hard stuff like proving Pearl Rosenblatt was faking her injuries. I didn't even need to find out whether she had intended to sue her doctor. If I could get Marie to agree to a reasonable settlement straight away, that might be sufficient.

I headed back to my office filled with resolve. Maybe Van Droop's pep talk had helped after all.

A few misgivings about the case still lingered at the back of my mind, like a headache that refuses to go away no matter how much aspirin you take. But I might have ignored those loose ends if it hadn't been for Emma. As I passed her desk on the way back to my office, she handed me a newspaper without saying a word. A younger version of Pearl stared up at me from the front page. My name and references to Universal were underlined in red felt pen.

I took the paper back to my office to read and reread the article in private. Some reporter was having a heyday. A poor invalid had been murdered, an invalid who had been fighting the big, bad insurance company. All she wanted was money that was rightfully hers. But the insurance company was dragging its organizational feet, refusing to acknowledge her distress with financial compensation. I was depicted as the main villain in the story, the mercenary face of Universal. No wonder Van Droop was upset.

The police also took a beating in the article. Two murders in one day, discovered by the same person, and the police hadn't arrested anyone. They didn't even appear to have a prime suspect. Although it was implied that if the police only stopped to think for a moment, they would realize that someone discovered on the scene of not one but two murders *should* be a prime suspect. Bruno was quoted as saying they were working on some leads but could make no definite statement at this time. Police doublespeak for "we don't know shit."

Although there was nothing libelous in the article, there was sufficient manipulation of facts to get my juices flowing. I stomped back and forth in front of my desk, ticking off each unfair statement in my mind. They said I'd been trying to trick the poor woman out of her money. Stomp, tick. Although they thankfully didn't mention the scattered nickels, they cast vague aspersions on my character. Stomp, tick. Pearl was a sainted woman who, but for her misfortunate accident, had a great future in store. Stomp, tick. By nature, all insurance companies were greedy institutions. Stomp,

119

tick. The stomping didn't accomplish anything, but it satisfied some primal urge to act upon unfair treatment.

Unfortunately, the story reduced any chance I had of coming to a quick settlement with Marie. She would undoubtedly see an offer as an attempt to avoid further bad publicity and try to use it to jack me around on the amount. Yet, what other course of action did I have? I needed to act quickly. Even if the police discovered the murderer or murderers, whether they were connected or not, the press might continue digging around. And it wouldn't take a Nobel prize-winning reporter to discover one or two more items that might not provide any answers but would surely make for good reading and reflect poorly on me and Universal.

Bruno was in his office that afternoon when I dropped by. He didn't seem particularly happy to see me. "What do you want, John?" he asked before I had a chance to even say "hello."

"Can't an old chum stop by for a chat?" I gave him my "good buddies" grin, the knowing locker room leer of one man to another, men who have gotten drunk together and swapped boasts about sexual prowess. But Bruno was having none of it.

"You still sticking your nose into the Rosenblatt case?" he challenged.

"Her daughter is pursuing her mother's claim, so I'm not 'sticking my nose' into anything. My nose was already there." There was something wrong with my statement, but I wasn't sure what.

"Stay out of police business, you hear?"

"I just dropped by as a friend, Bruno. Like Mother said, we don't see enough of each other." I was probably carrying the good buddy routine too far; the next thing you knew, I'd be losing money to him in a friendly poker game.

"Yeah," he said, his brown eyes clouded with thought. "It's just that you've never dropped by before."

"So, it's about time I did." I smiled. He seemed to relax, a smile teasing the corners of his mouth. "But since you mentioned it, how are things coming with the Rosenblatt murder investigation?" I kept the tone light, one good buddy to another inquiring about what's happening.

"So-so." He held up his hand and wiggled it from side to side.

"No leads then."

"What does that mean?"

"It doesn't mean anything. I'm just curious. After all, I did discover the body." Oh, oh, should I have mentioned that?

"That's what I read in the paper," he said with a grin. I grinned back, although my grin was totally fake. But that's what guys do, rib each other about stuff. This was a good sign.

"Yeah, I read that article too. We didn't come off too well, did we?"

"I noticed."

"That's why I'm here, actually." His eyes narrowed slightly. "I wanted to see how you were doing. After all, I know you're taking some heat because of me. And, well, we've been friends a long time." Surprisingly, when I said the words, I meant them. Bruno hadn't deserved criticism any more than I had. We were in this mess together.

"This off the record?" he asked.

"Of course. I'm not a reporter." I held up my arms. "And I'm not wearing a wire."

"Funny." He leaned back and emitted a huge sigh. Some of the papers on his desk fluttered in its aftermath. "We aren't getting anywhere. I don't have any leads. Not a one. And my butt's going to be in a sling if I don't come up with something soon. But no one saw or heard anything. Nada. Nothing."

"What about the gun?"

"Dead end so far." We sat in shared misery for a few moments. Then Bruno said, "I don't suppose you've given Zelda Gunnar's dying words any further thought?" The Rosenblatt affair had driven all thoughts of Zelda Gunnar from my mind.

"Sorry." That reminded me of something else, though. "What about the letter opener? Did you get any prints?" I didn't add "after you wiped off the vomit." That went without saying.

"No, no fingerprints." He was kind enough not to mention my involuntary obstruction of justice.

Should I tell him about Dr. Oliver, I wondered? If I told him everything, I would incriminate myself in a crime, but maybe a small hint was in order. "Bruno, have you investigated Dr. Oliver in the Rosenblatt death?"

"As much as anyone else she came in contact with. Why?"

"Mrs. Rosenblatt hinted to me that she intended to sue him for malpractice. He couldn't have been happy about that."

"That's what her daughter said, but it didn't happen, and there's no paperwork to suggest it was going to happen." I could attest to that. And even if there had been, it was likely destroyed by now. Thanks to me. Perhaps it was best to let things ride.

"What a mess," I commiserated.

"Yes."

I stood up to leave. "We'll pull through. We always have," I added, remembering youthful misadventures with a twinge of nostalgia."

"There's no 'we' about it, John," Bruno said coldly. "You stay out of it. Got that? There's some question as to whether I've been soft on you because you're an old friend." He glared at me accusingly. "Some people are saying you committed both murders."

I knew they were hinting as much, but not that anyone was actually saying it out loud. Like it or not, I was involved. I couldn't stay out of it. And I had no intention of sitting back and waiting for Bruno to take care of things. But I didn't have to tell him that. Nor could I stick my head in the sand and assume the reporters would no longer be able to see me. Mother always said things have a way of working themselves out, but I wasn't sure how her theory stood up in practice. If things weren't already bad enough, the onion I'd had on my hamburger for lunch was making a reappearance. It was time to go home.

Everything was quiet at The Haven. The row of mailboxes just inside the gate tilted crazily as though they didn't quite have their sea legs. I went over and reached inside my box, fingers sinking into gooey orange slime that had once been a popsicle. It was those damn kids again. Always up to something. I pulled out the stick and used it to scrape the mess onto the ground. It landed in tiny orange blobs at my feet, missing my toes by a fraction of an inch. Orange ooze clung to my fingers and drooled down my wrist. The goo had amazing sticky properties, connecting my fingers with sugary webs like a marzipan duck.

Cursing children in general and popsicle eaters in particular, I headed down the dock. In a few hours, the place would be hopping. It always was on Friday evenings. People threw parties, kids went wild, even the waves from passing boats seemed higher. I had nothing planned, but I felt a tingle of anticipation anyway. Maybe I'd be invited to partake in some revelry. The Rosenblatt affair could wait until morning.

My reverie was broken into by a dog barking, frantic yelping sounds interspersed with whines. As I drew near my front door, the sound grew louder and more insistent. I looked around but couldn't figure out where it was coming from. "Up there, mister," a small voice said. I looked up, and sure enough, there was a dog on the roof of my houseboat, head hanging over the edge, tongue lolling.

"What's he doing up there?" I asked. Really, popsicles in my mailbox was one thing, but a dog on my roof was going too far. I looked down at the young girl and noticed that her eyes were filled with tears. My resolve melted like a popsicle in the sun. "Is he yours?" I asked gently.

She nodded, her sad face splotchy from a combination of sunburn and specks of dirt. Could this vulnerable little girl be the same creature who tormented me by leaving chewing gum on my steps and dead fish in my mailbox? "I'll get him for you," I offered. It is, after all, better to give than to receive.

Luckily, I happened to have a ladder. It had seen better days, but it was a freebie from a neighbor. Free ladders aren't all that easy to come by. So, what if it wobbled a bit and always seemed to lean to the left? Some people climb coconut palms in their bare feet; I could certainly make do with some minor equipment deficiencies.

The dog became very excited as I set up the ladder. You'd have thought he was stranded atop the Empire State Building with King Kong after him. I mounted the steps and began my teetering ascent. If the dog hadn't leapt at me as I neared the top, things might have played out differently. But he did leap, landing on my shoulder, toenails digging into my skin through my shirt. It was at that instant that the next rung came loose as I grabbed at it while trying to maintain my balance. It was a miracle that I managed to hang on to the dog's tail to keep him from falling while scrambling down the ladder, landing hard on my left foot and slowly collapsing. The ungrateful mutt leapt off my shoulder and bounded off down the dock with his young master clamoring after him without so much as a yelp of thanks from either of them.

After ascertaining that just my pride was injured, I got up, eased the ladder down and examined the rungs. It looked like the rivets that held the top three had been sawed through to the point where they were barely capable of holding the rungs in place. If I had climbed all the way to the top, which I had intended to do if the dog hadn't taken matters into his own, er, paws, I most likely would have fallen. The roof wasn't that high, so I probably wouldn't have died from the fall, but I could easily have ended up with a broken bone or two.

My throat suddenly went dry. It was almost as if...but no, no one would deliberately do that to me, would they? The kids? They had never done anything dangerous before. Annoying, messy, and sometimes downright obnoxious. But they'd never done anything that resulted in harm to life or limb. A manufacturer's defect, then? No, that wasn't what the evidence suggested. And that dog hadn't climbed on the roof by himself. On *my* roof. And it was *my* ladder. A planned accident?

The question was whether I should call the police. But what could they do other than encourage me to make up a list of my enemies? To be on the safe side, now that it was too late to truly be on the safe side, I knocked out the other loose rungs. Then I searched the area. I don't know what I was looking for, a telltale footprint, perhaps. But I found just what I could have expected to find: nothing.

After unlocking my front door, I waited a moment before cautiously peeking inside, jerking my head back when it occurred to me that it might be asking for more trouble to stick my neck out like that. If there had been someone hiding behind my door, he could easily have karate chopped my neck...or worse. Next time I would have to be more cautious.

What was I thinking?! Did I really expect there to be a *next time*? No one was out to get me...were they?

Chapter Twelve

"The bacon cheeseburgers are excellent," I told Marie. She was studying the menu like someone about to take an exam on its contents.

"Cheeseburgers, yuk," she responded, making a face while running her painted nail along the listed items. "I'll have fish and chips. And a coke." Closing the menu with a flourish, she flashed me a look that told me *she* knew what was good to eat.

When I called her late Saturday afternoon to set up an appointment to talk about a possible settlement, she'd insisted that we talk over dinner. I assumed that since it was more business than pleasure—although there was always hope—I could charge it to Universal, especially if I got a reasonable settlement agreement.

Except for my phone call to Marie, my day had been unproductive. I spent considerable time worrying about the ladder incident. If someone was trying to get a message across, they would have been smart to either call or text me. My hearing's fine, and I can read, but I prefer to leave the deciphering of signs to fortunetellers and prophets of doom. Three damaged rungs on a ladder make me nervous, but they don't tell me what I should NOT be doing.

All day long I jumped at the least little noise, and I pulled the shades to keep boaters who motored past from looking in. They seem to think I'm there for their viewing pleasure. It didn't usually bother me much, but how was I to tell the innocent gawkers from an unknown enemy?

It was with considerable relief when the time came to pick up Marie for dinner. My relief turned to delight when I saw the way she was dressed—just barely. Her blouse and slacks were made of filmy material that hinted at transparency in the right light. Not that it was necessary to look *through* the material. And they had run out of cloth before the blouse was completed. It didn't quite reach around Marie's ample front, gaping open when she moved, revealing smooth, curved breasts. Once in the restaurant, she tormented me further by leaning forward when she talked.

To my surprise, she was extremely cordial. I was beginning to think she may have accidentally left me behind the other day. It *was* possible. For instance, I've occasionally forgotten where I parked my car in a parking lot.

"So, how are things?" I asked once our orders were placed, involuntarily glancing at her bosoms.

"Fine," she said. More than fine, I thought.

"That's good."

"Yeah."

"Well…" I began, striving to come up with a topic of conversation other than her mother's death and the reason we were sitting there. "Do you like cantaloupe?" I asked. I can't imagine why I asked; I don't care for it much myself.

"No."

"Me neither."

She played with the ice in her water glass while I shredded my paper napkin. When I could no longer stand the silence, I said, "I suppose you're busy getting your mother's estate in order."

"Not really."

"Oh?"

"She didn't leave much, except debts."

"Oh."

"But I haven't given up on the insurance," she assured me, smiling sweetly as she took a drink of water, her white teeth magnified through the glass.

"That's what I want to discuss," I reminded her.

"Some jerk lawyer tried to tell me I don't have much of a case. But what does he know? Mother had money coming to her, and I'm her daughter, so it should come to me." Her breasts bounced defiantly as she spoke.

"You will definitely get reimbursed for the damage to her car. And you'll get any medical bills directly related to the accident paid for. But money related to the operation and problems resulting from that are questionable."

"What about pain and suffering?"

"Well, it's difficult to know the extent of the pain since we don't have any medical reports. And she didn't have very long to suffer until she, ah, died."

She suddenly leaned across the table and looked me right in the eyes. "Do you get some sort of percentage on these claims? Or do you get something for keeping the payout low?" Her facial expression was hard, but her breasts remained soft and inviting. I wanted to reach out and stroke them.

"No, of course not. I'm salaried. I'm just trying to explain how it is. The way insurance works. I'm sorry for your loss, and no matter how it may seem, I really do want to help you." There were so many ways I could think of to help her through this time of sorrow. So many.

"I deserve the money," she continued. "While she was alive, all she did was try to get money off me. Well, now it's my turn to get some off her."

"She didn't leave you anything?"

"Her estate," she smirked. "That's a fancy word for what I got from my mother. The house is mortgaged to the hilt. She was behind on her car payments. She had a string of unpaid bills. And she owed all of her so-called friends. Some estate."

"No wonder she wanted the insurance money so bad," I observed.

"Yeah, she thought the accident was the best thing that had happened to her lately. She planned on living it up after she got her hands on all that dough."

The waitress delivered our food, and Marie fell to eating with enthusiasm. I like a woman with a good appetite. It's a sign she knows how to enjoy life's little pleasures.

"She would have blown through it in no time," she said between bites. "But with her dead, it will all be mine."

I sunk my teeth into my bacon cheeseburger, sauce dribbling out the sides and running down my chin. A hamburger, a glass of Coke, and thou, I thought happily. Of course, there was the question of Marie's attitude toward her dearly departed mother. Not exactly the good daughter. But then, it didn't sound like Pearl had been the perfect mother either. Besides the materialistic approach to her mother's death, the main thing that concerned me was whether I was lusting after a murderer. It wasn't clear why she would have killed her mother before the insurance claims were at least on record, although if she knew that Pearl was faking her injuries, it might have made sense to get rid of her sooner rather than later. And although the chances of a big recovery were slim, she hadn't known that before the lawyer and I told her. Looking at it that way, there was definitely a motive for murder. But I really didn't want to believe it had happened that way.

Marie dangled a piece of fish between two fingers. "I hate being poor," she said vehemently. "All my life, I've scrounged for money. For once, I want to have enough to enjoy myself a little. Mother owes me that."

"I don't know how much you consider enough," I tentatively said, "but perhaps we could work out a settlement." Her eyes lit up. "First, I need to know whether your mother initiated a suit against either Dr. Oliver or the hospital."

Fingering a French fry in a very sexy way, she said, "I thought she was suing both, but they say no."

"Of course, you can pursue claims against them on your own, especially if there is an issue of malpractice." Hint, hint. "That can be done separate from a settlement with Universal."

She popped a piece of fish in her mouth, chewing slowly and sensuously. "Let's talk about that later, okay?" She reached across the table and squeezed my hand. As she withdrew her hand, she noticed the sauce that had rubbed off on her, brought her fingers up to her lips, and slowly licked it off. Her pink tongue flicking in and out.

I suppose I should have thought more about the possibility that she was a murderer, but somehow my desire to get her in the sack seemed more pressing. I wanted that body. And I wanted it bad. The settlement could wait.

After dinner, we stopped at a bar for a few drinks. I carefully pocketed the receipt from dinner to attach to my expense reimbursement account, but the drinks were on me. I felt no shame plying her with liquor. We were both adults. And it was faintly possible that she wanted something from me as much as I wanted something from her.

Luring her back to my houseboat turned out to be a snap. Except for the brief visit to my place the other day, she'd never been in a houseboat before, and the thought of being on the water was "like soooo romantic."

"Yeah, yeah, romantic," I agreed as we drifted down the dark docks toward mutual bliss. For once, I was pleased that the kids had shot out all the lights.

Giggling and touching each other like teenagers, we worked our way up to my front door. Nibbling on her ear made it difficult to see which key I needed to put in the lock, but as eager as I was to get her inside, I was equally reluctant to forego one moment of pleasure. And the nibbling was definitely pleasurable.

The door finally opened with a squeak. We stood there in the doorway pawing each other, my hand finally inside her blouse, caressing a rigid nipple. Meanwhile, she was getting equally familiar. I knew it was going to be a night to remember.

When the porch lights came on, I felt like I'd been shot. There's nothing worse than instant sobriety unless it's having a tender breast jerked unceremoniously out of your hand. As Marie jumped away from me, I heard the sound of ripping material and experienced an overwhelming sense of loss.

"Hey, what is this?" Marie complained loudly.

"Sorry," another voice said, a familiar voice.

I squinted toward the other person, the sorry person that I intended to make a lot sorrier. "Mother," I grumbled. She was standing there in the doorway, one hand still on the light switch. "What are you doing here?!"

"This is your mother?" Marie said. "It figures." She stepped back, away from the circle of light illuminating the porch, clutching her torn blouse. Before I could say anything, she gave Mother a withering look and started to leave.

"Wait," I called, grabbing for her like a child reaching for a piece of candy. Mother just stood there, watching, her expression divided between embarrassment and curiosity. Mothers have certain rights. But surprising her adult son as he fondled a bare boob was going a bit too far. Even for her.

"Wait," I said again. "Let me explain." Actually, what I meant was let *her*, my mother, explain. See if she could come up with a reasonable excuse for shattering her poor son's hopes and dreams. At least let her say something to reassure Marie, to sooth her feelings and make a rematch possible.

Marie stopped, silhouetted in the shadowy light, one hand on her heart. "Go ahead. Explain."

"Go ahead, Mother, explain." She was eyeing Marie like someone considering a broodmare for her prize stallion. That's all she cares about, those damn nonexistent grandchildren.

"I came by to see you, John, and when you weren't here, I decided to wait." She raised both hands in appeal. Such an innocent-looking, well-intentioned woman. But I wasn't about to let her off the hook so easy.

"The door was locked," I pointed out. "How did you get in?"

"I knew you didn't lock it to keep *me* out." When I didn't comment, she added, "You left your kitchen window open."

The look on Marie's face said that all mothers should be locked up. I felt closer to her as a person than I had all evening. Perhaps I could call a taxi for Mother and salvage the evening. "Mother's leaving," I said. "How about a drink?"

Marie hesitated for a moment, then said, "No, I think I'd better be running along."

Mother quickly chimed in. "If you are taking her home, you can drop me off afterwards." Apparently, she'd decided she could wait a while on the grandchildren."

"I'll drop you off *first*," I announced.

"I want to go home," Marie interjected with a pouty frown. It didn't sound like there would be an invitation to join her.

Driving the two women home was definitely not how I had envisioned my evening. Mother interviewed Marie for the position of daughter-in-law while Marie politely, if reluctantly, answered her questions. I found out that she was a receptionist, didn't care much for her job, loved children—a plus that brought a smile to Mother's face—and looked forward to one day quitting her job and staying home to raise a family. Another plus. She also adored cats, hated to cook, always went to church at Easter and Christmas, and believed the President was doing a fine job.

Whenever I got the chance, I interposed my own view of the world: I love my work, hate children, despise cats, like to eat, never go to church, and believe the President is doing a lousy job. I was confident Mother silently pronounced us a perfect match.

When we arrived at Marie's apartment, she insisted that I didn't need to walk her to the door. I reminded her we still had some business to discuss, but even that couldn't get her to respond. She disappeared into the night, leaving the fragrance of French fries in her wake. Grumbling to myself about fate and relatives, I shoved the Saturn into reverse and roared out of the parking space. Mother wisely held her tongue for once.

"Nice girl," she said after I calmed down.

"Yes, Mother, very nice," I muttered with ill humor. Who wants a *nice* girl anyway?

"Make someone a good wife," she persisted.

"I'm not looking for a wife," I replied defensively. Let her figure out just what I *was* looking for.

"Of course you are. You just don't know it. A man needs a wife, a steadying influence on his life. You should start thinking about your future."

I *was* thinking about the future, wondering how soon I dared call Marie and how many drinks it would take to warm her up a second time. Should I offer to pay for the torn blouse?

"Somehow, her name seemed familiar," Mother said, breaking into my musings about potential future encounters with Marie. "But I can't quite place it." If she was hoping for some important family connections, she was going to be disappointed.

"Her mother was murdered recently," I announced with a touch of malice. "I discovered the body."

"Oh, yes, now I remember." I was pleased to note she seemed disappointed. But she quickly recovered. "It was the body with the trickle of blood."

Apparently, in this instance, murder trumped matchmaking.

"That's the one."

We arrived at her condo. I was about to unlock the door to let her out—Mother always locks the doors when in the car—when she suggested I might want a cup of hot chocolate before heading home. Why not? I shrugged. I certainly wasn't sleepy.

Once inside, Mother bustled about putting together a homey snack to go with the hot chocolate. It was her way of trying to make up to me. From past experience, I knew it wouldn't do any good to talk with her about what happened, but I resolved to make certain that next time I went out, I would secure all the windows.

"Tell me about them," she said as she placed the snacks and hot chocolate in front of me.

"About what?"

"The murders, of course. Is Bruno making any progress?"

"I don't know."

"Come on; you can't fool your old mother."

I don't know how she knows, but she always does. Maybe she really does have a sixth sense, at least where I'm concerned. There was no choice but to tell her about my talk with Bruno. Then when she started probing for details, I gave in and told her everything that had happened to me since I took on the Marshall case. I poured it all out, everything. I told her about Zelda catching me searching Conklin's office, about Pearl and Marie discovering that I was spying on them, and about the skirmish with the doctor's wife and her dog. Detail after detail came pouring out of my mouth. I was tired of secrets. And I wanted someone to reassure me, to tell me that my mistakes weren't so bad, that I'd done everything possible under the circumstances. When I finished, I turned expectant eyes toward Mother.

"They are hiding something," she said.

"Who?" I thought we were talking about me. Hadn't she been listening?

"Conklin, Marie, the doctor. All of them."

"A conspiracy?"

"Of course not." She scowled at me as if doubtful I was really her own flesh and blood. I wanted to shout that sometimes I, too, wondered the same thing. "They didn't report you when you played into their hands, did they?" *Played into their hands.* Was that any way for a mother to talk about her son? "There must be a reason. Or several reasons," she mused.

"What they are trying to hide isn't necessarily related to the murders," I said, feeling moody and picked on.

"Perhaps." She rubbed her hands together thoughtfully. "Then again, there may be a common thread linking their secrets." She stopped rubbing her hands, straightened her shoulders, and looked me in the eye. "What are you going to do about all this?"

"Well, I was working on a lead, but I was, ah, interrupted."

Ignoring my pique, she proceeded to pull out all the stops. "Your sainted father never would have let his name be dragged through the mud like this without a fight. You and your company in all the newspapers, and you in a position to know more about what's going on than the police. Where is your pride? Where is your initiative?" She was starting to sound like a fiery version of Van Droop.

Where are my brains, I asked myself? Why had I bared my soul to Mother of all people? Why didn't I just put an ad in the paper: "Blunderer seeks punishment. Anyone interested, come and throw stones." Then again, maybe she was right. I *was* in a position to know what was going on. I'd had a front-row seat for all the action. Besides, if I didn't get some answers by Monday, I might be looking for another job. I love my job. But I really do hate cats and kids.

—

134

Chapter Thirteen

There were no solid suspects, no one who obviously possessed the big three: means, motive, and opportunity. Of course, the murderer is always the least likely suspect. Everybody knows that. Someone who doesn't appear to have a compelling motive. Someone all sweetness and light on the outside and a smoldering volcano of hatred and deviousness within. Given that bit of folk wisdom, I went through the list of who might have killed Pearl Rosenblatt while scrambling eggs on Sunday morning. I assessed each person I had come in contact with. One thing stood out: there was definitely a shortage of innocence and sweetness among the contenders.

Mandy Marshall came the closest to meeting the criteria, but she had to be ruled out because she was too young to own a gun. Mrs. O'Lander might have been less obnoxious under different circumstances, but she hadn't tried to hide her bad side. Mrs. Marshall was a possibility, but I didn't want it to be her. She suffered enough having Mark for a son. Maybe Frances? Possible. But he didn't seem the type. That was the problem, though, wasn't it? Murderers are seldom a "type."

Okay, I said to myself, pouring my third cup of coffee. Who had absolutely nothing to gain by Pearl's death? Who was just outside the tangle of insurance claims and counter-claims but still connected? What I needed to do was to flex my imagination, direct my cleverness toward clues the police with their, ahem, plodding less innovative approach would fail to consider important. If it wasn't the butler...and it couldn't be since there was no butler involved. And it wasn't the husband...there was no husband around as far as I knew. And if it wasn't a random killing....

Finally, I made my choice. Someone who appeared to be only tangentially involved. Someone with no reason to hate Pearl Rosenblatt. Someone to investigate without stepping on any police toes. Mother, you are going to be proud of your son yet.

Dressing for the occasion, I chose a pair of jeans and an Indian print shirt I'd picked up on impulse at a street fair. It smelled like incense even after being washed. Maybe that was a good thing under the circumstances. It might be mistaken for weed.

To complete the look, I messed up my hair. Well, I messed it up differently than it was usually messed up. Then I tried to rearrange my features to look more "with it," sticking out my lower lip, James Dean fashion. No good. I looked like someone with messy hair and a lower lip disease. The outfit was on its own.

Frances Metzker was under an old car that was propped up on some blocks in his back yard. Mark was with him. Two minor players and, if my hunch was correct, two prime suspects. They supposedly assumed Universal was going to solve all of their problems related to the accident, so what possible reason would either have for murdering Pearl? That's what I was going to find out.

Neither guy paid any attention to me until I was within a couple of feet of the car they were working on. Then Mark looked up. "You mug some guy in the District for that shirt?" he sneered. His own threadbare denims and dark blue shirt branded him as a casual fellow who didn't care about clothes but who considered image everything.

Frances peeked from under the car. "Yeah, nice threads," he said. By being nice, he went to the top of the list.

"I just wanted to drop by and make sure you knew about Pearl Rosenblatt's death," I explained, closely studying their reactions. I was kicking myself for not waiting until Frances was through tinkering with the undersides of the car.

"Yeah, we heard about it," Mark said.

"Tough luck for her," Frances commented from below.

"Getting murdered is tough luck, all right," I agreed.

"The police catch anyone yet?" Frances asked, his voice muffled as he moved further under the car.

"Not *yet*." I emphasized "yet" to make it sound like they were about to pounce on the guilty party at any moment.

"Anyone I know?" Mark asked, sarcasm dripping from every syllable. He, for one, hadn't missed my hint.

"Might be," I said vaguely, looking away as if embarrassed to admit who it was to him. Maybe that would rattle his cage a bit.

"At least she won't be suing anyone now," Mark said.

"Her daughter will, though," I said loud enough for Frances to hear too.

"Her daughter?" Mark echoed, sounding surprised. "Can she do that?"

"Can and is," I assured them. They didn't need to know that her chances of recovering very much were slim.

"Does that change anything, like with Mark's insurance coverage?" Frances called from under the car.

"Weelll, yes and no."

Glaring at me, Mark asked, "What does that mean?"

"Yes, and no," I repeated. "Not substantially, but in some ways." Claims adjusters are masters of the vague phrase.

"Is Universal trying to welch on paying my coverage?" Mark sounded hostile. Not that I blamed him, but why hadn't I noticed that mean-looking wrench in his hand before?

"Universal doesn't 'welch' on their obligations," I said testily, keeping one eye on the wrench. "Of course, there might be complications as a result of Mrs. Rosenblatt's death."

"Complications?" Mark and Frances asked stereophonically.

"The police get wild ideas sometimes," I bluffed.

"Such as?" Mark apparently didn't scare easily.

"If, for example, they thought that *you* were involved in Pearl Rosenblatt's death, well, you can see how that might complicate matters." Complication was such a versatile word.

"Come off it. Why would I want to kill her?"

"Well, for one thing, she was causing you a lot of trouble."

"She was causing *you* a lot of trouble," Mark countered.

"But it would all come back on you."

"I'm underage," he boasted, probably for the first time.

"Well, it will come back to your mother then."

"Maybe Ma knocked the old bag off," he snickered.

Frances shot from under the car on his wheeled cart, using his foot to stop it in front of Mark. "That's nothing to joke about, Mark."

Mark ignored Frances and continued with his speculation. "I can see it now. The old lady sneaks off in the middle of the night, wearing an apron so she won't get blood on her clothes. Maybe she wears a pair of those rubber kitchen gloves. Anyway, she breaks into the cripple's house and bang, right between the eyes." As he spoke, he held his hand like a gun and tiptoed around the side of the car, shooting the winged woman hood ornament right between the eyes.

"Mark," Frances said, standing up. "This isn't funny." Actually, I had been rather impressed with Mark's use of the hood ornament as a prop. But Frances was right. It wasn't funny. Maybe I was wrong to suspect Frances. Maybe it was Mark, his young psyche warped as the result of a broken home at an impressionable age. Under his obnoxious teenage veneer, maybe he was the smoldering volcano.

"He's just kidding around," Frances said, wiping grease off his face with a dirty cloth he had taken from his back pocket. "He and his mother don't get along too well. And you know how kids can be."

"I suppose you have an alibi for last Wednesday?" The question was directed at Mark, but both young men looked taken aback.

"Sure," Mark said with less bravado than he'd previously displayed.

"Do you mind if I ask where you were?" If he was on solid ground, this is where he would tell me to buzz off, but he didn't.

"We went to a movie. Frances and me." Were they in it together?

"What did you see?"

"Ah, *Star Wars: The Last Jedi.*"

"What time did it start?"

"Well, we got something to eat before. Next to the theater. Not sure when it actually started." He definitely sounded like he was making this up as he went along.

"What about you, Frances? Know what time it started?"

"Around 8:00, I think."

"Good movie? Did you like it?"

"Yeah, lots of action."

"I've always been a Captain Kirk fan," I said.

The two looked at each other. Then Frances said, "You're thinking of *Star Trek*."

"Oh, right," I said. Then I paused. "But you two are going to have to do better for the police."

Mark wasn't ready to admit defeat. "What do you mean?"

"I mean," I said carefully, "you two better get your stories straight if you are going to pull off going to a movie as an alibi." Bruno wasn't going to be too happy with me coaching them on how to make their alibi solid, if and when his attention did turn in their direction. And, come to think of it, it wasn't probably too smart in general to reveal my suspicions about their actions to two such healthy, tool-wielding fellows. I had my own health to consider.

"I don't know about you," Frances said. "But I could use a drink." He wheeled about and headed for the house. Mark tagged along after him. I hesitated a moment, then decided to follow. They hadn't actually invited me, but they didn't tell me to go away either. "What's your pleasure?" Frances asked as he opened his frig and looked inside. I said a beer sounded great if he had any. He reached inside, pulled out a six-pack, and handed me a bottle.

The living room was cool and cluttered, but in a lived-in, masculine sort of way. We lounged around like old friends, quickly knocking off the six-pack, not talking much. I'd already made my point; the next move was theirs.

After a while, Frances asked me if I played poker. I admitted to playing a little, and in no time at all, he had a table set up, and we settled in for a cozy Sunday afternoon card game. I've always heard that playing poker is a good way to learn about people, so I didn't hesitate to join in. The police might be bound by more orthodox methods, but I wasn't. I would use my advantage, discover the truth, and astound Bruno and my mother. Maybe I'd even win a little money.

Eventually, I switched from beer to scotch and water. Late afternoon we sent out for a pizza, and I magnanimously paid for it since I'd been on a winning streak the last hour. If I'd known it had anchovies, I might have asked them to chip in. Mark gobbled up the ones I managed to pry away from the cheese, insisting that he had ordered a pizza without anchovies. In my opinion, someone who likes anchovies on pizza is capable of almost anything.

At one point, it crossed my mind that my winning streak could be a set-up. Maybe they were softening me up for the kill. That didn't sound too good. On the other hand, what the hell? I enjoyed winning.

Another guy dropped in just after we finished the pizza. Then another and another. The card game was becoming a major event. I hadn't discovered too much about either Frances or Mark, except that they were social and liked playing poker, but it had been a long time since I had hung out like this with a group of guys, plenty of booze, and an excess of backslapping male humor. Who says it doesn't pay to dress right?

Mark's mother called about nine o'clock. Mark was snickering and weaving back and forth while he talked, his cell phone not quite next to his ear. We all thought he was hilarious. What a card. What a load of crap he was feeding her. She would never guess he'd been drinking. Somewhere at the back of my brain, a voice said I should be trying to psych out Mark's ability to lie, but I stilled the voice. There would be plenty of time for that later. At the moment, the cards were falling my way.

It took two hours of steady losing and a head that felt like a prop for an aspirin ad before I began to lose interest in the game. Even then it took a fight to get me away from the table, a fight between two of my fellow players, that is. A guy everyone referred to as Pinkie got sore at someone called Jakes, and before you knew it, the two were hammering away at each other, making a mess of everything in the vicinity. My mind was dulled with drink, but I had sense enough left to pick up my glass and move out of the way. Mark was standing to one side, yelling, "Hit him! Come on. That's the way." He might have been Pinkie's manager by the look of pleasure on his face when

Pinkie landed a telling blow to Jake's nose.

Then a chair was smashed, and someone threw a bottle through a window. Another latecomer and Mark joined in the fracas. Someone else tried to unsuccessfully calm things down and got hit for his effort. He, too, jumped into the fray. A flying glass whizzed by my head, liquid spraying outward as if the glass were a lawn sprinkler gone berserk. What a waste of good booze.

Frances was next to me, looking excited in spite of what was happening to his house. "Almost as good as last Wednesday," he said. Last Wednesday, I repeated to myself. Wasn't there something important about last Wednesday?

"What happened last Wednesday?" I asked, my voice thicker than I remembered it being.

"Big game," Frances replied. "Lotsa money involved. Then we caught someone cheating...." His voice trailed off as he realized who he was talking to. "Look, there was some trouble, see? We beat up the cheater pretty bad. Mark doesn't want his mother to know about it. Got the picture?"

"Sure," I said. I wouldn't want my mother to know if I had beat someone up, not that I would, but I wouldn't want her to know if I had. So, I could understand.

"The other guys don't want any trouble with the police, and we don't want any trouble with *them*. They play rough. We all agreed to keep it quiet." I had no doubt he was suggesting that I either join in the pact to keep it quiet or someone might play rough with me. I shook my head and made a zipping gesture across my lips. No one would hear about it from me.

Then it hit me. Neither Mark nor Frances had murdered Pearl Rosenblatt. They had been involved in a brawl with some thugs on the Wednesday evening when she was murdered. So much for my theory.

Eventually, things settled down, enough chairs were recovered from the mess so everyone could gather around the table again, and the drinking and card playing continued. For how long, I don't know. When I couldn't read the little numbers on the cards anymore, I called it quits. That was a few minutes before I threw up in the corner by a pile of broken glass and debris.

No one seemed to notice my departure. They had my money; that was enough. Once outside, I had difficulty locating my car. Someone had hidden it in the driveway, and the driveway was much further from the house than I remembered. It crossed my mind that I'd had a few too many to be driving, but after I finally managed to get the key in the ignition, it seemed a shame to waste all that effort.

The drive home was uneventful, except for a couple of wrong turns I made where some fool had changed the landmarks. My head was a montage of aches and pains, and my stomach felt like it was due for the junk heap. Every couple of blocks, I stopped because I thought I had to take a leak, but each time I got out of the car, the urge went away. It took me four stops to figure out that my seat belt was too tight.

I missed The Haven the first time. Somehow it hadn't seemed familiar. In fact, nothing seemed familiar. The evening of drink and revelry had left me totally discombobulated. Not that I was capable of saying the word in my present state. It was like having an advanced case of cataracts in both eyes. I could see things around the periphery, but nothing looked right straight on. There was no way I could read the name on the parking stall. But I remembered it was at the end. All I had to do was find the end of the row of parking spaces.

When I passed the last parked car, I took aim and drove onto the platform. Had someone moved the tree closer? As I switched off the engine, I heard some creaking sounds. Then I had the sensation of falling, like being in an elevator that was descending. Unfortunately, my stomach wasn't descending at quite the same rate, and I felt incredibly nauseous. Movement ceased with a loud "thud" and a resounding crunching sound. I looked out my windshield. There was something wrong. There shouldn't be a house right in front of me. The parking area was elevated. It had a glorious view of quaint structures and water. I blinked. Then blinked again. But the blurry house refused to go away.

I took a deep breath to try and clear my head and settle my stomach. There was no getting around it. The house and I were on the same level, well, not exactly level. I seemed to be tilted forward. Not a very comfortable position, now that I thought about it. What was happening? Why was everything out of kilter, like looking in a Fun House mirror?

Lights and voices suddenly erupted from the house in front of me. Then someone opened my car door, and a familiar voice exclaimed, "It's John. Are you all right, John?" Someone else said, "His eyes are open."

I turned toward the voices. "I'm fine," I said. Why wouldn't I be?

"What did he say?"

"I couldn't tell. Maybe he's injured."

"Let's get him out of there."

"No, if he's injured, we shouldn't move him."

I listened to them arguing about whether it was safe to move me or not, unable to understand why they didn't believe me when I said I was fine. "Fine," I repeated. Why did it sound as though I was talking underwater?

"He's incoherent."

"Maybe he's in pain. We should call an ambulance."

Things had gone far enough. I leaned toward the door, my seat belt bringing me up short, pressing on my kidneys again. For some reason, the seat belt was almost impossible to remove. I jerked and twitched this way and that, trying to unsnap it. Every time I moved someone outside "oohed" and "aahed." By the time I managed to extricate myself, I was extremely irritated by the fuss everyone was making. Honestly! Couldn't a body come home a little late without causing a panic?

They were still arguing about whether to move me as I staggered out of the car. Then, suddenly, they all fell silent, staring at me as though I were an apparition.

"Good night," I said as I walked down the dock toward home. What had happened to the steps? And what was my car doing in the landlord's back yard?

Chapter Fourteen

"Ohhh my head," I moaned, trying to open my eyes, yet not entirely certain I really wanted to. It was bad enough, just being alive without having to look at the world. But I had to get up if I wanted to get an aspirin, maybe a dozen. And I had to answer the telephone. Each metallic "riinngg" was like a tiny bomb exploding in my brain. Why did I still have a landline anyway? And why hadn't I changed the ringtone? And why did someone keep calling? Couldn't they just leave a message?

"Yesh," I said. A faint pinpoint of sound came from the other end of the receiver. "Yesh," I said louder, rotating the phone until the other voice came in loud and clear, too loud and definitely with an unsettling clarity. Emma's voice boomed at me, each syllable jabbing me in the forehead.

After railing at me for several minutes, she finally paused and asked, "Are you alright?" Her tone implied that any condition short of death meant that I was totally responsible for my own actions. Unless I was dead, I'd better have a damn good excuse for whatever it was she was calling me about. I shook my head as I started to respond. That was a mistake.

"Ooohhhh," I moaned again.

"Mr. Smith, are you alright?" This time she sounded almost concerned.

"I'm not sure, Emma. I'll check and get back to you."

"Do you know what time it is?!"

"No, do you want me to look?" The world was gradually coming into focus, but I could only open one eye at a time.

"It's nine-thirty," she said crisply. If she knew the time, why had she called me to ask? "And you had an appointment scheduled for nine o'clock with

Mr. Van Droop." I felt another moan coming on. "Did you hear me?"

"Yes, I heard you." Every nerve in my body was quivering in pain. "Oh no," I said as the impact of her announcement hit home, "I had an appointment with Mr. Van Droop this morning."

"You most certainly did. He asked me to find out what happened to you. As soon as I hang up, I shall inform him." She sounded like she was looking forward to that.

"Emma, something came up," I said.

"It certainly sounds that way."

"I'll come in right away. Well, as soon as I can make it. Please tell him how sorry I am about being late. It was, ah, unavoidable." At least I could put together complete sentences even if it felt like they were being ripped out of my brain without anesthetic.

"I'll pass along your message." Click.

I stood there for a moment, hanging onto the receiver for support, disjointed recollections of Sunday afternoon and evening flitting in and out of my mind like moths seeking light. But there was no light, only some slightly disturbing images that didn't make any sense. But first things first. What was I going to tell Van Droop? There was no progress on a settlement. No progress on any aspect of the investigation. No progress, period. It would be a brief report. Perhaps his response would be equally brief: "You're fired."

I lurched off in the direction of the bathroom. It was tough going. The floor seemed to be rocking as if my houseboat was in the middle of an oceanic squall. The next houseboat I rented would be on solid ground.

The face in the mirror of the medicine chest looked like a cartoon image of me. I shook three Excedrin from a bottle, dropping a couple on the floor. On my second try I managed to get one more than I needed, but I didn't want to try putting it back in the tiny opening, so I swallowed all three with a few gulps of water from the faucet. Then I noticed that the "best before" stamped across the bottom of the bottle was from three years ago. In case their strength weakened once the expiration date had come and gone, I took two more.

Even after the Excedrin and a shower, I still felt dreadful. I got dressed anyway, changing jackets three times to find one that went with a tie that I hoped projected both professionalism and humility. There really ought to be a simpler way of putting one's neck in a noose. Then I remembered that there was—I was still a suspect in two murder investigations.

The part of my mind that wasn't dwelling on how horrible I felt was thinking about what I was going to say to Van Droop, so it was with considerable surprise when I got to my parking space to discover that it had been moved down into the landlord's back yard, platform and all. Squinting into the sun, I stared down at my car. It was almost fifteen feet below, tilting slightly forward, apparently intact, but surrounded by broken and smashed bits and pieces of platform debris. Slowly, very slowly, memories of falling through space came back to me. No wonder I felt so bad—I'd been in a car accident!

What a relief. A car accident. Van Droop would have to give me some slack with that as an excuse. All I had to do was get to the office and explain. But first, I had to figure some way to get my car out of the landlord's back yard.

"Excuse me," I apologized when the landlord's wife answered the door. She wears handmade clothes created out of exotic prints and unusual materials, and her long red-gold hair tapers outward in a series of small waves, stylish in an offbeat sort of way. This morning she had on a salmon-colored suede tunic that hung crookedly at an angle, the short end near her hip, the long end below her knees. "My car seems to be in your back yard," I explained.

"Are you okay, Mr. Smith?"

"As well as can be expected." The Excedrin hadn't kicked in yet, and I was obviously suffering from visual disorientation. I could have sworn she winked at me.

"Were you snockered!" she said, stifling a giggle.

"I beg your pardon?"

"You were feeling no pain last night," she said. "You got out of your car like some drunken lord and as dignified as you please wished us a 'Gud Niite.'" Neither her imitation of my leave-taking nor her interpretation of events

146

was reassuring.

"I had just been in a serious accident," I explained.

She suddenly grew thoughtful. "Yes," she said, "that's something we can't quite figure out." She pushed back a strand of hair that had fallen over one eye.

"What do you mean?"

"Well, last night, we attributed the platform's collapse to an act of God." How nice of him to act on my behalf, I thought irreverently. "But this morning, when we looked at things more carefully, well…." She hesitated. "You don't have any enemies, do you?"

Involuntarily I started, my eyelids protesting the sudden movement. "Enemies?" There was that question again.

"That wasn't an accident," she said.

"Huh?" I didn't like where she was going with this.

"The cross-braces had been removed. The entire structure had been weakened so that the platform couldn't support the weight of your car."

"Those kids…" I began.

"I don't think you can blame kids for this." She sounded defensive. One of my tormenters is her young son, an angelic lad in his mother's nearsighted eyes. "The cross-braces had been removed," she repeated. "That's not a prank."

It was all so confusing. And overwhelming. Who would want to do that to me? "I have to go to work," I said.

"We've notified the police. They will be here sometime this morning."

I started backing away. "Sorry, but I need to go to work. I'm late for a meeting with my boss."

"This was the work of professionals," she persisted. "The police will want to talk with you."

Professional "whats"? I didn't understand what she was saying. But what I did understand is that if I didn't get going, I would be making things even worse for what was left of my career as a claims adjuster. "Have them call me at the office." As I headed toward my car, I suddenly remembered what I had originally intended to ask. Turning back, I said, "Do you mind if

I drive through your flowers?" Her eyebrows went up like two pieces of toast popping out of a toaster. "That's the only way I can get my car out," I explained. "If I can drive across your flowers to where the embankment levels off a bit, I think I can make it to the road."

"But the police may want to see your car *in situ*," she complained, glancing at her carefully tended flowerbeds.

"I can describe it to them. And the collapsed platform isn't going anywhere. I have to go to work."

She continued to look as though I'd asked to drive through her living room, but reluctantly nodded consent. "Try not to damage the iris," she said plaintively. I agreed to avoid the iris, although I don't know an iris from a rutabaga. But I needed to get underway. And I certainly didn't want to be there when the police arrived.

I made my way through the pile of platform rubble. The Saturn appeared to be in perfect condition. Bee must have floated from the upper level to the lower level as the platform slowly tipped forward onto the landlord's yard below. There didn't seem to be so much as a scratch on the paint. If the inside was as pristine as the outside, I was home free. I got inside, put the key in the ignition, and turned it. The engine purred to life. I put it in gear and eased her off the pile of rubble. The landlord's wife watched from a safe distance, her cherubic son making faces at me from behind his mother's back.

It was a bumpy ride across the flowers, and I confess that I made little effort to avoid wiping out the entire lot. Her son puts dead fish in my mailbox, my parking space is sabotaged, and she is worried about a couple of flowers, I grumbled. Fair's fair.

My first run at the embankment was a fiasco. The Saturn stalled halfway up. It was steeper than I thought, but I was still convinced I could do it. I backed down, revved up the engine, and charged. The tires slipped in the loose earth, and for an instant, I had visions of shooting backwards down the embankment into the drink. Wouldn't the landlord's boy love that! I couldn't give him the satisfaction. I pressed the accelerator to the floor and leaned forward in my seat to encourage forward momentum. Just when I thought it wasn't going to work, the tires caught, and the Saturn lurched upward, flying over the crest of the hill as easily as Evel Knievel jumping thirteen buses.

The car came to a panting halt, stretched crossways on the road above. My head felt like one of those flowers I had run over. In fact, decapitation was beginning to sound like a pleasant option. Why didn't I just call Emma and explain that I had been in a car accident and was not feeling well enough to come to work?

I might have stayed there in the middle of the road indefinitely, trying to make up my mind what to do, but my thinking was helped along by several irate motorists whose horn blasts intimated I had no right to be in the middle of the road. As if I had driven there for the specific purpose of making their lives more difficult. For all they knew, I might be ill or injured, but no, their only concern was that an impediment to their progress be removed. The good Samaritans honked their horns and waved fists at me. If each horn blast hadn't felt like a spike being driven into my skull, I would have stayed there out of spite.

Once in motion, I automatically headed for the office. I arrived without incident, only to find the main parking lot at Universal full. And someone was in my spot. My replacement, perhaps? Desperate to get on with it, I finally found a narrow space and edged in between a brick building and a spotless Cadillac. If the Cadillac owner didn't have enough room to get in on the driver's side, it wasn't my worry.

My head still felt like a battleground. And the thought of what might be in store for me didn't help. So instead of heading directly for my office, I detoured via a small café for a cup of coffee. If ever I needed some caffeine fortification, it was now. I placed my order and got out my wallet to pay. It was empty! Even my secret compartment. I searched it again, hoping it was my eyesight and not the wallet that was deficient. Nothing. I'd been robbed.

"My money," I stammered uncertainly. "Someone...I...."

The cashier shook her head and gave me a look that said she'd heard it all before. "Come on, Mister, pay up or no coffee for you." I was hardly in a position to criticize her customer service skills, but I thought she was being a bit unreasonable. Although everyone behind me in line seemed to be taking her side. I heard someone mumble someone about "get a life" and another voice complained about "some people."

"But...." I felt like I was being judged unfairly and held up my empty wallet as proof. She seemed to think it was proof that I was a deadbeat.

"Hold that venti caramel macchiato," she yelled at the person making the drinks.

"No," I pleaded. Should I offer to leave my watch for security while I ran to the office for money? Maybe I had some money in my pockets. No, no such luck. Then I remembered my credit card. Just because I usually pay for my coffee with cash didn't mean I had to. "Here," I said, thrusting my credit card at her. "Use this."

She took the card from me and eyed it carefully. "You trying to be funny? John Smith, huh? First you have an empty wallet, now you give me a card with a phony name." Her loud voice shared my predicament with everyone in the store. Before she could accuse me of anything else, I whipped out my driver's license and my Costco card.

"That's my real name. See?"

She carefully scrutinized the pictures on my driver's license and the Costco card. Neither was flattering, and both had been taken several years before. For a moment, I thought she was going to say these, too, were phony. Instead, she signaled the barista that it was okay to make a cup of coffee for me. But it was clear she still had her doubts. She was only giving in because she was such a kind person, and I obviously looked like I needed a shot of caffeine.

On the way from the café to my office, I remembered a few more things about the night before. I wasn't robbed, well, not technically. I'd been playing poker, and I lost all of my money, every last penny. How was that possible?

When I reached Emma's desk, her reaction to my story about the car accident wasn't very flattering. She responded like the rich maiden aunt who long ago decided not to leave her money to her reprobate nephew. "Have you notified the police *again*?" she asked, her tone indicating that this was not only becoming old hat but very tedious.

She was right about my accidents becoming tiresome, and she didn't even know about the melted popsicle in my mailbox or the dog on my roof. But someone destroying my office, then my house, and now my parking space. It was not only tedious but downright irritating, even dangerous. "The police know about it," I replied. "They are coming by this morning to investigate." I pressed my fingers against my throbbing forehead and tried to think.

"Are you ill?" Emma asked, showing about as much sympathy as she would if inquiring about the health of the family pet. Well, maybe a bit less.

"I don't feel too well," I admitted. Then, hoping to get a little sympathy out of her, I added, "I think I hit my head in the accident." My head had definitely been involved in some kind of abuse.

"Maybe you should see a doctor." Her tone implied that if you aren't willing to see a doctor, you are probably faking your illness.

"I should have stayed home in bed." Let *her* feel some guilt for a change.

"What do you want me to tell Mr. Van Droop?" she asked, obviously immune to deflected guilt rays. It was game, match, set for the inimitable Emma.

"As soon as he can see me," I began.

"He left to attend a meeting downtown," she interrupted. "He won't be back until late this afternoon." From the gleam of triumph in her eyes, I could tell that she had been looking forward to dropping that little bomb.

Unwilling to acknowledge her victory dance, I forced a smile. "In that case, would you please let him know that I will be available when he returns and can see him at his convenience?" Still smiling, my teeth aching with the effort, I spun around and headed for my office. Apparently, one shouldn't spin around the morning after a late-night poker game and subsequent accident. I barely managed the long trek without falling or having my head explode. Once inside, I collapsed in my chair and put my head down on my desk. The exact same position I was in the day this whole mess started. I glanced regretfully at the empty wooden box peeking from the half-open cabinet drawer. What I wouldn't give for a drink of something stronger than a macchiato.

I finished off the macchiato, made two trips to the bathroom, and shuffled some papers on my desk. It was going to be a long day. I didn't want to go home and face the police. I didn't want to be gone if Van Droop returned early. But I didn't feel focused enough to actually do any work. And I couldn't even take a nap. Emma was bound to catch me.

There had to be some way to pass the time. Was there anything on the internet that wouldn't be flagged by our tech people as non-work-related activity? They would undoubtedly frown on playing games or browsing Facebook. But maybe there was a TV program that could be rationalized as relevant. Perhaps a rerun of *Leverage*. One of the main characters was a former insurance investigator. Or *Wipeout*. I could argue I was watching it to study liability issues.

I was still pondering possible TV programs that might help me get through the next few hours without getting me fired when Emma came in with a cup of tea. "I thought you might want something soothing to drink," she said in a neutral tone. Maybe I'd tickled her conscience after all. I used the tea to down two aspirin, wondering if it was all right to mix Excedrin with aspirin, but feeling too wasted to care. No side effects could be worse than the primary effect.

The call from the police didn't improve my day. The officer practically accused me of removing vital evidence from the scene of a crime. I pointed out that it wasn't the car that had been tampered with, but he didn't think that should have been my call. Maybe he had a point, but at the time, it had seemed important to get to work. I asked if they had made any progress. He told me that, of course, they'd made progress, but when pressed, he admitted they didn't have any leads. That was why he had called me—could I tell him if I had any enemies? I promised to compile an alphabetical list with a 1-to-5-star rating to let them know just how much each particular enemy hated me. He didn't think that was funny. And it hurt when I laughed.

During the lunch hour, Emma buzzed me on the intercom to ask if I was available to see a walk-in. It's a good thing she didn't ask if I was competent. Yes, I was available, alone in my office with only my pain to keep me company and, since misery loves company, I told Emma to send her in.

My heart skipped a beat when the door swung open, and I saw Zelda Gunnar standing there in the shadowy light. No, I told myself, it couldn't be her. She was definitely dead. But I couldn't bring myself to get out of my chair and move toward the apparition. That's what they always did in horror movies when the music got spooky, and you just knew that what they were about to do was a bad idea.

When the woman came closer, I realized she only resembled Zelda, but it was a striking resemblance. This version was slightly younger, not quite as grim, and a bit plump. A palatable knock-off of the officious Miss Gunnar.

"I'm Lizbeth Gunnar," the woman said, holding out a pudgy hand, forcing me to come out from behind my desk. Her name sounded like a vocalized lisp. I reached out and managed a flabby squeeze instead of my usual consciously firm handshake. It was too much like shaking hands with the past and not a very pleasant past. "I understand you were with Zelda when she died," the very much alive Miss Gunnar said.

"Yes. I was."

She smiled sweetly and sat down without being asked. I went back around my desk and sat down across from her. "Did you know her well?" she asked.

"Just a business acquaintance," I said carefully. "I didn't know her personally." I felt I should say something polite, perhaps offer condolences or something, but I've never been very good at that sort of thing, and I wasn't exactly up to operational efficiency at the moment. I sat there trying to appear sympathetic and receptive when all I really wanted to do was crawl into a hole someplace, like an animal that leaves the pack and wanders off when he knows his time has come.

"I hope you don't mind me dropping in like this, but I wanted to meet you." She smiled again, her robin's-egg-blue eyes glistening with grief.

"Of course not," I lied. "Nice of you to stop by." As long as she wasn't sent by Bruno to pump me about Zelda's last words, I could probably cope. But with eyes like those, she was a natural. Who could resist revealing their innermost secrets to them?

"Zelda's death was such a shock," she explained. She looked down at her hands. Her nails were bitten to the quick. "We lived together. Neither of us ever married, and it can be lonely living by yourself." She looked to me for agreement, and I quickly did so. It *was* lonely at times. "Zelda was a good companion. A bit, oh, impatient, but comfortable to be around." Was it possible that all she wanted was to talk about her sister? To pay homage to her memory with the person who was with her at the end?

"We had a small apartment near our places of employment," she continued. "I work in a small used bookstore, a nice place, not too busy. Zelda was the one with the important job." She bit her lip to hold back tears. "Poor Zelda. She was just about to become a manager. All her life, she wanted to be a manager. That man she worked for wasn't nearly as qualified as she." Her tone and manner had become confidential. Two friends chatting about the deceased, only I wasn't saying anything.

"She told me many times how he beat her out for that position simply because she was a woman." Leaning forward, she added, "She worked her way up the ranks, you know."

I only half listened as she rambled on, describing Hilda's finer qualities and earlier attempts to achieve success. An idea was struggling to surface, like a drowning man following the bubbles upward.

"She was about to become a manager?" I asked, interrupting her flow. She looked surprised but not particularly bothered that I hadn't been tracking. "Yes, I believe that she was."

"At some other office?"

"Oh, no. Zelda was going to become manager of the office where she'd always worked. I'm sure of that."

"What was going to happen to, ah, what about Mr. Conklin?"

She blushed slightly, and a finger went to her mouth only to be immediately withdrawn. "Bad habit," she murmured. "Trying to stop biting my nails. Zelda was always after me about it." Her upper lip quivered. Oh no, what was I going to do if she cried? Did I have Kleenex?

"What about Mr. Conklin?" I gently prompted.

"I probably shouldn't be talking about this," she said with the air of one who very much wants to do the thing they know they shouldn't be doing.

"Please," I encouraged. "I'd like to hear about it."

"Well," she began after glancing around to make sure the walls didn't have ears, "she believed Mr. Conklin was about to be fired." She blushed again, embarrassed to be sharing this bit of gossip while at the same time relishing the moment.

"Fired? Do you know why?"

"Zelda didn't tell me the details, but I think it was something about an insurance policy, for some hospital. Something like that."

I lurched forward, almost toppling off my chair. Then I coughed and hit my chest with my fist to cover my surprise. "Something in my throat," I explained.

"Poor man. Can I help? Do you need a drink?" I knew what she meant, but a real drink was what I needed.

"Ahem. Ahem. No, thank you. I think I'm fine now." Straightening up, I said, "As you were saying?"

"Oh, well." She seemed to have forgotten what she had been saying. "Zelda was so pleased she was finally going to get what she deserved," she concluded.

Zelda must have had something on Conklin, perhaps something to do with the Lady of the Lamp policy. That would explain why he was so vague when I tried to talk with him about it. In fact, from his point of view, it was possible Zelda had gotten exactly what she deserved. "Have you told all this to the police?" I asked.

Miss Gunnar fluttered her fingers in indignation. "Of course not. Hilda told me these things in confidence. I've only shared them with you because you were with her when she died." She glanced guiltily at her hands again. "Besides, those policemen don't understand what it's like to lose someone you are close to. They have questions they want answered, and that's all they care about."

So, I thought, Bruno or one of his compatriots was only interested in brief answers to specific questions and hadn't taken time to wade through Lizbeth's circuitous memories and tales of woe. They would be sorry if I was able to use this tidbit to find some answers to the larger question of "whodunit?" If only I'd done a better job the first time around when searching Conklin's office, Zelda might still be alive, and Lizbeth wouldn't be biting her fingernails. The good news—I still had a chance to redeem myself.

Lizbeth left all smiles and thank-yous. I was able to say with honesty that the pleasure was all mine. This bit of formal politeness made her blush one more time, and for a moment, I thought she was going to curtsy as she backed out of my office. It was hard to believe that this gentle creature was Zelda's sister. The resemblance that had seemed so strong initially had slowly faded with the unfolding of Lizbeth's guileless and mild persona.

After Lizbeth left, I informed Emma that I would be out for about an hour but would be back in plenty of time to meet with Mr. Van Droop before the end of the day. Her nonverbals left no doubt that she was skeptical. Well, I would show her. After a quick trip to Conklin's office, I would return triumphant.

My plan was simple. If Conklin was in, I would confront him and threaten to call the police if he refused to show me the policy immediately. If he wasn't in—which was what I secretly wished for in spite of my recent history with break-ins—then I would search his office until I found the policy and find out for myself what all the fuss was about. My headache had subsided, I had a plan, and I was feeling lucky.

To my extreme disappointment, there was a different receptionist this time, a wrinkled brunette with less shape than Keira Knightley after eating an entire pizza with the works. Someone's wife probably hired her. She informed me in a clipped voice that Mr. Conklin was unavailable and that she would be glad to take a message. "Glad" was obviously an overstatement; she had probably never experienced anything stronger than "mildly unhappy." I thanked her and said I'd wait. I meant it too. I would wait just long enough for her to leave the room on some errand or to go to the bathroom, whatever. Then I would slip down the hall and do what I had come for.

She obviously enjoyed trying to outwait me. I thought about offering to get her some coffee or setting off the sprinkler system, anything to get her out of that chair. I read an old newspaper that someone had left behind, studied my fingernails, checked for phone and email messages for the umpteenth time, and went through the newspaper again as if captivated by last week's news. She may not have needed to use the restroom, but I did. Urgently. The venti caramel macchiato I'd picked up on the way was taking its toll. When I could stand it no longer, I asked her where the nearest restroom was, and she pointed me down the hall in the opposite direction from Conklin's office. On my way back, I passed her in the hall. Perhaps she, too, had to make a pit stop. This was my chance.

To my surprise, I found what I was looking for right off. It would have taken me longer if I hadn't searched the bottom drawer of his desk first, hoping to find a bottle of something to swig for medicinal purposes. My headache had returned, not as bad as before, but a throbbing distraction that I could do without. There was no bottle, but there was a brokerage file on the Lady of the Lamp.

Wally walked in just as I finished perusing its contents. I was seated behind his desk, feeling better and better in spite of the lingering headache. When he saw me sitting there, he looked startled, then angry, and finally, fearful—all in just a few seconds. Then his face turned red, and he began flapping his arms like a chicken in distress. "You, you," he sputtered. "What are you doing in my office?"

I held up the file, label side out. "Just reading," I said calmly. "And it's very interesting reading, I might add."

"You have no right to be here," he said, lowering his voice as he shut the door behind him.

"I don't think it's a question of 'rights,'" I said, stroking the file suggestively.

"Would you please leave?" It was a last-ditch attempt to get rid of me, but we both knew it was futile.

"If I do, I'm taking this with me."

As quickly as his face had turned bright red, the color drained away like water from a sink, leaving him as pale and lifeless as porcelain. Then he suddenly went rigid and threw himself across the desk, grabbing at the file. "Give that to me," he gasped. As I pulled it back, he fell against the desk, his fingers just inches from the file. "Give it to me," he sobbed.

"It's too late," I informed him. "I know your secret."

He collapsed in a chair in front of the desk and put his still pale face in his hands. "No, no, no," he repeated in a desperate and pitiful way. "No."

There was a knock on the door, and seconds later, the receptionist appeared. Wally managed to pull himself together, but he was on the wrong side of the desk. She looked at me and demanded to know, "What are *you* doing in here?" Wally waved a limp hand to indicate that everything was okay and that she could leave. After plopping a few papers on his desk, she took the hint and departed, leaving the door open a few inches. I got up and closed it.

"Okay, Wally," I said. "Tell me about this." I pointed at the file. It contained a standard primary malpractice policy issued to the hospital about ten months ago, and, in addition, there were several very interesting items. The first was a letter from the hospital carefully outlining the excess coverage policy the hospital wanted, coverage for losses over and above the limits on the primary policy. The letter was dated shortly before the standard primary policy had been issued. Secondly, there was a copy of a binder sent to the hospital some months ago, assuring them that the excess coverage policy was in place. Third, and most intriguing, was a folder with copies of several letters and email messages from Wallis Conklin to a number of insurance companies requesting the excess coverage, all of them dated *after* the hospital had been told the coverage was in place. Conklin had issued a binder on coverage that did not exist.

Wally squirmed in his chair like a small kid waiting outside the principal's office. "Well, I...I...it's hard to explain," he said.

"Try," I prompted. "Start with how you obtained—or haven't obtained—the excess coverage for the hospital."

"I'm trying, I'm trying. You've got to believe me." *Please, Mr. Principal, I didn't put the dead rat on the teacher's desk, honestly, I didn't.* "All I need is a little more time."

"But you don't have it yet, in spite of what you told the hospital." It was a statement, not a question.

"I can get one. I'm sure of it." Like a hostile witness, he didn't want to admit to anything, even something obvious.

"But why?" I asked, truly puzzled. "Why not just admit you couldn't get it for them?"

"They wanted excess coverage, but the way medical claims have been increasing, it isn't that easy to get it these days. But I knew they wouldn't understand. And they're a big account, a really big account…." His voice trailed off, and his shoulders slumped. I knew how he felt, but I had to know the whole truth.

"You haven't told them yet, have you?"

"Please, I'm on the verge of getting the coverage. Please don't tell anyone."

"But claims-made insurance isn't retroactive. It's a question of when you become aware of a claim. Claims made during the period when the primary policy was issued, and the excess coverage policy is purchased won't be covered by the excess. You will have to tell them something."

"I know, but the primary policy has been sufficient so far. It's only the future we have to worry about."

Only the future, I reflected. A future without Pearl Rosenblatt to ruin his chances of covering his tracks. I might have discovered a motive for not one, but two murders. This was undoubtedly Zelda Gunnar's secret. She had probably threatened to reveal his deception to his superiors at Babcock-Chalmers. That had given her leverage over her boss. One way or the other, she could become a manager. Then he had probably found out that Pearl Rosenblatt intended to sue the hospital and that her claim might go over the standard policy limits. At the very least, her claim would call attention to the gap in time between the underlying policy and the excess policy. She, too, became a threat to Wally's future. And now I was in the way. Suddenly the only thing I wanted was OUT. Sitting across from a murderer with evidence in your hands didn't seem like a smart move. My brain must have been scrambled in the accident.

"You're right," I agreed. "Let's worry about the future and let the present take care of itself." I stood up. "Your secret is safe with me." Somehow it seemed all right to lie to a murderer.

"Oh, thank you," he said effusively, also standing up. "Thank you." For a moment, I thought he was going to hug me. Murderers are very emotional people. "I promise I'll take care of this right away, this afternoon." He reached out his hand, but I was already halfway to his office door. "I can't tell you how much this means to me," he said to my back as I exited.

The only thing it meant to me was a chance to escape. Once in the hall, I had second thoughts. Perhaps I should have taken the file as evidence. Of course, it would hardly do him any good to destroy it. He wouldn't be able to produce a legitimate policy that didn't exist. And any suit against the hospital might bring the policy gaps to the forefront. Conklin could be on the hook in so many ways.

This was a matter for the authorities. And as soon as I had done my duty as a member of the insurance community, I would stop by and tell Bruno all about it. But first, I wanted to inform the hospital of their situation. They had a right to know before the news hit the papers.

Unfortunately, I realized too late that I should have gone directly to the police.

Chapter Fifteen

"My name is John Smith. I'm with Universal Heartland Liability and Casualty Assurance Company of America...Incorporated," I said.

"Never heard of them," Byron Cheever rudely responded, looking down at some papers on his desk to let me know that he had agreed to see me, but that didn't necessarily include listening.

"What I've come to talk with you about only indirectly concerns Universal," I said to the top of his head. He had a tiny bald spot that would probably become larger within the year. "You see, I have a case in which the claimant was considering suing your hospital. But then, that's not what I wanted to talk with you about either." Talking to the top of his head was making me nervous. Who the hell did he think he was? I had come to save him from being surprised by a visit from a reporter or, worse, headlines about his hospital. And he didn't have the decency to look at me. Not that I was much to look at today with my bloodshot eyes and day-after pallor, but damn it, I had come out of professional courtesy to do the man a favor. "I'm in possession of some information about your insurance situation that I think you might find interesting," I announced. That got his attention. He turned a pair of cold, dark eyes on me.

"I beg your pardon?"

"I said, you have a problem with your insurance." That wasn't exactly what I said, but it was what I meant.

"And just how does that concern you?" His tone suggested that a peasant doesn't meddle in a king's affairs.

"Sorry to take up your valuable time," I said, rising. "I was trying to be helpful." But your mental butt-kicking is not something I have to put up with.

"Sit down," he ordered. My knees started to obey; I caught myself just in time.

"I don't think we have much more to say to each other." Even peasants have their pride.

He smiled. At least, I think it was a smile. The corners of his mouth twitched, and a couple of lines on his cheeks moved slightly outward. "I didn't mean to sound abrupt. But I have a lot on my mind. Now, what's this about some problem with insurance?"

Reluctantly, I eased myself back into the chair, knowing as I did so that it was a mistake. The only hunch I'd had in ages, and I ignored it. The "new" Nixon had been a lie; why did I expect the "new" Cheever to be any different? "Do you have a copy of your policy?" I asked.

"The hospital deals with a reputable broker. I'm sure everything is in order." His mouth twitched again.

"I'd rather not explain how I know, but it is my understanding that the hospital does not have the excess coverage policy you may think it has."

"I'm sure that will be taken care of soon," he blithely responded.

Astonished, I said, "You mean you know you are only covered by a standard primary policy at present?" Wally Conklin certainly hadn't acted as though the hospital was in the loop. Why had he begged me not to mention it to anyone if Cheever already knew and was okay with the way things were?

"Mr. Conklin recently informed me that he was having difficulty obtaining the excess coverage we want, but he has assured me that it will be taken care of soon."

"Recently? How recently?"

"Fortunately, we have no large suits pending, so our insurance coverage has been sufficient. In fact, many hospitals operate with only a standard policy. However, we at Lady of the Lamp believe in being cautious by preparing in advance for the unexpected. That's why I asked Mr. Conklin to find an excess coverage policy for us."

It all sounded so simple, yet I could swear there was something wrong somewhere. If Conklin had killed Zelda because she knew about the problem with the excess coverage for the hospital, then he had killed her for no reason, because the head of the hospital didn't seem to care. If Cheever wasn't worried, why was Conklin so upset? And, more importantly, why should I care? I should go talk to Bruno, dump all of the bits and pieces of info in his capable hands, and let him figure it out.

"Fine." I stood up. "As long as you are aware of the situation, everything's fine. I was concerned that you didn't know, and when the police start asking questions, well, the reporters are never far behind."

"Police?" He sounded genuinely surprised.

"Yes, your policy may be evidence in a murder investigation. It may not be, but that's for the police to decide."

"Sit down," he ordered again. Did he think I'd come to talk to him for the exercise? After a brief knee dip, I remained standing.

"I don't see that we have anything more to discuss."

"I think we do." His tone suggested that he had a secret file on me, one that would have made J. Edgar Hoover blush. I couldn't figure the guy out, but I finally sat down anyway. I was tired.

"When you first mentioned this insurance matter," he said, "I didn't realize you were here as a friend. Now I appreciate that you are concerned for any adverse publicity that the hospital might be subject to as a result of our, ah, little problem." Now it was "our little problem," was it? "But I can assure you that it isn't a police matter. And even though everything is under control, it would be awkward if the public were to discover that we weren't as fully covered as we would like to be. As I'm sure you know, the public has a way of misinterpreting such things, always seeing it in the worst possible light." He paused and regarded me with those dark, unfathomable eyes.

If everything was so fine then why was he suddenly all smooth talk and mouth twitches? All he had to do was tell the police what he just told me. Maybe he could even persuade the reporters that things were hunky dory.

When I didn't respond, he said, "As someone in the insurance business, I'm sure you agree." It wasn't a question.

163

"But you just got through telling me there's nothing to worry about, so why try to hide the facts?"

"As I just explained, people can create problems where none exist. And minor issues have a way of taking on a life of their own if you let them. The best thing for everyone involved is to simply say nothing about this." He paused, then asked, "You understand, don't you?" This time it was a question, but it felt a bit like a threat too.

"The only thing I understand is that the police frown on having evidence withheld in a murder investigation."

"Are you talking about the murder of that woman at Babcock-Chalmers?"

"Yes." If he didn't bring up Pearl Rosenblatt, I wasn't going to. Things were complicated enough.

"But what makes you think that our policy has anything to do with it?"

"It probably doesn't," I agreed, standing. All I wanted to do was get out of there. "Sorry for any inconvenience."

His demeanor suddenly grew hard as marble. "Either sit down and listen to what I have to say, or I'll turn you in to the police for breaking and entering. In case you didn't know, Conklin is prepared to swear out a complaint."

That stopped me in my tracks. Wally had begged me to keep quiet and then had obviously bared his soul to Cheever before I could take my information to the police. That squealer. Could he make the charge stick? And was he talking about the first time or both times? Maybe the police would give me a break if I gave them a good lead. Then again, what did I actually have to offer the police? If Cheever was threatening me, then he probably wouldn't hesitate to do whatever it took to keep the hospital's situation out of the press. What if he and Conklin got together on a story—could they pull it off? I sat down.

"That's better. All I ask is that you wait a few days. Mr. Conklin and I have discussed the matter and believe that everything will be resolved shortly. Allowing us a little slack in this matter is in *everyone*'s best interest." His emphasis on "everyone" reminded me of something the Godfather might say to an underling. "Do we understand each other?"

This time I understood perfectly. I was to keep mum until Conklin and

Cheever had time to cover their tracks. Then I was free to tell the police whatever I wanted to; only there wouldn't be any evidence to back up my story. Maybe Conklin would even twist things to make it look like I was trying to create a diversion to cover my own criminal acts. If my first break and entry came to light, it might look as though I had a good reason to kill Zelda. Maybe Conklin was not only a murderer, but smarter than I thought. He'd played on Cheever's weaknesses, and between the two of them, they had me right where they wanted me.

"We've got a deal," I agreed, not standing up right away, just in case the interview wasn't over. Then he gave me a papal nod and maintained eye contact without blinking for what seemed like an eternity. Was I supposed to kiss his ring to seal the deal? I dragged myself up and out of his office, feeling totally drained of energy and ethics.

By the time I got back to Universal, I was exhausted, and my headache was making another comeback. But Emma didn't care. She pointed out that I was behind on my emails, had several calls to return, and, furthermore, my jacket did not go with my pants. Then she added that Mr. Van Droop wouldn't be able to see me until tomorrow afternoon. There was at least one thing to be thankful for.

After browsing my emails and staring at the flashing light on my telephone console, I decided to go home. I waited until Emma stepped away from her desk, then sneaked down the hall and out of the building. I felt rotten. Really rotten. In that moment, I thought there was no way I could possibly feel any worse. Unfortunately, I was wrong.

It wasn't easy finding a parking place at The Haven. I could hardly put the Saturn in another tenant's stall, and the surrounding area was peppered with businesses and threatening signs that said "Unauthorized Vehicles Will Be Towed." I considered driving back down the embankment and across the flower beds to my parking platform's final resting place, but I finally opted for a nearby restaurant parking lot that was hopping with customers. I parked right up front as if I had nothing to hide, then slinked past the entrance and walked down the road to The Haven.

The way my day had gone, I should have known better than to check my mailbox. At the very least, I should have had sense enough to look inside before exposing my tender flesh to the snapping claws of a live crayfish. Those kids were working overtime. I pulled my hand out of the mailbox with the crayfish dangling from my finger. He refused to let go. Finally, I put him back in, closed the door on his claw, and jerked my finger out. It took about a quarter inch of skin off the end of my middle finger. Swearing, I slammed the box shut. There would be time enough tomorrow to collect my bills and dispose of the crayfish. Although maybe I should attach him to the tail of the landlord's dog. The kids liked their dog.

As if he'd heard my thoughts, the landlord suddenly appeared, a cunning smile on his usually sullen face. "Well, John," he said. "It's good to see you up and around."

"Yes, thanks." I tried to slip past him, but he sidestepped, so we were face-to-face.

"We need to talk about the damage to your parking space."

"Can't it wait?" I immediately felt defensive. The landlord hasn't liked me since I moved in. The first week I was there, he had invited me to drop by and "smoke one," and I'd asked, "One what?" Not long after that, his kid started plaguing me.

"No, I need to know who is going to pay for the damage."

"What do you mean? Don't you have insurance?" My stomach began to churn in time with my throbbing finger and pulsing headache. I was a veritable rhythm section.

"It seems there's some question about coverage with you being drunk and all."

"Who says I was drunk?" And even if I had been, how could they claim I was responsible for what had happened?

"Come off it, John. It was obvious."

"Did you give me a breathalyzer? Did you consider the fact that I might have been in shock? I should sue you for not calling a doctor. You didn't even check to see if I was injured." I couldn't actually remember what they had said or done, but by the look on his face, I had hit a homer with my comments.

"John, you smelled like a distillery. You can't honestly claim you weren't drunk."

I sidestepped to the question of liability. "You can't possibly think that I personally caused the damage to your platform." I was starting to get angry, real angry. Why did everyone assume they could push me around?

He smiled, tugging at the sweatband that held back his stringy hair. "You better think about it, John. It might be easier for everyone involved if you just coughed up some cash. You wouldn't want that fancy firm you work for to find out you have a drinking problem, now would you?" He really was a nasty piece of work. Maybe it was him and not his son who put things in my mailbox. And why did everyone think they could blackmail me? Do I have "easy target" printed on my forehead?

"Don't you think it would be best if you let your insurance company investigate before you start making threats? In case you didn't know, blackmail is illegal."

"Hey, easy, man. Who said anything about blackmail?" Then he smirked and said, "Your word against mine. And I haven't been caught drunk in public lately." He rocked back on his Birkenstocks and crossed his arms. "And, as you may know, finding a good houseboat rental isn't easy these days. Lots of people want them."

If he hadn't been so right about how hard it is to find houseboat space, especially one in a choice location like mine, I would have told him where to get off right then and there. As it was, I managed to calm myself and offer a compromise. "Perhaps it's best if I deal directly with your insurance company," I said. He didn't look pleased. Maybe he was thinking of double dipping.

"Think it over," he warned as he stalked off.

As soon as I reached my houseboat, I went inside and poured myself a drink. All I wanted was to sit there on my comfy sofa and relax, my head immobilized, insurance problems set aside for the moment. Let the crayfish and blackmailers and murderers do their worst, but to somebody else. I desperately needed a little peace and quiet.

When I came to, it was dark outside. Apparently, I had dozed off. My head felt better, just a dull ache to remind me of Sunday night's poker game. And I was hungry. That was a good sign. I was headed for the kitchen when I heard someone on the porch. Maybe the landlord with more threats. It wouldn't be Mother at this hour. And I seriously doubted it was Marie. Did Girl Scouts make the rounds selling cookies after dark?

Perhaps they would have broken in even if I hadn't opened the door for them. I'd like to think that's the case. I'd hate to think what happened next was my own dumb fault.

They didn't bother with small talk. They just pushed me back, away from the door, and shoved their way inside. They were wearing masks. One of them had a gun. My knees turned to jelly, but I held my fists up in boxer fashion and prepared to defend myself. I would go down fighting.

And I did…almost immediately, my arms flailing about as they knocked me off my feet. I didn't have a chance. It was two against one, the two of them standing and me on the floor being kicked and jabbed and kicked some more. All without a word being said. No, that's not quite accurate. I think I yelled, "Don't!"

Eventually, I forgot about the dull pain in my head. Every square inch of my body hurt. Then everything became very hazy and slowly turned to oblivion.

Chapter Sixteen

Everything was white and shiny, like a glossy overexposed photograph. An antiseptic odor assaulted my nose. A river of pain flowed through my body. I was laying on a hard surface covered with a white sheet. There was a man on a bed to my right with tubes running from a clear plastic container hanging above his head and into his arm. His arms looked like ancient parchment. Except for his nose, his gaunt face was splotchy red. He looked awful. Like I felt.

My mind jumped from fact to fact: white walls, antiseptic smells, a sick man, pain— Aha! I was in a hospital.

Waking up to find yourself in a hospital and in terrible pain is only a small step away from ending up in a morgue. But it is a very important step. I felt momentarily reassured. Then the moment passed, and I began to worry about my condition. Did I look like the living corpse on the next bed? Was my body still intact? I wiggled my toes, raising my head slightly to see if the sheet moved. Somewhere I had read that people with amputated limbs still claim to feel the missing appendages. But the sheet moved when I wiggled. My toes were all right, but wiggling them wasn't such a smart move after all. A couple of them felt like they might be broken.

Next, I tested my fingers. They, too, moved. If I could move my toes and my fingers, I figured the body in between must still be there. I only felt like I'd been chopped into tiny pieces. I laid back on my Lysol sweet pillow and tried to think.

Two men with fists like Golden Gloves Champions wearing brass knuckles instead of gloves had paid me a visit. I remembered being on the floor with the two of them dancing the flamenco on my ribs. They had also kicked me with their metal-toed tap-dancing shoes even though Queensberry Rules expressly forbid kicking. Maybe the rules don't apply to dancers.

My aching mouth brought me back to the present. I couldn't seem to make my lips work properly. Visions of black gaps in what had once been a nice set of even white teeth flashed before my eyes. Gingerly I opened my lips and directed a stiff and sore finger toward my stiff and sore mouth, jabbing where I thought my teeth should be. "Ouch," I muttered as my finger misfired and poked a tender spot on my lower lip. Just then, a lovely young thing dressed in virgin white appeared. Her presence washed over me like a soothing ointment.

"We're awake, are we?" she said, smiling. Ignoring her grade school teacher singsong voice, I started to return her smile, then, remembering that I might be missing a few teeth, I abruptly closed my mouth. "Do you think we're up to eating a little something?" she chirped. She had large luminous eyes, all warmth, and no depth. My eyes slid over her uniformed body, and I immediately forgave her for a lack of depth. Her surface more than made up for it.

"Yes," I croaked. I did feel hungry, or at least I was experiencing some sort of discomfort in the region of my stomach. And I vaguely remembered heading for the kitchen to get something to eat. Before the fight. Or before those two thugs mopped up the floor with me.

"Good." She leaned over to plump my pillow, her round, firm breasts brushing against my arm, her hospital perfume tickling my desire. I loved having my pillow plumped.

She was gone before I had a chance to ask about my condition. At least I knew one thing—my sexual drive had not been diminished. Determined to find out just how bad off I was, I propped myself up on one elbow to survey the damage firsthand. The effort was excruciating. The throbbing in my head threatened to confuse seismographs for miles around. But I persevered, raising the sheet to peek at myself. Things looked okay, if not a bit worse for wear. Then I remembered my mouth and the possibility of months of dental work ahead. I tried to run my tongue along my gums to count my teeth, but my tongue felt like a dead weight. What I needed was a mirror.

After trying to focus on the reflection in the gleaming metal table arm attached to the bed, I discovered that the table contained a pull-out mirror. Anxious but determined, I flipped the mirror up and looked in it. The Frankenstein face that stared back at me couldn't possibly be mine. It was all patchy and mottled looking, with stitch marks holding everything together. How awful!

I was so absorbed with my new image that I didn't hear the nurse return. "There, there," she said as she pushed the mirror away. "We mustn't indulge our vanity, must we?" She was going to have to do something about the "we" talk if we were going to have a relationship.

"Awful," I muttered, leaning back. "Awful."

"Oh, not so bad," she said. "The doctor says you were lucky. It should all heal nicely even without plastic surgery."

Plastic surgery? My god, I hadn't thought about that. Maybe while they were at it, they could add a rugged-looking cleft in my chin. I'd be willing to pay a little extra. Or had she said that I wasn't going to need plastic surgery? "No plastic surgery?" I asked. The question came out as a squeak. I felt cheated. No Kirk Douglas cleft, and my vocal cords had been damaged, returned to their pre-pubescent state. Was I going to be a male soprano?

"No, you'll be your normal handsome self in no time."

"My voice?" I said as she placed a plate of institutional food in front of me.

"You will be just fine," she answered vaguely. She put a fork in my hand and pointed at my plate of food. I still didn't know if I had enough teeth to chew with, but I doubted I'd need too many for the lifeless stuff before me. It had no aroma or color. It just was.

She left me to my meal, admonishing me one last time to "Eat up." After a couple forkfuls, I could stand the suspense no longer. I removed the plate, pulled out the mirror, and examined my face, or what was left of it. Actually, it wasn't quite as bad as I had thought at first. There was only one jagged row of stitches that started near my right temple and meandered up and across my forehead. The blotchiness seemed to be due to a series of bruises and superficial cuts. The swelling was what gave me the monster look with bulging brows and elongated jowls. That was bound to go down eventually. At least no one could accuse me of being nondescript for a while.

Encouraged by the assessment of my facial juries, I slowly pulled back my lips like a chimpanzee showing off. Somehow my teeth had survived, a row of gleaming enamel in a broken body. If all someone saw were my teeth, they'd never guess I'd been in a fight.

Turning back to my meal, I poked around for something to chew on. It seemed like a waste not to use my one good asset, but only the applesauce offered any challenge. After working my way through about half of my meal, I was exhausted. I pushed the plate away, lay back to rest, and dozed. Thoughts of what all this was costing prevented me from falling into a deep sleep. Would my health insurance cover everything? Were there exemptions for bodily harm brought on by my own stupid acts?

Suddenly a voice pierced the fog of my half-asleep musings, bringing me back with a jolt into the world of sickness and discomfort. "See, he's awake," the voice was saying. "I won't stay long, but I know he will want to see me." I caught a glimpse of my nurse's disapproving glare as she turned and left with my breakfast tray. Bless her. Next time I would be a good boy and eat everything on my plate.

"Hello, Mother," I managed, my voice high-pitched but audible.

"You're certainly a mess," she said in her motherly way.

"My teeth are okay," I said.

"You're a mess," she assured me. "Now, what's this all about?" She pulled a chair next to my bed and sat down, shoulders straight, not touching the back of the chair as though she feared contamination.

"How did I get here?" I asked. I'd been wondering who had found me.

"You were lucky, that's how."

"What does that mean?"

"It means that you could have died; that's what it means. But some child found you."

"Child?"

"Some sweet little girl was out looking for her dog. She said that the dog sometimes hangs around your houseboat, so she went to see if he was there.

Your door was open, and she peeked in. That's how you got here."

I didn't have to ask who the girl was; I knew the one she was talking about. But I wasn't buying the dog story. She probably noticed my open door and saw a chance to put a dead fish or a live crawdad in my bed, but I wasn't complaining. The accommodations here weren't half bad, especially when compared to the alternative, coming to on the living room floor without so much as a pillow to plump or someone to plump it.

"Do you know about my injuries?" I asked.

"You were lucky," Mother said again. I didn't feel all that lucky, but I let her explain. "No broken bones, no internal hemorrhaging, no concussion, no…." She continued to tick off what wasn't wrong with me as though she were going through the index to a medical text. I finally couldn't stand it any longer and interrupted her list of medical calamities.

"So, what IS wrong with me?"

"Someone beat you up," she said, apparently astonished that I should ask. I tried one last time.

"But how bad are my injuries? Will I have to stay in the hospital long?" If she'd sneak me a sandwich and some beer, I wouldn't mind hanging around a while, but I wasn't going to last long if I was limited to hospital fare.

"As I understand it, you have contusions over most of your body, abrasions and lacerations on your face, and resulting trauma to your system. There is nothing else of consequence wrong with you."

"In other words, I'm covered with cuts and bruises. Is that what you are trying to tell me?" Nothing of consequence as long as you weren't the one experiencing the aches and pains, I said to myself.

"Well, you might put it that way." She seemed disappointed that I hadn't been impressed with her candy striper depiction of my medical issues.

"What about the two men? Did the police catch them?"

"Oh, I almost forgot. Bruno is going to stop by for a chat later. He's handling that end of things." She gave me a sick room smile, not too hearty, but sincere and encouraging. Then the look vanished, and Mother leaned toward me and lowered her voice. "Who did this awful thing to you, John?" she asked, sounding like an actor in an afternoon television serial.

173

"I don't know," I admitted.

"But you saw them."

"They were wearing masks. And they didn't waste much time on talk."

"Masked men. My, how thrilling." She actually clasped her hands together like she was enjoying herself. What kind of mother gets a vicarious high from her son's misfortune?

"I wouldn't exactly describe the incident as thrilling," I complained. "More like painful." Where were the tender words of maternal consolation?

The nurse came in and stood with her hands on her hips across the bed from Mother. "I really think he's had enough excitement for this morning." If I couldn't stand any more excitement, I thought, then you'd better leave right away.

Mother sputtered something about being my mother, but the nurse wasn't impressed. In the hospital, excitement is rationed out like pills, and mothers are no exception.

I slept, this time deeply, dreaming about my pretty nurse, only to be awakened by a new face. With cool efficiency, a hairy arm swung the table in front of me and plopped down a tray. Then I was informed in no uncertain terms that it was time to eat. No smile. No words of encouragement. It was *time to eat.*

"Where's the other nurse?" I asked.

"I only have time to keep track of myself," he informed me, eyeing my pillow as though considering whether to plump it. I poked at it a few times to relieve him of the duty and sullenly attacked the mound of bland food set before me. Why did they bother handing out silverware when a straw would suffice? And what about the menus and updated cuisine hospitals were supposed to have these days?

After lunch, Mother came by again but said she couldn't stay. There was this absolutely wonderful garage sale she just had to go to. I made some comment about her not needing a garage, and she informed me with jokes like that the hospital would boot me out in no time.

When she was gone, I felt lonely. The fellow in the next bed was either asleep or dead, and everything was unusually quiet for a hospital. Only the drip, drip, drip of IV bags punctuated by an occasional blipping sound from a machine. There was nothing to do but try to sort out what had happened to me and why.

Someone, two someones, had beaten me up. There had been one unsuccessful "accident" and one successful one. It was a miracle I hadn't ended up in the hospital before now. Somebody was definitely trying to put me out of commission. But not necessarily permanently, unless the doctors and my mother were right and I had just been incredibly lucky.

But *why* was someone after me? If I couldn't figure out the why, then how was I going to avoid more accidents and beatings? And why didn't they try bribing me instead of getting physical? Or why didn't they send some luscious female to persuade me to their point of view? The least they could have done was to threaten me so I could have had the option to stay out of their business. If I knew what that business was.

I stabbed the bell next to my bed and waited impatiently for someone to respond. When the nurse with the hairy arms rushed into the room, he seemed disappointed to see me sitting there breathing normally. If he wanted near death, he should take a look at the guy in the next bed. "I need a pencil and some paper," I explained.

"Oh, I see. You rang for room service." His sarcasm didn't escape me, but I persisted.

"I have to occupy my time in some way."

"You could watch television," he retorted. Then he glanced around and said, "Oh, this is one of *those* rooms." He left no doubt that one of those rooms meant cheap. I hadn't noticed before, but there was no television. My only source of entertainment was listening to the raspy breathing and machine noises from my roommate's side of the room. "All right, I'll see if I can find some writing materials."

Actually, it didn't take him long to locate what I'd asked for. I was surprised because pencils aren't used much anymore. But I like the feel of the wood and the primitive quality of graphite on paper. With high hopes, I pulled the hospital table in front of me, positioned the lined tablet, and picked up the freshly sharpened pencil with the plastic flower taped to the eraser. I was ready to think.

I spent the first ten minutes doodling. Slowly, very slowly, random thoughts started penetrating the hospital haze. I decided to start by identifying everyone with even the remotest reason for wanting to hurt me and then go from there. The first person who came to mind was my landlord. Then I remembered a kid in the sixth grade whose steely I'd stolen in retaliation for him taking my lunch. After that, it was more difficult to add to the list. Perhaps FooFoo had a relapse, thereby angering Dr. Oliver and his wife. Oh my God, what if I was in the Lady of the Lamp Hospital and Dr. Oliver was my attending physician? Maybe he arranged to have this happen so he'd have another chance at me.

A gurgling noise from my roommate distracted me for a minute or so, but once I ascertained that his chest was still rising and falling rhythmically, if in a somewhat syncopated fashion, I returned to my list. Reluctantly I added Marie's name. Then Mark Marshall's. In spite of his somewhat nasty disposition, he seemed like a longshot. But he undoubtedly knew a few ruffians who would enjoy punching someone's clock. Maybe even someone from the card game. They had certainly been ruthless. For that matter, Frances might resent my prying into his life, and he and Mark seemed to share some questionable contacts. I wrote down his name and tapped the pencil against the tablet to encourage thought. Perhaps even Vivian Marshall should be on the list. She might be confusing the message and the messenger related to her insurance problems.

Looking at the names I had written down, I realized that, with the exception of the first two, I had compiled a list of possible murder suspects. Feeling guilty about including my landlord and the kid from grade school in a list of potential murderers, I drew a line through their names. My real troubles had started with the Rosenblatt case. If I wanted to figure out who was trying to shut me up, I had to figure out who had murdered Pearl and possibly Zelda. With that in mind, I added Wally Conklin and Byron Cheever to the list. Then, to round out the usual suspects, I squeezed Lizbeth Gunnar's name in at the bottom of the page. I hadn't anticipated having such a long list.

Then, at the top of the sheet in the left-hand corner, I printed SUSPECTS. In the middle of the page, I wrote MOTIVE, and to the right, OPPORTUNITY. If I could determine motive and opportunity, perhaps I could also prevent future opportunities for the perp to come after me. Perp. That sounded so cool. Like I knew what I was talking about. Maybe I could write a screenplay for a mystery based on my experience. It would be nice to see my name in the credits.

SUSPECTS MOTIVE OPPORTUNITY
Leon Oliver Malpractice suit
Mrs. Oliver Revenger for FooFoo
Marie Rosenblatt $$$
Mark Marshall General orneriness
Frances Metzker ??
Vivian Marshall Protect savings
Wally Conklin Project his job
Byron Cheever Prevent unfavorable publicity & cost to employer
Lizbeth Gunnar The grieving sister

I left the OPPORTUNITY column blank. Bruno might be able to fill it in when he came by. I'd promised Mark and Frances I wouldn't reveal their secret about what had happened at their poker game the night of Pearl's murder. But their names still needed to be on my list; after all, I only had their word for their alibi.

As for motives, all I had was a list of unspectacular and unlikely motives for murder. Whatever happened to grand passion? How plebian to kill for financial reasons or to prevent unfavorable publicity.

One the basis of motives, I preferred Mark. Orneriness was at least an emotion, if not a very grand one. But Dr. Oliver was the clear winner of the "strongest motive" award. With Lizbeth probably the least likely. Although, if she hid a simmering volcano of emotional magma beneath an exterior of sweetness and apparent vulnerability, that should make her the number one suspect. Still, I couldn't imagine why either Dr. Oliver or Lizbeth would think they had a reason to silence me. Dr. Oliver knew I hadn't found the evidence I'd been searching for in his home, and with Pearl dead, I was no threat to him. As for Lizbeth, I had offered her a sympathetic ear in her time of need. Nor was I a prime suspect in her mother's death. She had no reason to hate or even dislike me.

As for Marie, well, she knew she didn't need to get tough with me. All she had to do was blow in my ear. I'd even be willing to ignore the fact that she adores cats.

Mark, Frances, and Vivian all seemed to fall into the same category. They might have reason to resent me, but they didn't have much to gain by calling a halt to my investigation. Their roles in what had happened weren't going to change. Although perhaps Vivian was striking back blindly, like a cornered animal. First she kills Pearl to protect her security, then she turns on me. Maybe she even enlisted Mark's help in setting up my accidents. It was a possibility.

Conklin and Cheever were a couple of tricky bastards, but why bother attacking me when they had already defanged me with blackmail? Overkill? And Cheever hadn't known about the insurance problem until Monday, so he couldn't have caused my first two accidents. Conklin might have, if Zelda had told him about me breaking into his office the first time around. But that still didn't give him motive for my recent incident.

There was, of course, always the possibility that I was concentrating on the wrong murder. Maybe someone believed Zelda had given me a meaningful dying clue and feared that I would eventually figure it out. If that was the case, then I needed to make a mental leap and decipher "Argghh" before they made their next move. "Argghh." Maybe I should be looking for a pirate wearing an eyepatch with a parrot on his shoulder.

The more I thought about it, the more worried I became that the person wishing me harm was Zelda's murderer, hence a stranger. Someone I wouldn't see coming until it was too late. Once that thought lodged itself in my consciousness, each person who peered into my room seemed suspicious. And now that it was visiting hours, a steady stream of people roamed the halls, squinting at the tiny cards posted next to the open doors in order to identify their occupants. "Sorry," they would say before moving on, their plastic smiles glued over appropriately solemn faces to conform to hospital etiquette. Often they carried flowers—a way to smuggle in a gun?

By the time Bruno showed up, I'd worked myself into a lather of nerves, fears, and suspicions. "Bruno, am I glad to see you," I practically shouted when he appeared. His eyes were fastened on my roommate. "Contagious?" he asked as he took a seat. Then, "Yeah, well, it's good to see you too." He took a second look. "You look awful."

"Thanks."

"That's one of the things I'll never get used to," he said.

"Huh?"

"The ugliness of my job." His eyes roamed over my face.

"You don't have to look," I said defensively, as if my battered appearance was my fault.

"Hey, don't take it personally. It's just that, well, I've never liked the sight of blood. But you learn to cope."

Changing the subject, I asked, "So, have you caught them yet?"

"Who?"

"The truck that ran over me, who else?"

"Oh, them. No, we don't have anything to go on. That's why I'm here." He reached into his jacket pocket and pulled out a notepad and pen. "Okay. Who did this to you?"

"That's what *you* are supposed to figure out," I complained, tossing him the chart I was working on. "Maybe it has something to do with either Pearl Rosenblatt's or Zelda Gunnar's deaths. Maybe you can add some names to the suspect list and fill in the opportunities column."

He studied the list, then looked at me. "What makes you think your problems are connected to these murders?"

"Was I robbed?" I asked anxiously. How happy that would make me! If they had nicked my television and my Mickey Mouse watch, that meant they wouldn't return. Perhaps if I hadn't put up a fight, they might have left me alone.

"No, you weren't robbed...as near as we can tell," he added.

"Damn it, Bruno, I'm not in a joking mood."

"Me neither," he said. "Let's get down to work."

Chapter Seventeen

Bruno and I spent hours going over my list, getting nowhere. First, we'd decide on one person and consider all the pros and cons, then move on to another, like a couple of hungry dogs going from one meatless bone to the next. Bruno made a big show of telling me how he couldn't reveal any police information about possible leads or suspects. That made me think he didn't have any more to work with than I did.

Apparently, most of the suspects had alibis, including Lizbeth Gunnar, who wasn't a serious contender by police standards. However, none of the alibis was airtight. That didn't surprise me. Modern murderers know better than to come up with the perfect alibi; that immediately draws attention to them.

In spite of our best efforts, no one rose to the top of our list and stayed there.

My partiality for Dr. Oliver and then Marie wavered, ebbed, and returned with gale force. Then ebbed again. For a time, my money was on Lizbeth as the least likely, but I eventually gave in to Bruno's conviction that it had to be Vivian. Then, when Bruno read my landlord's name through the smeared pencil lines, he promptly changed his vote. I fell back on an earlier belief that Conklin was the guilty party. Bruno, in turn, went after Mark, Frances, and Cheever, but I dug in my heels and stayed with Conklin. At the end of Round 1, it was one vote for Vivian and one for Conklin, with a six-way tie for second place.

After I'd given Bruno the benefit of my thoughts and hinted at some of the evidence I hadn't previously revealed, without actually admitting to doing anything illegal, only then did Bruno inform me the matter was police business and I should keep my nose out of it. I argued that I had legitimate business and personal reasons to be involved. First, I had a boss to appease. Second, I was tired of having an accident every time I turned around. And third, putting a voice to a thought lurking at the back of my mind, I expressed my concern that the next time it was possible, an accident might be fatal. When Bruno didn't disagree, my mouth got very dry, and I could feel my heart beating. Ker-chunk, ker-chunk. There was a spike in my heart rate on the monitor that was tracking my vital signs. If I wasn't careful, just talking about having accidents might do me in.

Dinner was a beige and green rerun of lunch, but I managed to force it all down, and, in turn, I was rewarded with a visit from my doctor. Not, thank heavens, Dr. Oliver, but a bent preoccupied man with thinning hair and a receding chin. He mumbled something, shook his head, wrote on a pad, and started to leave. "Hey, Doc," I called after him. "When do I get parole?" He turned back with an expression that said the animals weren't supposed to speak. I repeated my question anyway.

"Tomorrow if you'd like," he responded, as if it was solely a matter of personal preference.

"Then I'm okay?"

"Medically, yes." I wasn't sure what he meant by that crack, but I didn't ask. The important thing was that I was being released; I could go home. But before I left, there was one thing I wanted to do.

When my hairy armed nurse came by to give me a pill to ease my pain and help me sleep, I began bombarding him with questions. Did the nurses have regular shifts? How often did they change? What about days off? Why did they only have first names on their nameplates? Were their identities secret?

"As interesting as I find this conversation," he said with a sardonic edge, "I don't have the time to continue this discussion at present. May I suggest you either subscribe to the American Journal of Nursing...or get to the point."

Stammering about how kind the other nurse had been, I explained that I just wanted to thank her but didn't know her full name or how to get in touch. He crossed his arms and shook his head in disbelief. Feeling that I'd been rude, I babbled on about how he, too, had been kind, and I appreciated all he had done for me.

"You can leave a tip under the pillow when you're discharged," he interjected. He added, "Her name is Nancy Nevensky, she's not married, and if you want, I can probably get her telephone number for you." I managed a weak "please," and he gave me a "you're pathetic" look and departed.

That evening as I drifted off to sleep, my mind was filled with visions of Nurse Nancy reaching out to me through a white mist. Just as our fingers were about to meet, two masked men leapt out of the shadows. In spite of the pain pill, I had a restless night, awakening each time some muscled creep was about to bash me over the head or shove me off a cliff. If I was going to get a good night's sleep in the future, I needed to figure out who was trying to send me to my final resting place.

The next morning, I informed the person who came in to check on me that I was told by the doctor that I could leave any time, and I wished to do so immediately. Nancy wasn't due to return until the following day, and I had her phone number tucked away in my wallet, so I had no reason to linger. As the doctor had said, I was medically okay. I was prepared to argue with the staff about my departure, but they didn't seem that sorry to see me go. They quickly processed the paperwork and were preparing my bed for the next patient before I even had my pants pulled up. I waved goodbye to my unresponsive roommate and left.

I didn't call Mother to tell her I was leaving; I didn't want her fussing around or coming to the hospital to accompany me home on the bus. I suppose I could have called someone with a car, but I wasn't feeling particularly social. It seemed easier to hop on a bus and find my own way home. Everything went well until I had to transfer. My entire body protested, having to stand there at the bus stop. If I'd had a bullet handy, I would have put it between my teeth to keep myself from screaming. It didn't help that the other people at the bus stop kept glancing surreptitiously in my direction. Perhaps they were wondering if they should recognize me from some horror movie.

Once on the bus, I sank gratefully into the only empty seat. Let the woman behind me with the bag full of groceries stand; she hadn't just escaped from a hospital bed. Unfortunately, she didn't know about my body's protest against physical activity. She pointedly glared at me before grabbing an overhead strap next to my seat, glowering and shifting her weight from one tired foot to the other, letting me know that if the death squad came by to pick up my body, she wouldn't bother pointing out that I wasn't quite dead yet.

Seldom have I been so happy to see The Haven. Of course, as exhausted as I was, the sight of an empty park bench would have made me happy.

My return was inauspicious and uneventful. No one came running out to welcome me with open arms. My front door was standing open a couple of inches, as it supposedly was when the little girl discovered me lying prostrate on the floor. Great, I thought. All the cats in the neighborhood were probably making my home their headquarters now. And any kid who wanted to could have left a calling card.

Boldly pushing open the door, I paused in the doorway to reconnoiter. Suddenly it hit me that with the sun at my back, my silhouette made a perfect target. A rush of adrenaline enabled me to leap aside. Unfortunately, the sudden movement jarred every bruised muscle in my body. Even my still intact teeth hurt.

Slowly, ever so slowly, I peered around the edge of the doorway into my vacant living room. Then I tiptoed inside, leaving the door open in case I needed to make a fast exit. Assuming I was capable of doing so. Only after assuring myself that I was indeed alone did I close the door and pour myself a drink. Breakfast could wait.

The phone rang like a mechanical conscience before I had a chance to take a single sip. It was Mother. She wanted to know if I'd made it home all right. I'd answered the phone, hadn't I? Then she asked if I wanted her to bring over some chicken soup. Chicken soup? When had she ever made chicken soup? I told her I didn't need anything except rest and hung up.

The pain pill went down smoothly with my second drink. I vaguely recalled the nurse warning me not to mix alcohol and pills, but I decided that was only if I intended to drive. And I had no plans to go anywhere. Then Emma called. She wanted to know where I'd been and snorted with disbelief when

I told her, "in the hospital." She informed me that Mr. Van Droop had about had it with my shenanigans, and if I wanted to keep my job, I'd better shape up. I suggested she call the hospital to confirm my story, and I had no doubt she would do so the instant she hung up. Then I informed her that I wouldn't be in until tomorrow and asked if she would check my calendar (she already had) and do whatever needed to be done in my absence (she already had). She might be critical at times, but she was efficient.

After refreshing my drink, I laid down on the couch to plan my next move. Unfortunately, planning seemed conducive to sleeping, and I didn't wake up for several hours. By then, I was ravenous. I poked through my empty cupboards, rejecting a can of cream of shrimp soup and some ancient Twinkies. Why would anyone in their right mind buy cream of shrimp soup? And those Twinkies, I know they supposedly have a long shelf life, but I didn't remember buying them. It crossed my mind that the children might have left them for me, probably laced with laxatives.

There wasn't anything edible in the refrigerator either. I had to settle for a couple of slices of dry toast made with stale bread. Hospital food served through a straw was beginning to sound pretty good.

Eating produced another drowsy spell, but after a short nap, I felt almost alert. In my opinion, I was on the road to recovery. But in order to make certain the road didn't dead end, I needed a plan, one that would assure my continuing good health.

In spite of Bruno's suspicions about Vivian Marshall, I still leaned toward Conklin. Perhaps I just didn't want it to be Vivian. She had served me coffee and had two dependent children. Granted, one of the children was old enough to survive on his own and might even be a murderer, but it would be much nicer if Vivian was innocent.

A simple plan, that's what I needed. Simple plans were always best. Easier to think up. Easier to execute. And fewer things to go wrong. Yes, what I needed was a simple plan.

A strategy was just beginning to take shape in my mind when there was a knock at the door. My heart started beating so loud that I was sure whoever was out there could hear it. The last time I answered the door, I ended up in the hospital. Could it be the gruesome twosome returning for a rematch? Well, this time, they wouldn't catch me unarmed. Picking up the nearest weapon—a monkey pod statue of a naked woman a friend had brought back from the Philippines—I crept over to the window and peeked out. A man in a suit was standing on my doorstep, one hand raised in a fist.

He knocked again, this time louder, while I stood there and watched. He had neat, short hair and large ears. His suit was immaculate, conservative, and tasteful, and he was wearing a white shirt. Either a banker or an insurance man...or a well-dressed mugger.

Still gripping the monkey pod statue around the ankles, I hesitantly opened the door a couple of inches. The man immediately moved his face close to the opening, making him appear all nose and teeth. He wasn't a banker. "I'm from Pacific Farms Insurance," he said smoothly, slipping his card through the space. I took it with my free hand. "We don't insure farms," he chuckled mirthlessly when I didn't ask.

"Harrumph," I said, refusing to open the door further. He hadn't proved his bona fides yet, although I doubted any self-respecting crook would make such a stupid joke.

"I'm here to talk with you about the damage to your parking space." He showed me a few more teeth. I could see his molars in back, one had a gold crown.

What the hell, I thought. Might as well get it over with. "Come in," I reluctantly invited, opening the door and stepping out of the way, still gripping the monkey pod statue, just in case. He came inside, surreptitiously looking around, evaluating my assets, no doubt. "Can I get you a drink?" It seemed the hospitable thing to do since my drink was very visible on the side table.

"Well...." He seemed to waver.

"I'm drinking scotch," I said, sidling over to the side table, not wanting to turn my back on him. It was then he noticed the statue in my hand.

"Ah..." he began, eyeing my makeshift weapon. "It's a little early for me." However, it sounded like he thought he might need that drink.

As we settled in, he made a few complimentary remarks about my view and how nice it must be to live on the water. Then he broached his reason for stopping by. "I understand that you'd been drinking the night of the, ah, accident."

I didn't reply but toasted him with my glass.

"I understand you'd been drinking quite a bit," he added. He gave me a cozy grin between lads to let me know that it was okay to drink a lot. I didn't grin back. Nor did I reply. He shifted in his chair, careful not to wrinkle his trousers. "Let's be honest," he said. "There are witnesses."

"Witnesses trained in medical evaluation?"

"Medical evaluation?" he echoed.

"Yes, witnesses who can tell the difference between the effects of shock and drunkenness? Witnesses willing to testify under oath? Witnesses who will stand up to cross-examination by medical experts?" Now I grinned back.

"Really, Mr. Smith. Why force us to investigate your movements on Sunday evening? It would be simpler for everyone if you would stipulate to your drinking, and we could then work out a settlement right here and now."

"What kind of settlement?" I was going to force him to put all his cards on the table before making any admissions.

"Well." He coughed uncomfortably. We were obviously getting down to the touchy stuff. "We'll agree not to sue you for property damage if you'll have your insurance company pay for repairs. You do have insurance, don't you?"

He knew damn well it was doubtful my renter's policy would cover something like that. What he hoped was that his implicit threat to sue would frighten me. Well, it wasn't going to work. In fact, I was insulted by his lack of subtlety. "Your file on me must not be very complete," I said evenly. He shifted in his chair again. I wasn't following his script. "You do know my occupation, don't you?" He didn't respond, but I could tell by his face that he didn't. Savoring the moment, I announced, "I'm a claims adjuster." He lost his composure for a second but quickly recovered.

"Then you know we'd just as soon sue as pay for the damage."

"And you know that I'm going to let you go ahead and sue."

It was a stalemate.

He abruptly stood up and perfunctorily thanked me for my time. I walked him to the door. Before stepping onto the porch, he turned to me and said how much he hated to sue a fellow insurance man, but he was sure I understood how it was. Then he walked away. I knew how it was, all right, and I'd take my chances in court. I didn't damage those damn braces under my parking spot, and their condition was definitely not an act of God.

After polishing off the rest of my scotch as a chaser for two aspirin, I resumed thinking about my nice simple plan to trap Wally into confessing he was a murderer. It had the advantage of only requiring me to leave my home once and then only to trot next door to ask my neighbors for a favor. I combed my hair, trying not to look at my face in the mirror, sucked in my stomach, and made my neighborly way next door. Erin's expectant look turned to disappointment when she saw me standing there on her doorstep, then disappointment turned to shock.

"Oh, John, how awful," she said, overtly cringing at the sight of my face. It wasn't an impact I enjoyed making on an attractive young woman, but I swallowed my pride and explained what I wanted. "It's a joke I'm playing on a friend," I lied.

She hesitated. "We're expecting company." Out of the corner of my eye, I saw her roommate off to one side, mouthing the words "humor him." When she realized that I had seen her, she turned away, obviously embarrassed. As neighbors, we have a cordial but not close relationship, so it wasn't surprising they weren't eager to participate in my little subterfuge. But I was willing to accept being humored as long as I got what I needed.

Erin sighed and obediently picked up her cell phone, like someone being asked to take a seat in the dentist's chair. I handed her a piece of paper with her part of the dialogue. She took it, skimmed the page, and murmured, "Strange." Then, "Is this all? Just say this and hang up?" She politely didn't add, "And then you'll go away?"

"Yes, that's all." As she punched in the number, I noticed the table was set for four, and the aroma of bubbling tomato sauce wafted from the kitchen. It made my mouth fill with saliva, and it was with difficulty that I listened to Erin read her lines over the phone. I had to hand it to her; she played her part beautifully. Not that it was a particularly challenging role, nothing to get her an Oscar nomination. But she baited the hook like a pro. All I had to do was go home to my empty refrigerator and wait for Wally to snap at the bait like a hungry fish. If he did, I'd accomplish several things. I'd be able to show my boss how smart I was. I'd make Bruno happy with me, after he yelled at me for interfering with police business, of course. And I'd be able to sleep nights without fear that my sleep might be made final.

I went back to my houseboat, poured another drink, and got ready for my visitor. First, I closed the curtains but made sure the side window was left open. I didn't want him to actually have to break in. Then I turned off all the lights and positioned myself in a corner, out of sight.

My phone rang right on cue. It rang and rang and rang. I'd switched off the message function. I didn't have to look at my caller ID to know it was Wally. Good old predictable Wally.

I drank and waited. Then I drank and waited some more.

After another fifteen minutes or so it occurred to me that I wasn't exactly being smart about what I was doing. My plan had a flaw, a serious flaw. If Wally bought Erin's story and thought I was away for the evening, that didn't necessarily mean he would come unarmed. I wasn't going to be able to leap out of the shadows and subdue him with an empty drink glass, and I was in no shape to do much subduing anyway. And what if he sent the two thugs back in his place?

Frantic, I dialed Bruno's number, suddenly starting to sweat like I was in a sauna. While I waited to be put through to Bruno, I thought I heard a noise. Was Wally here already? Maybe he didn't live that far away.

"Thank god, Bruno," I whispered when he finally answered.

"Who is this? Speak up. I can't hear you."

"Bruno, it's me, John," I hissed.

"I can't hear you," he repeated.

"John," I squeaked. "It's me, John. Come quick, Bruno. It's a matter of life and death."

"Do you need something, John?"

"Yes," I said louder. "Come quick."

"Right away, John." He hung up.

My body went limp with relief. I sneaked over to one of the windows to try and figure out what was happening without calling attention to the fact that I was there. It was almost dark, and most of the dock lights were out again. I couldn't see much. Listening for all I was worth, I stood there in the dark, waiting. When nothing happened, I returned to my chair, not quite as confident as I had been, but still hopeful that Wally would show up and things would go as planned. Besides, good old Bruno was on his way. I had backup. Whatever happened.

Then it hit me—good old Bruno didn't know I'd left the hospital. He could be racing off in the wrong direction at this very moment.

My fingers shook as I punched in his number again. A dispatcher answered and said he thought Bruno had just left, but he would try to get a message to him. I urged him to hurry.

My head was spinning with fatigue, fear, and drink. I slumped into the chair, too weary to think about what else I should do. When I heard distinct footsteps coming down the dock, I managed to rouse myself, grabbed the monkey pod woman again, and prepared for the worst. When the knock came at the front door, I was surprised. Then it occurred to me that it might be Wally checking to make certain I wasn't home. If I answered the door, maybe I could avoid being attacked. On the other hand, if I didn't let him break in, my plan would fail. I held onto the statue and waited, my fingers pressing into the thick ankles, a splinter of wood poking into my palm.

The knock came again, this time insistent. Moments later, the door crashed inward with a loud crunching sound, and Bruno blasted into the room, his massive body turned sideways like a human battering ram. "Bruno, for god's sake, what are you doing?" I yelled. Momentum carried him halfway across the room, where he tripped over a chair and knocked a lamp to the floor as he fell.

"Damn," he exclaimed, quickly leaping to his feet. Then he turned to me, saw that I was alive, and demanded, "Is this your idea of a joke?"

"I was just trying to see who it was before I answered the door," I explained, staring at what was left of my lamp. "That was expensive," I added peevishly.

"What did you expect?" Bruno said angrily. "You call and give me the life-and-death routine. Then you have dispatch follow-up for good measure. And you expect me to take the time to pick your lock?" He stormed over to the door to look at the damage. He'd pulled one of the hinges right out of the door jamb. The door was hanging crazily at an angle, and there was a jagged crack along one edge. Would my insurance cover the damage, I wondered? Didn't my tenant's policy have a three-hundred-dollar deductible? Somehow I had the feeling that was just about the cost of a new door.

Bruno helped me shove the door back in place. Then I explained the situation to him. He cursed me for trying to take the law into my own hands. Then he cursed me for being half drunk and not thinking clearly. Then he cursed me for calling him at the last minute. Then he cursed just for the hell of it. He was really upset. Finally, he said, "When I found out the hospital had released you, I knew something like this would happen." I didn't point out that he had no way of knowing any such thing would happen since I hadn't even thought up the plan until a few hours ago. Instead, I fixed him a drink and the two of us settled in to wait for Wally.

He came right on schedule.

Chapter Eighteen

"I didn't do it," Wally cried. "I didn't do it."

"Come off it, Conklin," Bruno said in his tough cop voice. "Why else would you sneak over here to look for that log?"

Wally sniveled, a pathetic figure, tie askew, sweat rolling down the side of his round face. "I didn't do it," he mumbled, almost incoherent.

"Do you want to tell me about it here, or do I have to take you downtown?" The way Bruno stressed "downtown," conjured up visions of rubber hoses and glaring lights. Wally looked panic-stricken. He didn't seem to realize that what he needed most of all was a lawyer. Bruno had, of course, advised Wally of his rights, but quickly, a stream of monotone phrases, so as not to interfere with his psychological upper hand.

Wally turned to me. "Are you in on this?" he asked. He seemed to be a little slow catching on. It was my place, and I was there with the police. Did I have to spell it out for him? Then it struck me that Wally might decide it was time to make good on his threat to turn me in for breaking into his office, especially if he thought I'd ratted on him.

"Police," I shrugged. "They use you. You know how it is." I appealed to him with my eyes, although I was having difficulty focusing. He nodded as if he understood, while Bruno looked on with a bewildered expression on his face.

"Well, are you going to talk, or are we taking a trip?" Bruno demanded. Wally looked from me to Bruno and back to me again. Then his shoulders drooped, and he sank into my favorite chair.

"When I realized the police were looking into the possibility that I...I...

killed Zelda, I admit I began to worry." His hands were trembling, and he had to press them together to keep them still. "I felt like they were trying to pin it on me." He glanced nervously at Bruno and continued to address me. "When Lizbeth called and told me she had given John a log that belonged to her sister, well, I started worrying even more. She said it was filled with stuff about the office, and that I was mentioned frequently. I've always known Zelda resented me for becoming the regional manager. She felt that she deserved the position. So, when I found out she had been keeping a log, I was afraid there might be something in it the police could use against me, to accuse me of her…murder." His voice grew soft and raspy, like his energy was draining with his hope for a reprieve.

The lump that had settled somewhere in the depths of my stomach began to gyrate with indecision. For some reason, I believed the klutz. Would a real, honest-to-God murderer be so inept? First, there was the blatant mismanagement of the hospital insurance policy. Then he breaks into my home through the front door, using a battered credit card to pry open the lock, almost tearing the door off its remaining hinge. And the door hadn't even been locked.

"Maybe he's telling the truth, Bruno." Wally gave me a grateful look, his hangdog eyes thanking me for the strokes. Bruno, on the other hand, gave me a mind-your-own-business glare. "Is what he said about the police breathing down his neck true?" I asked.

"He's one of the suspects in the Gunnar homicide," Bruno acknowledged in his official voice. "He worked with her. We have to investigate him. And if that makes him nervous, well, maybe he has something to be nervous about." Wally seemed to be getting smaller and smaller, like he'd taken a swig from a bottle marked "Drink Me." My sympathy for the nerd was conversely growing.

"Come on, Bruno, what are you going to charge him with? Damaging my door?" I didn't bother pointing out that he had done most of the damage before Wally arrived.

"You—" Bruno stopped and glared at me. "This was *your* idea. You called me and said it was a matter of life and death, dragged me all the way over here, and now you tell me it's a mistake? What's the matter with you, John?"

"Sorry, Bruno," I apologized. I was sincerely sorry. "I thought I had the right guy, but now that he's here, I don't think so. Look at him." We both turned to look at Wally, huddled in my chair, looking pathetic and wretched, not anything like a wild-eyed murderer.

Bruno wavered a moment, then came back with a counterargument. "You know that murderers never look like murderers. Well, not usually, anyway. Take Elsie Borden, for instance."

"Elsie Borden's a cow, Bruno."

He thought for a minute. "Are you sure?"

"You mean 'Lizzie.'"

"Oh, right." Well, you know what I mean." I did.

"The question is what you're going to charge Wally with if you haul him downtown. Since I don't care to press charges...." I left the sentence hanging, hoping Bruno would change his mind and leave before Wally had a chance to recover his wits and decide to press charges against *me*.

Bruno paced back and forth, mumbling to himself about ingrates and blunders. Finally, he told me not to bother calling him the next time my life was in danger and not to expect flowers at my funeral. Then he made his exit, not too gracefully since the door toppled over on him when he pulled it open. He kicked at it and left it lying where it had fallen.

"Thank you," Wally said as he helped me prop my door up again. "Sorry about the door." He seemed to be recuperating, but he apparently hadn't quite grasped yet that I was the one who had lured him to my houseboat and that Bruno had been the one to break the door down. Still, I was surprised when he said, "Can I look at the log now?"

"Huh?"

"The log. The one that Lizbeth gave you."

"There isn't any log, Wally."

"No log?" He seemed truly puzzled.

"No, no log." Then after a pause, I added, "It wasn't Lizbeth that called you. It was a trap."

"Oh." For a moment, he remained confused, then somewhere in his brain, a connection was made, and a light came on. "You tricked me!" he accused. "You…YOU tricked me."

"That was the idea," I admitted.

"Why you…you…you…." He apparently couldn't find a word that labeled the level of disgust he felt for what I had done.

"You walked into the trap with your eyes wide open," I pointed out. "And if it hadn't been for me, you'd be headed for the police station right now." I was beginning to wonder if it wouldn't have been better to let Bruno haul him off. Even if he wasn't a murderer, he was a very irritating person. And my head hurt. As well as the rest of my body. The painkillers were obviously wearing off. "Want a drink?" I asked, heading for my almost empty bottle of scotch.

He hesitated, then acquiesced when he heard the sound of ice cubes cascading from the ice maker chute into my glass. We all have our triggers. Pouring his drink brought me to the bottom of the bottle. I had obviously been drinking entirely too much whiskey for medicinal purposes.

We sipped our drinks in an uneasy silence. Finally, he said, "I didn't do it."

"I believe you."

"She wasn't an easy person to get along with," he confided. I believed that, too. "I don't think she had any friends other than her sister." He seemed to want to talk, so I let him, too tired to contribute much to the conversation. "I know she felt she should have had my job. Not that she ever said so to my face, but there were hints. A lot of them. And she watched me like a hawk. Then, when I was struggling with that hospital policy problem, I tried to hide it from her. But I think she found out."

That got my attention. "You think she knew about the policy?"

"Yes, I'm pretty sure she did."

"Why?"

"Well, she was acting like the cat that ate the canary, and as far as I know, I was the only canary she was after." Wally smiled, obviously pleased with his use of metaphor. Drink can make you clever. "You see, the company was her life. I never saw her express happiness about anything not related to work. And there she was, humming and being secretive. I was sure she'd found out about the policy problem. My other work was above reproach."

"You sure that was the only thing you screwed up?" He didn't like my phraseology, but he assured me the rest of his work was in order. Then he went on talking about Zelda and Babcock-Chalmers while the wheels in my head went spinning on and on.

"The head office had been dropping hints about a possible promotion," he was saying when I broke in with a question.

"What would she have done with the information?"

"Who?" he asked as if we'd been talking about dozens of people.

"Zelda. What would she have done with the information about the policy issues?"

He thought a minute. "I'm not sure. Probably tell the people in Chicago."

"Would she have done some checking on her own first? I mean, if she was going to accuse you of incompetence and fraud, she'd want to be sure of her facts, right?" I felt like a long-distance runner about to break the ribbon at the end of the race, weary but exhilarated.

"Fraud? I don't think my actions constituted fraud," Wally protested, obviously not keeping up with my train of thought.

"I don't care about that now. Just answer my question." He looked at me, blinking as if trying to figure out what he was doing there talking to me about all this. "You didn't leave a signed confession lying around, did you?" I asked irritably. "So, what would she have done to verify her assumptions?" I already thought I knew, but I wanted confirmation.

"I'm not sure."

"Isn't it obvious?" I was practically shouting at him. How could he be so dense?!

"I don't understand what—"

"If you wanted to find out about a policy and you had already checked with the broker, who would you try next?" I was on the edge of my seat, about to leap up and throttle him for being such a schmuck.

"I suppose I might go to the insured."

"Right." Finally. "So, what did Cheever say to you when you told him about me breaking into your office?"

"Huh?" Wally definitely wasn't going to win any awards for his ability to use his little gray cells.

"Cheever," I prompted. "How did he react? What did he say? Start at the beginning and tell me everything."

Wally did not have a photographic memory, not even a halfway decent one. At the time of his conversation with Cheever, Wally's sole concern had been what Cheever was going to do to him when he learned about the policy issue. The finer points of the exchange had been given short shrift, barely managing to survive in the recesses of Wally's brain. I had to open another bottle of scotch and show more patience than Job ever needed to pry the story out of him.

Helped along by my questions, Wally did kind of remember that it had seemed odd at the time that Cheever so readily agreed to help him out. If a claim was made, the hospital would have a good case for a countersuit against Babcock-Chalmers, so they might not have been on the hook for any payments. Of course, the prestige and reputation of the hospital were at stake, and Cheever was understandably very sensitive about that. Nevertheless, he had been surprisingly amenable to working things out off the record.

With a little more encouragement, Wally also remembered that it was Cheever who suggested blackmailing me about the illegal entry. The idea was that I would have to promise to keep quiet about the Lady of the Lamp policy until after Wally had a chance to obtain the excess coverage and put things in order. Cheever had explained that this approach was best for everyone concerned. At the time, Wally had no reason to question this rationale—he was getting a reprieve; that was all that mattered to him.

As Wally talked, all the little pieces fell into place. But since this was the second time in twenty-four hours that all the little pieces had fallen into place for me, I was cautious. Still, it's hard not to convince yourself that you're right about something when you can't think of any better explanation. When I finally spelled it out for Wally, however, he was convinced I was insane. Why would Cheever, a very important and powerful man, soon to be named Director of the Lady of the Lamp, risk everything by murdering Zelda? What motive could he possibly have?

Cheever's lack of motive gave me pause, and I was about to confess to being insane when Wally sighed and said, "Then I suppose I shouldn't have told him about Zelda's log."

That was a show-stopper. "You what?" I yelped. Yes, I actually "yelped," like an excited Schnauzer about to be attacked by a Doberman. "You told him about Zelda's log?" I was trying to get to my feet when the telephone rang. Wally and I froze in place as the phone rang and rang and rang. "That could be him," I whispered. Wally nodded weakly in agreement. I staggered over to the light switch and flicked off the light. "We don't want him to know we're here," I said. Standing there in the dark, I could feel my heart racing—pit-a-pat, pit-a-pat—my mind a muddle of drink, conjecture, and fear.

Turning off the lights had been a reflex action, an attempt to hide our presence, not an invitation to Cheever to come aboard. Yet, when I heard a noise at the front door a few minutes later, I wasn't surprised. I flattened myself against the wall, praying for a flash of inspiration.

None came.

The door fell inward. A figure loomed in the doorway, holding something aimed in our direction.

Chapter Nineteen

"**M**other!" I exclaimed as she switched on the lights with her elbow.

"Your mother's the murderer?" Wally said. "And such a sweet-looking woman."

"What's going on here, John?" Mother asked, sounding peeved. "What are you doing here in the dark?" She was holding a pot in front of her. "I brought you some chicken soup."

"Oh my god, she's threatening you with chicken soup." Wally's speech was slurred. He sounded a bit tipsy.

"My mother's not the murderer," I assured him.

"You've been drinking," Mother said.

"He certainly has," I agreed.

"What is she doing here if she isn't the murderer?" Wally folded his arms across his chest and leaned back. "Explain that."

"I'll just put this in the kitchen," Mother said, stepping gingerly across the door.

"Chicken soup," I said to Wally. "She brought us some chicken soup."

Wally sniffed the air. "It does smell good."

"It *is* good," Mother rejoined. "If you want some, come along." She headed for the kitchen.

Wally and I somehow managed to prop the door back in place one more time. Then we switched off the living room light and joined Mother in the kitchen. She sat us down and ladled out hearty portions of broth with meaty chunks of chicken floating alongside plump dumplings. Not even Wally's noisy slurping interfered with my appreciation of the meal, my first food in a while. It was delicious. Being sick wasn't half bad.

It was Mother who noticed him. "Who's that with the flashlight coming in through the window?" she whispered.

I squinted into the darkness of the other room. He saw me at the same time I saw him. But Mother was quicker than either of us. She flicked on the living room light before Cheever had a chance to make his getaway. He must have thought the light in the kitchen was intended to deter burglars. Little did he know we were in there having a chicken soup party.

Even caught in the act like that, Cheever seemed unperturbed, looking very dignified in his expensive suit and dark gloves. "I didn't know you were home," he said calmly.

"Sit down," I ordered as I stood up. It was a difficult maneuver, like chewing gum and walking at the same time. Wally sat there in a semi-comatose state, chicken soup dribbling down the side of his mouth.

"I'm afraid I don't have time for a chat. I must be running along." Cheever turned toward the front door.

"Stop," I yelled, feeling gratified when he obeyed. As he turned back toward me, I said, "I think we need to take the time for a little chat." Cheever's eyes flicked over me as if I was little more than some flotsam he'd come across at the water's edge. But he sat down, crossed his legs, removed his gloves, and folded them across one knee, waiting patiently while I tried to remember what it was I wanted to chat with him about.

"Wally, come in here," I called to buy a little time to think. Mother helped Wally to his feet, and together they tottered into the living room. After depositing him in one of the chairs, she took a seat on the sofa, out of the way, but close enough to be able to put her two cents worth in without raising her voice. "Now then," I began, but before I could continue, Wally jumped in with an apology.

"We didn't mean to trick you."

"It was my idea," I offered, feeling like it was my duty to take the blame, but unable to remember what I had done. I felt tired, very tired. My brain cells were on dim. And my vocal cords still weren't functioning properly.

"Yes, it was all John's idea," Wally agreed. "He made up the log to lure the murderer here." He nodded toward Mother. "She came just after I did." Mother thrust out her chin and lowered her eyebrows. I knew that look well. Wally had better watch what he said.

For a while, no one spoke. Then Mother asked Cheever, "And what do you do for a living, Mr...?"

"Cheever, Mother. This man is Byron Cheever, Assistant Director at the Lady of the Lamp Memorial Hospital." Apparently, I could remember *some* things.

Always quick to size up a situation, Mother said, "And I suppose you hope one day to be *the* Director?"

Cheever nodded.

I felt like something was going to happen, but I couldn't predict it. My stomach was acting up. It was becoming a tossup whether I'd pass out or hug the white pagoda first.

"And you, Wally, you're the insurance broker who fudged on the hospital's insurance?" Mother asked. I'd forgotten I mentioned that to her. I really had to learn to keep my mouth shut.

"Yep, that's me," he said cheerfully.

Mother looked around at the players in our improvised drama and narrowed her eyes in contemplation. All she needed to complete the picture was either a Sherlock Holmes cap or some knitting, a.k.a. Miss Marple.

Cheever suddenly rose with the air of a dandy about to leave the party, his gloves held daintily in one hand. "I'm afraid I must be going."

"Not so fast," Mother said, standing to her full, intimidating mother-sized height.

Cheever paused to draw on his gloves, snugging down each finger with care. I tried to get to my feet to defend my mother if she needed it, but it was a struggle.

"You didn't drop by to chat, did you, Mr. Cheever?" That was an understatement, given he had entered through an open window.

"That's none of your business," Cheever replied rather rudely.

"Hey," I yelled somewhat indistinctly. "You can't talk to my mother like that."

"No, you can't talk to our mother like that," Wally cried, somehow managing to stand up. I was impressed.

Cheever started toward the door. "Just one minute," Mother said, stepping squarely in front of him. "I have a few more questions."

Cheever hesitated, trying to jostle past her. When she stood her ground, he tried to shove her aside. After that, things got crazy. I vaguely remember a chorus of voices yelling, "You can't treat our mother like that." Then Wally and I threw our drunken arms around Cheever, pinning him under us as we crashed to the floor in a collective heap. Cheever fought back, but Wally and I were feeling no pain. The last thing I remember before passing out was hearing Mother say, "Hello, Bruno? This is Heloise Smith."

You would have thought Bruno would be happy to have a murderer handed over to him like a fully cooked Thanksgiving turkey on a platter, but he didn't seem to be. After greeting Mother politely, he turned to me and yelled, "What kind of a crazy stunt were you trying to pull? And with your mother here! Don't you ever use your head?"

Mother came to my defense by asserting, "But that man's a murderer." She pointed at Cheever. He was looking a little less dapper and none too happy.

"How do you know you have a real murderer this time?" Bruno addressed the question to me, but Mother answered.

"I never trust a man who tries to hide a bald spot," she said, rolling her eyes at Cheever's head. His hand involuntarily darted to the few long strands of hair he had carefully combed over his balding pate. It was the first time I'd seen him lose his cool. I was convinced, but Bruno still looked doubtful, perhaps wondering how that argument would stand up in court.

"I can only guess about the Rosenblatt murder," Mother continued, "but I can tell you all about the Gunnar affair." She didn't stop to ask if anyone was interested in her theory. Cheever definitely wasn't, but he was in no position to protest. And Bruno knew better than to try and stop my mother once she got hold of an idea. "I only know what John has told me and what I've read in the papers. But it seems rather obvious." Bruno winced, but he didn't interrupt. "I know the Pearl Rosenblatt type," she said proudly.

"I thought we were talking about Zelda Gunnar," Bruno said, sounding confused.

"We are," Mother insisted. "Now, as I was saying. Pearl was a pushy, selfish woman. When she found herself involved in an auto accident, and her with no accident and health insurance, she saw right away how she could make a few bucks. She contacted the Marshalls' insurance agent immediately, and he, in turn, passed on the problem to John. Pearl wasn't about to let the insurance company off easy with a small settlement. Not her. She was entitled to compensation, a lot of compensation, and she intended to get what was her due. The $100,000 on the Marshall policy was just the beginning. So, she went ahead with an operation she'd been needing and then tried to draw Dr. Oliver into the potential suit.

"How do you know that?" I asked. My words didn't sound that clear even to me, but Mother understood me just fine.

"You told me, John. Don't you remember? You said that Dr. Oliver was having insurance problems and that he had made inquiries about getting new insurance. Why would he do it at that particular time unless Pearl had threatened him with a lawsuit?"

It did seem obvious, the way she explained things.

"Who else would she call?" Mother paused briefly to let her audience catch up with her logic. "The hospital," she said when no one responded. "John, you told me that her daughter—that nice girl you had over here the other evening—she thought her mother intended to sue the hospital. Of course, she did. Why would Pearl Rosenblatt let them off the hook? Now if she had talked directly with Mr. Cheever here, there probably would only have been one murder committed. But if you ask around, Bruno, I'm sure you'll find that some admin at the hospital gave Pearl the name of Wally's insurance brokerage." I remembered that was how I'd gotten Wally's number. Mother was onto something.

"So, Pearl Rosenblatt talked to Zelda Gunnar," Mother continued. "And Miss Gunnar, hoping to inherit Wally's job, and suspecting the status of the excess policy, saw her chance to make him look bad. Unfortunately for her, she called Mr. Cheever to confirm the coverage problems. But the problem wasn't just Wally's, it was also Cheever's. He should have caught on to what Wally had been up to long before then. He'd been sitting on Wally's binder for three months, hoping a policy would appear and the problem would go away. But it didn't. Such negligence on his part wouldn't look good for an aspiring director. And," she concluded, "we all know what happened next."

Cheever's left eyelid had developed a twitch. "I want to talk with a lawyer," he said.

Chapter Twenty

C heever continued to deny everything right through his trial and even after his conviction. Mother and Bruno weren't the least troubled by his tenacious refusal to confess, but I admit to some feelings of uneasiness. After all, I had set the trap that caught him; I didn't want the responsibility of putting an innocent man behind bars. Mother, on the other hand, had an explanation for everything and was confident in her interpretation. She has a tidy mind. And the jurors agreed. I suppose that's justice.

Ironically, Zelda's last words did help convict Cheever. Not what she said to me with her dying breath, but what she wrote in her log, the real one that Lizbeth discovered when she was boxing up Zelda's things to give to the Salvation Army. Just like I'd said when I was making things up, Zelda had detailed all of the petty wrongs committed by Wally on a day-by-day basis. Sooner or later, she would have had enough evidence to get him fired. So, in a way, Cheever had done Wally a favor, two actually. Not only did Wally retain his job, but he got a new assistant, a cute young thing who thinks her boss is "the best."

Overall, Wally was incredibly lucky. The press more or less ignored what the log had to say about him. A headline proclaiming "Employee Hates Her Boss" probably didn't sound like the kind of breaking news that would sell more newspapers. They concentrated instead on sensational headlines, like: "Victim Reveals Name of her Murderer" and "Blackmail, Insurance Fraud, and Murder." Wally had been lucky, but Cheever wasn't. There was a line in Zelda's log that noted he was coming by to talk with her about the hospital's insurance on the very day she was killed. She'd probably thought he was her savior; instead, he was her nemesis. But she got even by pointing a bony finger at her murderer from the grave.

I wasn't so lucky, either. Bruno refused to believe I didn't know about the log all along. He couldn't accept that I had been clever enough to dream it up out of thin air, very thin air if I remember that day correctly. Nor did he give me any credit for helping him solve the case. Rather, he told me that it was only out of respect for my mother and our past history that he didn't charge me with obstruction of justice.

Although Cheever was convicted of Zelda's murder, he was never even charged with Pearl's. They didn't quite have sufficient evidence. But the way Mother figured, he killed her for the same reason he killed Zelda—she wouldn't relent on the insurance matter. Most likely, he tried to stall for time in order to obtain a new policy that would cover Pearl under the claims-made provision, but, according to Mother's theory, Pearl didn't want to wait. Why should she? From her perspective, there was no reason to wait; the hospital had money, *all* hospitals had money. If there was a problem with insurance coverage, that wasn't *her* problem.

Unfortunately for Cheever, the hospital was on the verge of exceeding its insurance limits, and without the excess coverage policy, Pearl's claim would have pushed them over the top. But if Mother was right, money was never the issue for Cheever. It was a question of reputation, Cheever's reputation. Too much time had elapsed since the binder had been issued for Cheever to pawn off all the blame on Wally. Not only was the hospital in a position to lose a good deal of money, but Cheever's sloppy handling of the situation wasn't going to aid him in his campaign to be named director by the hospital's Board. The promotion was anything but a done deal. Still, in spite of this one misstep, Cheever might have been appointed director anyway, but we'll never know. One thing we do know, however, is that his life jail sentence eliminates him from the running.

During the investigation and subsequent trial, Cheever never admitted any responsibility for my "accidents." But Mother and Bruno agreed that he was the most likely suspect. And when the first two attempts didn't slow me down, he probably hired the two thugs who beat me up. Bruno assured me there were plenty of bent individuals out there who were more than willing to rough someone up for a little cash. Some would even do it just for the fun of it.

As for Zelda, her sole purpose had been to gather sufficient evidence to expose Wally's connection to the hospital's insurance difficulties. Even though Babcock-Chalmers was most likely liable if one of their employees issued a phony binder, for once the company's interests did not directly coincide with Zelda's. Confirming Wally's role in the affair would have sealed his fate. Mother thinks that's why Zelda broke into my home and office, to see what I had on Wally. Perhaps she also wanted to keep my investigation alive by making me think Wally was the one doing the searching. After all, he had the most to lose. If that was her plan, however, she had overestimated my deductive abilities.

Insurance! People always feel they're owed. Mark and Frances hoped to get their insurance companies to pay for their mistakes. Vivian believed that Universal, a large company with considerable assets, had an obligation to cover her son's accident and thereby protect the poor divorcee who faithfully paid her insurance premiums, if sometimes a little late.

Pearl also believed she was owed something for nothing. Why not? If insurance companies can pay outrageous sums to other people for all sorts of wild claims, certainly they could pay for her pain and suffering. She did have pain, and she had been suffering. It just wasn't directly linked to either the accident or the operation as she wanted everyone to believe.

Unfortunately, the insurance companies aren't in business to oblige everyone. Someone always loses. And in this instance, two paid with their lives.

As for me, I'm not naïve; I don't expect to make money off insurance. But I did feel I was entitled to compensation for out-of-pocket expenses incurred during the investigation. Unfortunately, my health insurance only covered seventy percent of my hospital bills. It seems their rates exceeded those my insurance program considered to be "reasonable." Then, neither my auto nor my tenant policy insurers were willing to defend me against my landlord's suit for damages to his parking area. They jumped on his argument that my drinking was somehow responsible for what happened. Go figure. To top it all off, I'm also having to fight for the forty-five dollars above the three-hundred-dollar deductible I feel my tenant policy insurer owes me for my door. They claim the police department is liable, and the police, of course, deny responsibility.

I am fortunate in one respect, however. I still have my job with Universal. Van Droop proved they really are "The Company with a Heart" by forgiving me for the trouble I'd caused them. He did point out, though, that in the future, I was not to consider myself on loan to the police department. He also hinted very strongly that I should start wearing more professional attire and consider investing in an automobile more appropriate to my station in life as a Universal employee.

Although I am reluctant to give up Bee, I decided to test a potential new look by asking for a bright red Mustang as a loaner when I took my Saturn in for some repairs. As I drove it off the lot, the sun was shining down on my new image, my face was almost back to normal, and I happened to know that it was Nancy Nevensky's day off. Maybe I would give her a call to see if she wanted to have a cup of coffee with me. I could impress her with my new wheels, and she would magically fall into my open arms. Life was good.

Heads turned as I sped toward my rendezvous with fate. I didn't see the battered old Gremlin until it was almost on top of me. I swerved off the road to avoid a collision but, as if attracted by magnets, the Gremlin stayed with me. As the two cars came together, I caught a glimpse of the Gremlin's driver, a middle-aged woman surrounded by dogs and bobble-headed children. She didn't even seem to notice that we weren't two ships passing in the night, but two cars making bodily contact. Then, without even slowing, the Gremlin careened off down the road, children and dogs leaping and cavorting as if nothing had happened.

I suppose I should have turned around and chased her down, but I was in shock. It was a hit-and-run, and I was the victim. I pulled over to check the damage. The red paint along the entire side of the car looked like it had been attacked by an enraged animal with three-inch claws. And there was a long dent where some part of her vehicle had bumped into mine. Those old Gremlins are tough…and mean.

After everything I had recently been through, I couldn't believe this had happened to me. It wasn't fair. I got back in my wounded car and returned to The Haven. Nancy would have to wait until another day. I had to call my insurance agent.

"It was a hit and run," I explained, waiting for him to tell me everything was going to be okay, that my insurance would pay for the damage. After some bodywork and a new paint job, the Mustang would be good as new. Maybe I'd give up Bee and keep it.

"I'm sorry, Mr. Smith," my agent said in a clipped, punctilious voice. 'You obviously haven't read your policy carefully. On page twenty-eight, section 4, subpoint 3B, it distinctly says that you are covered in a borrowed car but not a loaner, unless you have informed us of your intention to temporarily change vehicles. Your premiums needed to be adjusted for the difference in the cost of coverage. And you, Mr. Smith, did not adjust your premiums."

It seems I hadn't been insured to the hilt after all.

Acknowledgements

Insurance is serious business. And death is nothing to laugh at. So, writing a murder mystery with a claims adjuster as the protagonist is not something that is automatically funny. In addition, I'm very aware that we don't all laugh at the same things. Nevertheless, I live in hope that readers will enjoy my strange sense of humor that I try to firmly ground in credible plots.

My apologies to the inner klutz in each of us, to claims adjusters who have to deal with greedy clients on an almost daily basis, and to any reader who finds my protagonist's lust for curvy women more pathetic than funny.

Finally, I want to thank Harriette Sackler for giving John Smith a chance. And Shawn Reilly Simmons for her patient editing and a cover that captures the fanciful mood of *In$ured to the Hilt*. With a special "thank you" to my readers. Without you I wouldn't be an author.

About the Author

Through the years, Charlotte Stuart has taught college courses in communication, left a tenured faculty position to go commercial fishing in Alaska, spent a frustrating year as a political speech writer, enjoyed time as a management consultant, and survived several years as a VP of HR and training.

She started her writing career with a PhD thesis that had the distinction of being stolen from the University of Washington library. After getting a number of serious academic articles published, she turned to penning humorous stories about boating. Her current passion is for writing lighthearted mysteries that are grounded in real situations and relationships.

Charlotte lives on Vashon Island and appreciates its rural atmosphere while being only a 20-minute ferry ride from Seattle. She is the past president of the Puget Sound Chapter of Sisters in Crime and a member of the Mystery Writers of America. www.charlottestuart.com

SOCIAL MEDIA HANDLES:
https://twitter.com/quirkymysteries

https://www.facebook.com/charlotte.stuart.mysterywriter
https://www.instagram.com/cstuartauthor
https://www.goodreads.com/author/show/19305587.Charlotte_Stuart

AUTHOR WEBSITE:
https://charlottestuart.com

Also by Charlotte Stuart

Disastrous Interviews: the Comic, Tragic and Just Plain Ugly - 2013

Survival Can Be Deadly (A Discount Detective Mystery) - 2019

Campaigning Can Be Deadly (A Discount Detective Mystery) - 2020

Shopping Can Be Deadly (A Discount Detective Mystery) - 2021

Moonlight Can Be Deadly (A Discount Detective Mystery) - 2023

Why Me? Chimeras, Conundrums and Dead Goldfish (A Macavity & Me Mystery) - 2019

Who, Me? Fog Bows, Fraud and Aphrodite (A Macavity & Me Mystery) - 2021

Not Me! Speluncaphobia, Secrets and Hidden Treasure - 2022

Bogged Down (A Vashon Island Mystery) - 2020